WILDRAITH'S LAST BATTLE

Jokan picked up his sword and the baby and went to the door. The noises of people and animals had increased, the dance of flames looked to be bursting out everywhere, the smell of blood was strong, but the wildcat and the badger seemed to have deserted the street in front of this house and gone for other prey. Jokan took the baby into his left arm and ventured out.

A bear rose up at him from the shadows. Jokan screamed and swung up his sword in defense. The bear dropped on all fours, sniffed at the child, and lumbered past them towards the center of town. Shaking, Jokan followed at a safe distance. The town was burning and filled with enemies, and outside was the dark and forest, with teeth and claws, quills and talons, and sharp curved beaks that came tearing from all directions . . .

Wendy Adrian Shultz

WILDRAITH'S LAST BATTLE

PHYLLIS ANN KARR

ILLUSTRATIONS BY WENDY ADRIAN SHULTZ

FANTASY
ACE BOOKS, NEW YORK

An Ace Book

ISBN: 0-441-88969-7

First Ace Printing: September 1982
Published simultaneously in Canada

Manufactured in the United States of America

2 4 6 8 0 9 7 5 3 1

ILLUSTRATIONS
by Wendy Adrian Shultz

"They proposed to shorten their wait with a game of chess.".. 8

"She had no companions except forest creatures.".. 26

"Such bodies as she found were picked clean from the bones.".. 60

"Senerthan's best warriors gathered with him in the high-roofed bower.".............................. 78

"Stinging gnats rose from the river and muffled Gilmar's army.".................................... 104

"Gilmar was easy to pick out, riding his silver-gray stallion.".................................... 140

"They stood staring at each other across the remaining steps.".......................................160

"Their swords and hand-axes rang for nine minutes—in later tales nine hours.".............. 203

"Hooded onlookers held hounds that greatly resembled wolves.".................................... 246

"A sudden lurch downwards, a sound of falling stones.".. 277

PART I

Chapter 1.

At about the time Gilmar the Old entered the war between Senerthan of the Long Forest and Dulanis Butter-hair, a widow who lived beyond what was then the farthest reach of the fighting lost her child to the god of the woodlands. . .

A generation or two earlier, hunters from the eastern forest and herders from the western plain had begun to crowd each other in the valley of the Copper River. A few farmsteads were burned, westerners and easterners found unflattering names for one another, and the more peaceable folk followed the river north, where Gilmar the Old (then the Young) made them welcome in his warm and ocean-bounded territory, or south into the foothills of the Whitepeak Mountains.

The people of the east had had many petty leaders, but Seneth of the Sure Bow was becoming supreme in the Long Forest, thanks to her hunting talent and to her claim that her son Senerthan had been fathered by the moon god Ormrathe. Senerthan grew up handsome and hardy, with a cleft chin and a skill in weaponry that came to surpass even that of his mother-teacher. When his hair sil-

vered early, the last dark strands gone before his
twenty-third year, it was taken as final proof of his
paternal descent. With the revelation that her god-
ly spouse had called her to join him forever, Seneth
Sure-bow disappeared into the deepest woodland,
leaving few hunters who would not follow her son
wherever he led.

The people of the west enjoyed a looser and
earthier, but older and more firmly settled, central
government. All were members of one family, however scattered; and the headship of this family,
passing from parent to eldest child, had been preserved for generations in one ancient branch. It
seemed providential for the peace of the border between east and west that Dulanis should have been
born in the same year as Senerthan. The easterners,
with their different fashions, said unkindly of the
Butter-hair's trait name that it signified not the rich
color of her long braids but rather their im-
moderately oiled appearance; but none could find
any other fault with her beauty or her mind. When
her father, from whom she inherited the Cauldron
of the Ancient Hearth, died prematurely with a suf-
fusion of blood in the brain, Dulanis herself jour-
neyed east to meet Senerthan on an island in the
Copper River.

The valley farmers had learned to build in wood,
clay, and stone; but for the meeting between their
leaders they raised a hall combining the older styles
of west and east, with domestic hides stretched
over a framework of boughs still leafy. Senerthan
came first to this hall, and waited three days, cutting holes in the hide walls to let in more air and
watching the summer leaves wither on the framework. On the fourth dawn he came out of the hall

determined to return to the forest's heart and leave his farmers to their own machinations, and saw in the glow of the sun through dissolving rain clouds that the daughter of the western plain had arrived at last.

He retreated inside, gave orders that fresh boughs and leafy vines be brought to deck the interior, and watched through one of his window-holes as Dulanis stepped upon a raft and was carried to the island, the morning light crossing the sky to shine on her long golden hair and the greens and russets of her woven garments, until some rocks and trees above the island's shoreline hid her raft from sight. Only then did Senerthan turn from his vigil to the chair set for him on one side of the firepit.

At length Dulanis appeared in the open doorway. She was flushed from her climb, and she blinked in seeming displeasure at the holes which made the place less dark than it would otherwise have been. Then she blinked at Senerthan's nine attendants, who were weaving fresh greenery into the dry branches. "Help them," she said to the nine members of her own household who followed her inside. She herself sat in the chair placed ready for her and gazed at Senerthan across the firepit.

"Woman, First of Herders," he said.

"Man, First of Hunters," she replied.

She had green eyes and he had grey. The storytellers were later to sing that they sat and looked at one another unblinking for from nine hours to nine days, and that the fire in the pit between them blazed brightly all that time without needing to be replenished. In fact, the fire had not yet been kindled, and it was barely nine heartbeats before Dulanis spoke again.

"The gods might have provided me worse," she said.

"Indeed," he answered, "though I am half a god myself, I find Dulanis of the Plains as fitting a mate as my father Ormrathe found my mother Seneth Sure-bow."

"We of the plains owe nothing to your gods of the forest," said Dulanis.

"Ormrathe shrinks and stretches his silver circle over all the world," said Senerthan, "forest and plain, shore and mountain alike."

By the end of this speech Dulanis had had time to remember who the easterners meant by the name Ormrathe. "We call the moon god Ellisa," she said, not mentioning that the westerners also called the moon god female. "But until the gods themselves write their names in the sky, Senerthan Supple-finger, I think we need not quarrel on their behalf."

His people believed that the gods actually had written their names across the night sky. But there was some argument among his people as to which letters certain stars helped form, and with this, perhaps, in mind, he did not contradict Dulanis. "We will agree," he said, "that all our gods are good."

They called their oldest advisors. Within an hour it was settled that they would be wed first by the sunlit ceremony of her people and second by the nocturnal ceremony of his, but before all else they would begin with a new ritual, unique to themselves and the situation: they would make a stew of herd meat, wild game, and barley flour, cooking it in the Cauldron of the Ancient Hearth and stirring it with the Moon Spear that Seneth had fashioned of bronze and silver for her son.

While their companions brought up the Cauldron, filled it with water, minced the meat, ground the barley, and kindled the fire in the pit, Dulanis and Senerthan retired to a cool, shaded place outside the hall, where they proposed to shorten their wait with a game of chess.

Both easterners and westerners played this game with ten pieces to a player, on a board of one hundred squares. But the westerners gave the principal piece, the Head or Leader, a move of any number of squares in a straight line, while the easterners limited it to four squares but allowed it to turn corners during the move. When Dulanis saved her Head from capture by moving it seven squares to threaten her opponent's last Runner, Senerthan protested. Dulanis could have saved the piece with a move according to hunters' rules, but she could not have threatened any of Senerthan's pieces. She refused to take back her move, upon which he overturned the chessboard.

Dulanis stood, brushing jet and amber chess pieces from her lap. "I might strike you," she said, "and pay you for this at once."

"To strike a god's son," he replied, "is an insult that can never be paid in full."

"So be it," said Dulanis, turning and walking away from him to the hall, where she kicked the Cauldron over so that the water spilled into the pit and drowned the fire. Then she took her people and her Cauldron to leave the island.

Senerthan had set the chessboard up against a tree and was shooting arrows into it. As Dulanis and her companions passed on their way to the

Wendy Adrian Shultz

raft, he shot an arrow into the arm of her uncle Jokan Round-face instead.

That evening Dulanis sent half of her people to the river's eastern bank in an effort to trap Senerthan on the island; but he and his hunters broke through. Senerthan's people and Dulanis Butterhair's, those who had come with them and those who had been living in the valley, left between fifty and a hundred dead and six farmsteads burnt before the two young leaders turned back into the hearts of their separate territories to gather their forces. Had they had armies to bring with them to their meeting, this first battle would have been more bloody.

They had borrowed the chess pieces from a farmer of the valley, one whose home survived. Two days after the fighting, his servants rafted to the island and gathered up what they could find, but three figures of jet and two of amber were missing. As the years went by, searching for the lost chess pieces became something between a sport and a ritual: some folk searched because fine little statues in jet and amber had their value, others because a kind of belief grew that finding the pieces would somehow help win the war for Dulanis or Senerthan, even though no one else could say for sure which player had used which color. . .

In the first full summer of the war Senerthan's people struck often and with telling effect, until it seemed likely that the next summer he would fulfil his threat of defeating Dulanis utterly and carrying her into his woods by force. His hunters were already skilled with bows and spears, and they shot from a distance, killing their enemies with little loss to themselves.

But in the winter Dulanis gathered and trained her armies. Jokan Round-face planned fortifications, both standing and movable, and the Butter-hair's cousin, Ytran Crook-tooth, devised bows that required two and three men to draw, but that sent great arrows over much longer distances than those of Senerthan's hunters. Dulanis taught her people to shoot from behind large shields of wood and hardened leather, until the farther range of their bows forced the enemy to close with them; and herders had equal or superior skill with sword and axe. Seeing that her armies, though better protected, could not move so quickly as Senerthan's small, unburdened attacking parties, Dulanis also sent many of her people to newly built towns with thick, high walls of earth, wood, and stone.

When the fighting season came again, and Senerthan crossed the Copper River in the pride of his strength and confidence, he found Dulanis prepared not only to hold him off, but to drive him back and to threaten that she would have him caught, bound, and brought by force into her favorite walled town.

That winter Senerthan organized his raiding parties into larger armies and adopted some of his enemies' war tools: large shields to form moving walls, and more powerful bows. In the third summer of the war, Senerthan seemed again to be winning, but not by so wide a margin as the first summer.

In the fourth winter, both Dulanis and Senerthan began removing women from their armies. They realized the struggle was likely to be long, and each summer had seen an increasing loss of fighters. New armies must be bred.

Senerthan at first removed all women from his army, hiding them in deep forest havens and building strongholds for them on the far edges of his territory. Had he not been known as the son of Ormrathe and Seneth, he might have been unable to make good such a command; even with the power he held over his followers, women remained in border raiding parties where loyalty to the moon god's son was weaker than lust for plunder. As the summers went by, Senerthan studied the matter with more reason and a keener eye to his immediate need, and brought back into his armies all women known to be sterile. Tales sprang up of women who made themselves barren in their desire to fight.

Dulanis began by removing only the young and obviously fertile from her armies in the field. The youngest she sent to refuges on her farthest western borders. Women of doubtful fertility or approaching the end of their childbearing age she assigned to command and other relatively safe duties in the new walled towns. Older and sterile women continued as before, but whenever any of these proved fertile after all, which happened more frequently as fewer women remained with the main bodies of fighters, she and her inner burden were brought with care to the nearest refuge.

Both peoples had been monogamous, the hunters mating each spring and autumn, usually with the same mates as the previous season; the herders mating in theory for life, though rules of divorce existed. Now, with the sanction and encouragement of the leaders, polygamy became the western standard and free mating the eastern, with liberal variations everywhere. Babies born to wom-

en who survived battlefield rape were accepted into
the mother's people as gifts from the gods, and the
more strong children a woman bore, to whatever
father or fathers, the higher was her honor. Only
Dulanis and Senerthan themselves escaped censure
for refusing to mate. The hunters understood that
the moon god's son, who could with a few
statements of divine decree concerning the needs of
warfare change a whole people's mating customs,
must guard against squandering his own half-
divine seed. And the herders regarded the chastity
of the Butter-hair as a symbol of the more conti-
nent past and a promise of future return to the old
ways.

In the north, Gilmar (now the Middle-aged) had
been bribing his people to produce more babies
since the first year of his neighbors' dispute. In the
sixteenth summer of the war, a few years before the
first of Dulanis or Senerthan's new crop of children
was ready, Gilmar swept southward with an untouched army.

Chapter 2.

Old Ironstead was slowly crumbling in some northeastern woodland that Gilmar might have claimed had he yet needed the area for his increasing numbers of people, and that Senerthan might have come to protect had he not been so much occupied with Dulanis to the south and west.

Gilmar would, perhaps, have been more in the right since Ironstead had been built by northerners, Rol and Arria the Much-loving, who came southeast in search of metal for the fighting which had made Gilmar's grandfather Gudmar the Sullen supreme in the north. True, Rol and Arria had lived originally under the rule of Gudmar's chief rival, Ilsa the Crafty. But Rol's and Arria's second loyalty had been to business (their first being to one another), and they sold impartially to Ilsa, Gudmar, Sorum the Old, and—when her agents could travel so far—Ylith Short-tongue.

The quality of Ironstead weapons may have given rise to the common northern boast: "My sword was forged on the anvils of Hell," though some scholars claimed it had been heard even before Arria's birth. But by the time Gudmar had married Ilsa, subjugated Sorum, and slain Ylith in single

13

combat, the lode at Ironstead, whether it had fallen from the sky, been left by the ancients, or grown in the earth like underground mushrooms, was nearing depletion. Arria and Rol stayed on nevertheless, as did many of their workers. Prosperity had enabled them to raise fine, comfortable buildings; the more prudent had trade reserves stored up in their thick walls and deep cellars; and they were well content with their home.

Once, during the early years of the northern war, either Sorum or Gudmar had sent a battle force to secure Ironstead with its resources for himself, but the settlers had kept the invaders at bay until Ilsa's warriors arrived to finish the rout, and after that all leaders had left the community in peace, finding it better to allow their enemies Ironstead weapons than to expend the force that would have been needed for conquering and keeping the miners and forgers. So Ironsteaders had grown accustomed to independence.

In the last years of this war and the first years of Gudmar's undisputed rule over the whole of the northern coastlands, Ironstead became a refuge for deserting warriors and former followers of Gudmar's rivals, so that the settlement reached its highest populations at about the same time its original reason for existence was running low. As the deposits of metal finally gave out and the community became impoverished, many folk departed again, either trusting Gudmar's promises of leniency to all and returning to the improving life of the north, or distrusting them and seeking homes farther south. Those who stayed at Ironstead turned to farming, hunting, and gathering.

Rol and Arria went at last into the woods to-

gether and were never seen again, but this was due
to their natural age and determination to die un-
parted as they had lived. They left a village that
had by now levelled into a small, poor, but proud
little knot of decaying large buildings, small new
ones, and fierce minds in sinewy bodies.

Ylsa Tender-face was born in Old Ironstead
twelve years before Senerthan of the Long Forest
overturned the chessboard into Dulanis Butter-
hair's lap. When Ylsa was fourteen, and it became
obvious that the trouble between the hunters and
herders to the south was no mere summer's thun-
dershower, half Ironstead entered a great effort to
find any metal that might have been missed in
former times and forge it into weapons for this new
war; and Ylsa's father, Horj the Black-arm,
worked himself to death at furnace and anvil trying
to get new iron from old earth. Ylsa's mother, Ria
the Lank-chest, grown careless after Black-arm's
death, was killed hunting a bear. One mate
seldom outlived the other very long in Ironstead.
All folk cherished their legends, but Ironsteaders
even more tenaciously than most. Filled with the
example of Arria and Rol, unaffected by the new
breeding customs that Dulanis, Senerthan, and
Gilmar introduced among their neighbors, Old
Ironstead clung to lifelong monogamy, with certain unsanctioned but deep-rooted variations.

When she was nineteen Ylsa married Forn of the
Riverlands, who had come up from the Copper
River valley to escape the fighting. She did not love
him, but she wanted children. Though a woman of
some property, she had had no success previously
in finding a mate as Ironsteaders called it a bad

omen for both parents to be dead before their child's wedding; and then, too, Ylsa was very pretty and Ironsteaders preferred plain partners in marriage. But Forn was as willing to give to Ylsa children as to any other woman, and for the first year they lived tranquilly together—she in hope and he in the division of his nights between Ylsa and Dob Tanner's son. The second year, still childless, Ylsa made so many demands on her mate that he had little strength left for Dob's son and the youth turned elsewhere, discovering that Iama the Impartial had her attractions too. Toward the end of this second year, Ylsa's body began at last to swell, and she allowed her husband some rest.

Guessing that his labor would start again soon after hers had ended, Forn used his respite for drinking, gambling, and trying to win back Dob Tanner's son, who had now broken with Iama and was persuading Arria Large-ear into marriage. One cold night while Ylsa was giving her child suck, Forn lay down outside in a stupor, between Goran Red-nose's tavern and the necessary, and froze himself, despite all the cheap local wine and ale in his stomach, into the first of a series of chills and fevers that stiffened him permanently within ten days.

Unlike so many Ironsteaders, Ylsa refused to give up all interest in life. She had what she had wanted all along—a son, Horj of the Brown Eyes. She yielded to custom far enough to put on a show of grief, discussing all of Forn's good traits whenever the subject arose. Sometimes she even brought it up herself. In time she came to believe that he had in fact been a good and loving mate, and to look back tenderly on their few years together, but the life she led alone with her child suited her. Like Iama the Impartial, she kept her other relationships quiet and brief, and she bore no more children.

Then, in the sixteenth summer of the southern war, young Horj Brown-eyes went deep into the forest, in answer to a challenge issued by one of his playmates, and did not return.

The lad was now seven years old and of an age to spend whole days running and gathering with his friends, so he was not missed until evening. Then all Ironstead searched the forest from first dusk to full nightfall, and many continued the search by moonlight, though they did not carry torches, because the season had been dry. The next day, too, they searched, but then the community as a whole returned to its own rest and work. Ironsteaders, both young and grown, had lost themselves in the forest through the years, and food must still be farmed and gathered against the winter for those who were not lost. Nevertheless, Ylsa persuaded Dob Tanner, Goran Red-nose, Tark the Crook-fingered, Iama the Impartial and a few others of whom she had made lovers or friends, to search on during the second night and part of the second morning.

At last all but Ylsa herself gave up. She gave them insults for farewells and wandered on, stumbling in her weariness, until they decided she, too, was lost.

She came out of the woods again in the middle of the night, made her way to the home of the child who had challenged her son to find some red-tipped stickmoss, and began to beat him in his bed.

His screams soon woke his parents and sister, who
pulled Ylsa away to her own dwelling and left her
with a cup of drugged wine. She did not drink it.
She pulled her old goat Comely into the moonlight
and poured the red liquid over her back in a crude
shape meant for the sign of the Tree: single trunk,
nine limbs, nine roots. She led Comely, thus
marked, to the edge of the forest and with pushes,
kicks and shouts drove her away between the trees.

Some Ironsteaders blamed Ylsa for not offering
the customary sacrifice to Wildrava, god of the
woodlands, at once; others, more traditional in
their religion, maintained that such a sacrifice
would do more harm than good since the goat was
flawed by a broken left horn and a limp in the right
hind leg. But Comely was the widow's last
possession of value, who had provided milk to
wean young Horj and had given Ylsa a measure of
companionship that neither husband, nor lovers,
or even her son (for a child's thoughts turn around
itself) had given her. The widow wept to watch her
go—and whether she wept for her son, her goat, or
herself, none could say.

Next day Arria Large-ear's children and Sarn
One-arm, looking for berries, found what a wolf
had left of the goat's corpse, recognizable by a few
wine stains on the hide. A few hours later some
hunters brought in Horj Brown-eyes. He was stiff,
undecayed, and some bits of poisonous mushroom
were between his teeth.

Ylsa had fallen asleep after sending her goat into
the forest. Her neighbors did not wake her, but
Goran Red-nose sat in her dwelling, beside the
boy's body, until she woke of herself, at sunset.

She sat up and stared at Goran across the room.

She could see that her son was dead. "When?" she said.

"Last night, maybe, this morning? Acid mushrooms."

Ylsa crawled to him on hands and knees, took the small, thin corpse with its bloated belly, and rocked back and forth for a long time, without moaning.

When the first stars began to appear, she whispered, "And Comely? And my goat?"

Goran shrugged. "Wolves."

"Wolves. Wildrava's hounds." Ylsa laughed like the crackling of brittle-thunder. Still gripping her son, she got to her feet. "Then I curse you, Wildrava of the Woodlands! I curse you, god who takes the pay and holds back the purchase! Do you hear me, god of the forest? I curse you, robber and cheater!"

She carried her son's body to the bedstraw, knelt, and arranged him carefully, tenderly, while Goran squinted at her in silence. When the task was done, she rocked on her heels, staring up through her one small window at the night. "I curse you, Wildrava!" she shouted as if there had been no pause in her unprayer. "Now strike me, lying god! Aye, strike me!"

The tavern keeper stood and moved away, as if expecting wolves or lightning to spring through the window. But the god gave no sign of having heard the curse. Ylsa waited for a few rapid heartbeats, then uttered a wordless cry, turned, and ran to the door, disappearing into the darkness beyond.

Chapter 3.

Gods are accustomed to the curses of mortals, as also to the bereaved sighs of the newly dead. They know that most curses are soon repented in guilt or terror, most sighs swallowed in the continued mysteries of existence. But sometimes a mortal's cry rings a chord in the god's own self-awareness, and the music raises a kind of bruise or blister, a minute eddy in the spreading circles of the infinite, scarcely to be seen from even a little distance (as distances are reckoned in those planes), but painful for a time to the god in question.

Ylsa's son, Horj Brown-eyes, was still too young at his death to feel either his own loss or his mother's very deeply. He puzzled a little at her desperation, but the excitement of excarnation overpowered all. Wildrava kissed him, put him upon his old nurse-goat Comely, and watched them off into the beginning of their journeys, which would not again touch Ylsa's life until her own death.

Then the god of the woodlands put itself into the Overgod for consideration of Ylsa's curse.

The goat was blemished, said the god of the woods.

It was the woman's last and only possession to sacrifice, said the god of domestic animals, who, like all the gods, was in some measure an individual, in some measure one more aspect of each compeer, and in some measure one particle of the Overgod.

I neither rejected nor accepted Ylsa's sacrifice, said the god of the woods. *I merely allowed my creatures to obey their hunger.*

But the widow cursed you, said the god of the weather.

The boy did not, said the god of the woods. *The boy is content.*

His mother is not, said—unexpectedly—the god of soldiers.

I should have expected that reminder to proceed from our sibling of birth, said Wildrava, *god of the home.*

The god of soldiers, who had been called into individual existence more recently than most of the others, gave a metaphorical shrug.

And his mother is searching the same plane for him even now, said the god of the woodlands, mixing tenses in the way gods tend to do among themselves, verb tenses being so vague in their own language.

His mother will not be searching the same plane for a very long while, according to her own present perception, said the god of soldiers. *Unless in her recklessness she cuts short her life expectancy.*

We are not required to fulfil prayers, said the god of the woods. *And no more are we required to heed curses!*

The boy and the goat were the only creatures this woman had left to value, said the god of the home.

If this is cruelty, said the god of the woods, *have*

I not been cruel countless times, in all our aspects?

And have not others of us passed over the grindstone? echoed many gods at once.

And if I fail? said Wildrava. *To die and fall lower than any dead mortal, with farther to climb through ages unguessed by mortals with their little cyclical measurements of passing years? Not to regain my place again before there is a new world and a new universe?*

Do you fear? said the Overgod.

Yes, said Wildrava, *I fear. And I am eager.*

We will be diminished, said the Overgod. *And at your return we will be enlarged. If you fail, another will be personalized for your woodlands, until the new world and the new universe.* (But the Overgod said all of this in a single word.)

The last hand Wildrava touched before falling was the hand of the soldiers' god.

Chapter 4.

Only a few nights after Ylsa the Widow departed, war came once again to Ironstead.

Edrik Short-shoulder and Birn Nine-toes were not among the first harvest of Dulanis' wartime seeding, but they had been three and four years old the summer of the overturned chessboard, so they knew the former long peace of the western herdlands more from their grandparents' memories than from their own. Bred to warfare, Edrik had earned command of three hundred before his eighteenth year. Birn had newly inherited leadership of the remnant of Ulkan Lack-tooth's three hundred when Ulkan and half his force died in battle with a few hundred of Senerthan's hunters. Birn charged the defeat to the dense eastern woodland in which the battle was fought. Ulkan, he said, deserved to be slain for foolishly leading his party so deep into the hunters' own ground.

While trying to bring the survivors back to open land, Birn met Edrik, whose party was still whole except for a few losses to accident and sickness. With much argument—Birn was a year older and would not always yield to Edrik simply because Edrik had the more fighters—they turned southwest, but found a large army of Senerthan's people massing between them and the Copper

River. So they turned and slipped northward, hoping to get back into their own lands that way.

One night as the two leaders were debating whether to cut west in the morning or to follow the skirts of the forest a little farther in search of a stream that might flow into the great river and provide them a sure supply of water for the march, Slurm Split-brow brought a girl about nine years old to Edrik's tent.

The child was sobbing uncontrollably and, in spite of her youth, bore the marks of Slurm's lust. They questioned the girl, who, if she was hardly capable of coherent speech, was still less capable of lying or withholding answers and they learned that had they gone a little more to the east that day, they would have come in sight of Old Ironstead.

"Smiths and weaponmakers," said Birn. (Ironstead's reputation had outlived its supply of metal.)

"A town of Senerthan's?" said Edrik.

Birn smirked, as always when Edrik asked for his knowledge or opinion. "It's in the hunters' lands, I think? And where do Senerthan's devils get their iron-barbed arrowheads, if not from this rotten place?"

Edrik rubbed his beard. "Then the Butter-hair would thank us for stopping the supply."

The child sobbed out some words that might have held a denial of Ironstead's owing any loyalty to hunters.

Edrik looked at Slurm and said, "Strange her people would let her wander the woods alone."

"The one-armed dung bait who was with her is free meat for wolves tonight," Slurm answered with a grin.

Edrik laughed. "Well, they're enemies now, Senerthan's people or not. We can't leave them at our backs."

They did not think of themselves as cruel, and they did not kill the child. They left her tied to a large old tree, a water skin within reach of the arm that was free from the elbow down.

Then they groped through the night toward the settlement. On the way they found Wem the Old, father of the child Slurm had taken, and he bartered information about the settlement eagerly enough for news of his child. In this manner Birn and Edrik learned that about two hundred men, slightly more women, and seventy or eighty children inhabited the old town—Edrik accepted round numbers rather than wait for Wem to reckon up everyone by name on his shaking fingers —and that many of them were searching the woods that night for his child. Birn and Edrik led their warriors on, leaving Slurm behind to finish off the old man at his leisure. Waiting would not bring them an hour more ripe for the attack. Indeed, delay might cost them the surprise.

A woman neither Ironsteader nor hunter was also walking in the forest that night. She had no companions except forest creatures: two wolves on one side, a stag on the other, bear, badger, and a few foxes following, a family of rabbits hopping ahead, an owl and numerous moths flying in circles above her, and some mice scurrying around her feet. She wore dull brown trousers, a dull green tunic, and, hanging unheeded from the dull rope belt at her waist, a sword with a sheen that all but

Wendy Adrian Shultz

glowed in the moonlight. Her head and feet were bare, and as she walked she looked down at her hands as if they were a greater mystery than the truce between predators and prey around her.

A scream brought her out of her thoughts. She looked beyond her hands and saw a child bound to a century-old oak and cringing from the wolves, though they kept their distance.

The woman went forward to squat beside the child. One of the rabbits hopped along, staying well within the woman's moon-cast shadow, and sniffed at the child's leg.

"You will be safe," said the woman, speaking as if unused to her tongue. "I will untie you." Clumsily at first, but with growing skill, her fingers worked at the ropes. But the knots were tight.

The woman became impatient and pulled the sword from her belt. She balanced it for a moment, making a gleam of moonlight chase back and forth along its edge, then used it to slice the rope, well away from the child. She took another second to brush her fingers over the scar left in the tree's bark. Inept as she was with the sword, it had not cut her.

Still sobbing, the child clutched her arm and stared at the unnatural collection of animals around her.

"They will not hurt you," said the woman. "You see, they do not come near you. And they are not hungry."

"When . . . when they get hungry?" whispered the child.

"Then they will leave me and find their food, and others may come to me instead."

The child rubbed her tears away on the woman's tunic and took a drink from the waterskin when the woman held it to her lips. "Who are you?"

"Wil . . . draith," the woman said, and smiled. "Who are you?"

"Yma. The . . . the . . ." But Yma buried her face in Wildraith's sleeve again without bringing out her trait-name.

"You are Yma the Bloody now. You are smeared very much with blood, child. Are you hurt?"

Then the girl, gradually and with many incoherences, brought out what had been done to her and what she understood of the things happening around her.

"How long have I . . . ?" said Wildraith at last, when Yma paused. "Yma, how many were these people who left you here?"

"Hundred . . . hundreds and hundreds."

"And they go to destroy Ironstead?"

Yma clutched Wildraith and sobbed.

"And they left you here, when?"

"Hours ago. Hours and hours ago."

"But this same night?"

"It . . . yes . . . I want my mother. I want my father. I want Sarn One-arm."

Wildraith put her palm on the child's forehead, curving her fingers up over the wet, greasy, tangled hair. She held her hand steady a few moments, until Yma quieted. She lifted her other arm, and the stag stepped forward, timidly but trustingly, to lie down beside the child. Wildraith put her free hand on his head, between the antlers.

"Nothing will hurt you, Yma," Wildraith said slowly. "Sleep. When you wake the deer will take you to a stream. Wash your body and your clothing, wash all the blood clean. Then wait. Wait all the day and all the night. Rabbits and squirrels will bring you food—though if a squirrel brings mushrooms, do not eat those. The squirrels can eat mushrooms that you cannot. The second morning, if no one has found you, follow the stag and he will lead you to Ironstead. But if you see it is smoking and destroyed, go back into the forest.''

Yma nodded. Wildraith took her hands from their heads, and the child curled up against the deer. He sniffed her uneasily at first, but lay still and let his body warm hers.

Wildraith stood. Her face was drawn, her lips compressed. She turned and started after the western warriors. Her movements were those of walking, but the two wolves loped to stay at her side.

She found Slurm Split-brow and Wem the Old. Wem was dead, his blood still bright on Slurm's blade. Wildraith came upon the westerner before he was aware of her or the animals. Knocking the warrior to the ground with an awkward, but effective, blow, she straddled him, seized his hair and pulled his head back so that he was staring at her face upside-down.

"Are you one of these people who want to destroy Ironstead?" said Wildraith.

He choked.

"Your companions. They have gone forward?"

He seemed to try to scream, but the sound strangled in his neck.

"How many are you?"

"Four . . . hundred . . . and . . . and about . . . thirty . . . I think."

Wildraith looked at his face. For the second time that night, she pulled the sword from her belt. She held it awkwardly—it took her three strokes to cut through his neck.

"I am clumsy," she muttered, looking curiously at the sword. "Good. The widow will be clumsy too. But this way all goes slowly!"

She dropped Slurm's head and strode on, taking no further interest in the bodies. The owl and a number of the insects remained behind to nibble. Ravens and other scavengers less shy of dead than of living humanity would come later.

She caught sight almost simultaneously of Ironstead and of seven attackers creeping into position around it. Looking to right and left, she soon made out more attackers on each side. So they meant to ring the settlement in, then close upon it at some signal, perhaps a battle shout. Light showed in four windows. Many Ironsteaders would be away in the forest tonight, searching for Yma as—a few nights ago—for young Horj the widow's son, and friends would be waiting for them in the town, with food and drink, companionship and a place prepared for their rest, when they returned tired and empty. But most of the buildings were dark.

Ironstead had held off an attack during the northern wars, but then the community had been young and prosperous, its daily labor the making of weapons, and its people perforce skilled to some degree in the use of their manufactures. And they had only needed to hold the invaders back until The Crafty's army could come and relieve them.

"There is always the chance of mistake," Wildraith whispered. "Whatever course, there is the chance of mistake. These brains . . ." She paused in her reverie, smiled, and shrugged. "These brains are slow and this time is fast. Nothing stranger."

The smaller animals—the rabbits, foxes, mice, skunks, a porcupine—left her shadow and scurried towards the settlement. The birds—for many night birds had joined her—the insects, bats, snakes, lizards, and toads, all hastened forward. Even the badger made a start, but turned back as if by command.

A few of the western warriors noticed some creature brushing or slithering past or flapping overhead. They assumed their own advance had roused these animals. A few toads were squashed, a few rabbits spitted by fighters who thought it good opportunity to provide for their stewpots. But more animals slipped through the circle unheeded. They caused little wonder among Edrik's and Birn's people, who were working their way into position, waiting for three hoots like an owl followed by a shout of "The Cauldron!" as their signal to attack. No single group of warriors could know that the same small, quick movements rustling between them were being repeated everywhere along the circle. Not only from around Wildraith, but from all sides of the forest, the animals converged.

Several rabbits chased each other through Eris the Fertile's dwelling until all her seven children were awake. A toad hopped on the faces of Dob Tanner's son and Arria Large-ear. A skunk came into Goran's tavern and released just enough of its scent to penetrate the brains of the one or two late watchers who nodded over their sour brew. Four mice and a pair of nightjars harried Dob Tanner's cat into a yowl that woke the sleepers in two houses. Several porcupines curled up next to every dog, asleep or prowling, that they could find, and quilled them until growls, yelps, and howls chorused through all the town.

The noise carried to the ring of crouching warriors. Lights appeared in more and more windows as embers were stirred up, lamps and tallow-dips kindled. Edrik, who was to have given the first owl-hoot, hesitated. But Birn, on the other side of the town, took the strange commotion as a sign that no more time must be lost and gave the first hoot himself. When Edrik did not reply at once, Birn added the second and third.

Wildraith, waiting among the trees, smiled to hear it. "A human thinks to sound like an owl?"

As if in answer to the mock hoots, the howling of wolves rose from every part of the forest.

Then Edrik shouted. His first shout was word-less, like many of the shouts that came from other warriors in the circle. But he shouted again, "The Cauldron! The Cauldron! Dulanis!"

The warriors rushed forward. Sixteen summers of fighting had schooled them to a measure of dis-cipline. Besides, the howling came from behind, and if the wild animals were about to attack—many westerners could not scoff with complete sin-cerity at Senerthan's claim of descent from a god—the town would be safer than the woods.

Wildraith rushed forward also, darting between two of Edrik's men and skimming on towards the town. The westerners could see at once that she was not one of them, for her hair streamed out long, black and unbound while their own was cut short to be out of their way.

One of Edrik's men drew back his spear arm and took aim. The badger sank teeth into his heel be-fore he could throw. All the larger animals, who had waited while the smaller ones were waking the town, now followed after Wildraith, covering her charge. The wolves joined the badger to bring down the would-be spear hurler, then turned to find other opponents. A boar was breaking the circle to the left. To the right, Edrik himself narrowly escaped the bear's paw.

Meanwhile, Wildraith gained the nearest building. Sword in hand, she sprang in through the doorway and looked about the lamplit room. "Ylsa!" she cried. "Ylsa Tender-face!"

A woman and a man, their nerves already tightened by the birds that had waked them with light pecks at their foreheads and the wolves that howled around Ironstead, stared back at the stranger. The man threw a clay water jug, which missed aim by a finger's length. The woman wrestled down from the wall an experimental type of weapon, a fire-hardened ashwood sword with sharp-ground stones inlaid along the edges to form a blade.

"No, you are not Ylsa," said Wildraith.

"Tilis the Supple," replied the woman, trembling a little.

"Keep yourselves. Enemies come." Wildraith turned from the doorway and ran deeper into Ironstead.

Next instant Edrik and a companion burst into the room. Edrik's shoulder dripped blood. So did both his comrade's legs, and this man's left hand had been half bitten away. Their wounds were maddening them, fear of the animals was driving them on, yet some memory of their original purpose remained, and they lunged for the Ironsteaders.

The man snatched up a hoe, but soon fell beneath their onslaught. Tilis swung and hacked her way into the street. Here she met another western warrior, half his face gone. She could see him by firelight—one of her lamps had fallen into her bedstraw.

He gave a great bellow and struck his axe at her.
With an answering cry, she dodged the blow and
swung her weapon into his side at the waist. He
toppled and rolled, and she saw that some long,
thin animal—a stoat or weasel—was clinging to his
back, having gnawed a blood-smeared hole
through his shirt, and seemingly trying to burrow
into his ribcage.

The town was full of the screams of strange
warriors pelting in from all sides with beasts at
their heels or dragging at their flesh. Ironsteaders
came tumbling out into the streets; flames started
up here and there where other houses were fired by
accident or design. Tilis glimpsed the dark-haired
woman far ahead, leaping deerlike toward Dob
Tanner's house, that showed fire at the window.
Tilis ran after her. Two wolves jumped out at the
young woman's side, and she half veered; but they
went past her to grapple with an invader she had
not seen in the shadows. She ran on to the tanner's
house.

When she reached the door, she found the dark-
haired woman pulling Dob into the street. He
seemed to have been overcome by fumes from
some of his hides singeing in the heat; the stranger
and even Tilis—who caught only a weakened draft
of the stench—coughed heavily. Dob's cat minced
and darted about them as Tilis helped the stranger
haul the unconscious man to a cooler place.

"Ylsa—" said Tilis, pointing at the widow's
former home. "Ylsa Tender-face—gone."

"Gone?" The stranger gripped Tilis by one
shoulder.

"Left—a few nights ago—gone crazed, we
think."

"No!"

Tilis shrank away at that cry of despair, and crouched above old Dob. The stranger turned and ran toward the widow's empty house.

On the other side of the town, a fifteen-year-old boy named for Dulanis Butter-Hair's kinsman Jokan was dashing and scrabbling away from a badger and a wildcat. Whimpering in terror, he nevertheless managed, by whirling every few steps to slash at them with his sword, to keep them a few paces at bay until he could dodge into a house, swing shut and bolt the door.

The lower part of the dwelling was empty save for two dead bodies, one an invader and the other a partially dressed settler. In the half-loft above, a woman was shrieking, a man grunting, and at least one child crying. Jokan recognized the man by his harness as a fellow westerner, and wondered whether he, Jokan Greenstick, could ever pump his seed into an unwilling woman in the midst of fighting and turmoil.

Then there was a crash as of pottery, the woman's hand came up and struck into the man's back before Jokan could cry a warning. The man screamed and pulled away, groping at his back. The woman thrust at his front. He tried to stand, slipped on the edge of the half-loft, and fell to the floor below, clawing at something that protruded in a splay of blood from his stomach.

It was Gam Squint-eye. Jokan seized the thing and yanked it from Gam's guts with as little thought as possible. Gam gave his last and ugliest cry, thrashed over, doubled up, rattled and was dead. Jokan glanced at what had been in his stom-

ach and saw it was a toasting-fork that the woman
had thrust deep. He shuddered and looked up at
her.

She had risen, all blood smeared, her long tunic
falling back down, unbelted, covering her to the
knees. She stared at Jokan. He dropped the fork
and gripped his sword with both hands, as when he
had swung it at the wild animals outside. She threw
a lamp at him—its flame went out in midair, but a
few drops of hot grease spattered him as it broke
on the hard-packed earth floor.

He started for the ladder. She had one more
burning lamp in the loft with her, and this one she
used to fire her bedstraw. She laughed as the flames
caught and shot up; the children's wails redoubled;
and Jokan retreated a few steps, cursing. To be
driven back into the street was to be driven back to
wildcat and badger and the gods knew how many
more beasts by now. He glanced once more at
Gam.

The woman was now on the ladder, coming
down. He rushed forward and kicked it sideways.
It fell, the woman with it, and her head struck hard
on the floor. Not knowing whether she was dazed
or already dead, he thrust his sword into her stomach. Her throat rattled and her eyes became fixed.

He felt as if Gam's death rattle had sent him into
a panic and the woman's had brought him out of it.
He laid his sword on the floor, replaced the ladder
against the edge of the loft, and began to climb. If
he could not engender children in battle for the
Butter-hair's cause, he could at least rescue them to
carry home across the river.

One of the children was maybe two years old, the
other less than half a year. Jokan's appearance did
not quiet them. The older one screamed even

louder and tried to get away, but there was hardly anywhere to scrabble, so it shrieked, wiggled, and struck out with its little arms and legs. After a few moments, Jokan gave up trying to make this child trust him, and picked the baby up out of its boxlike crib. This brat, at least, was too small to do much that the young man could not counter by the mere strength of his hold. The older one beat at Jokan with its fists. He shouted at it—it found room to run towards the back of the loft. But the fire was spreading from its parents' bed, catching in the dry old beams and floorboards. The child burned its hand, shrieked, and drew back.

"All right, you little turd, stay here and fry!" Jokan screamed, starting down the ladder with the smaller child curled tightly in his left arm. The two-year-old stared around from him to the fire. A flame jumped out of some old wood near enough to scorch one small buttock. Then at last the child came whimpering to the edge of the loft. Children learned to climb young when they lived around rungs, and though the brat was shaking so hard it might have made the ladder fall if Jokan hadn't been just below to steady it, and though the young westerner took several kicks in the face and shoulders during the descent, they reached the ground before the loft timbers began cracking.

Jokan put the infant down, found some rope, caught the two-year-old after a chase around and over the corpses, and knotted a dragline between its waist and his own. Then he picked up his sword and the baby and went to the door. He put the baby down again, unbolted and opened the door a crack. The noises of people and animals had increased, the dance of flames looked to be bursting out everywhere, the smells of blood and excrement were strong, but the wildcat and badger seemed to have deserted the street in front of this house and gone for other prey. Jokan took the baby into his left arm again and ventured out. The fingers of his right hand twitched on his sword hilt, the two-year-old jerked at the rope, and he had no clear idea of what to do next.

A bear rose up at him from the shadows. Jokan screamed and swung up his sword for defense. The bear dropped on all fours, sniffed at the children, and lumbered on past them towards the center of town. Shaking but vaguely reassured, Jokan followed at a safe distance. The town was burning and filled with enemies, but the animals did not seem to be attacking Ironsteaders, and outside was the dark and the forest, with teeth and claws, quills and talons, and sharp, curved beaks that came tearing from all directions.

Ethaan and Arileth of One Another were in their late twenties or early thirties that summer. (Their branch of the forest people lacked a keen appreciation for the strict reckoning of years.) They had hunted alone in their pack of two since coming of age. They had never joined Senerthan's war. The forest god Wildrava, the earth god Oma, and the wind god Oriloth received more of their homage than the moon god Ormrathe; and they refused to risk their lives or change their mates—for their coupling had proved sterile—on command of the moon-god's son.

They sensed something abroad in the forest that night. The creatures were moving with a purposefulness beyond the usual search for food, and it promised ill for the night's hunt. Once Ethaan aimed at a stag, but it broke into a run, leaped over him and disappeared, not as if it had scented danger but as if it had heard a summons and the hunter was an unimportant obstacle in its path.

They spoke of retiring deeper into the woods. But they felt no urgency. The strangeness affected them as it seemed to be affecting the animals: with restless energy rather than fear. They decided to steal another look at the western warriors who were blundering their way north along the edge of the Long Forest. "If we shot a few arrows into their camp," said Arileth, "they would think Senerthan come again to halve their number." The thought of so many herders scurrying about timorously in the dark, combined with the curious mood in the forest, made the two hunters laugh like squirrels.

Their gaiety changed when they found Sarn One-arm's corpse. They had gone into Old Ironstead now and then over the years, for company or small trade, and they recognized One-arm as a man who had known the forest well—for a house-dweller—and could find his way about for almost a full day's walk in any direction from the town. He had been killed by an axe swung through his bowels, sometime between midafternoon and twilight.

"Herders' work," said Ethaan.

"Some of Senerthan's fools use axes now," said Arileth.

"Herders' work, none the less." Ethaan clenched his fist in disgust.

"Or the work of one of his own neighbors." Arileth clenched both her fists. "When have either herders or hunters struck at Ironstead?"

They spread Sarn out for the scavengers and went on, soberly. They saw two search parties of Ironsteaders—Iama the Impartial with Goran

Red-nose, Onar the Freckled with Ydissa the Skillful—but avoided them, suspecting everyone.

They found where the westerners' camp had been, and they read the signs of this group's departure toward Ironstead. They also found the oak tree with a fresh scar in its bark, the ropes and the imprinted ground which told them that a child had been cut free by someone who walked barefoot, that the child and a deer, after lying close for a time, had risen and gone in one direction, the Barefoot and a bewildering variety of animals in another, after the western warriors. Arileth touched one of the prints left by a bare human foot, and shivered.

They looked at the two trails—of the child and the deer, and of the warriors, the animals, and Barefoot. They looked at one another in the moonlight, joined hands, and began to follow the broader trail, moving warily toward Ironstead. They did not feel personally menaced; but someone or something was menaced tonight, and the threat lay taut and heavy about them.

It was sprung at last when they were within a shout of Ironstead. They heard the cries and noises of the onslaught. A few moments later, they glimpsed the smoke and glare of the first fires.

"We could have warned the Ironsteaders," Ethaan murmured.

"Until we found the camp," Arileth replied, "we could not have known which to warn. Even now, the Ironsteaders may have drawn away and entrapped the herders."

"And the animals?" said Ethaan.

Arileth shivered again. "And Barefoot. Does Barefoot fight with the westerners, or with the Ironsteaders, or against them all?"

They started forward again at a run. Here a badger, there some wolves, overhead a hawk or an owl sped past, but the hunters paid no more attention to them than they to the hunters. On reaching the last trees around Ironstead, the creatures hurried on into the town, while Arileth and Ethaan climbed a tall oak and watched.

Buildings burned—not so many as to show the success of any concerted plan of destruction, but enough, and sufficiently widespread, to show this was no accident of everyday house-life; and flames spread quickly in the dry wood and thatching when people had no effort to spare for dousing them. Ironsteaders and westerners fought in streets and houses, their shadows glimpsed at doors and windows. The townsfolk fought half-dressed, with whatever had come to hand, hoe or tongs or old, rusting weapon-model. The attackers fought in leather harness, with well-sharpened swords, spears and battleaxes, but they had the beasts and birds to fight as well as the Ironsteaders.

"Barefoot!" Arileth touched her mate's arm and pointed. The stranger could hardly be seen for the surrounding animals and westerners, but while in the other knots of battle the animals came at the invaders from back and flank, helping townsfolk only incidentally, around this one fighter they formed a circle of defense. And while elsewhere western warriors fled from the wild creatures, here they faced them, trying to close in, urged by two or three heroes.

Ethaan and Arileth cared nothing that the westerners were Senerthan's enemies, and little that the Ironsteaders were in some measure their own friends. They had always practiced what they conceived to be the neutral indifference of the gods.

But they did feel a bond with the animals they hunted. They began loosing their arrows.

Jokan Greenstick had taken advantage of another unbolted door. The house was not visibly in flames, and because of his own rush through the noise, confusion and glare on all sides, he hoped at first to find it a deserted refuge. He found instead another battle, and another fire.

One of his fellow westerners was fighting against two Ironstead women. The westerner had sword and axe, and blood gushed from his leg. The women had flails and household tools, and fought with unskilled desperation. None yet noticed Jokan or the crying children.

He made his decision before they did, stepped in behind, and drove his sword through his countryman's back.

It stuck, and the man, falling forward, jerked it from Jokan's hand. The women jumped out of the way. One of them screamed. They then faced Jokan.

He choked down panic and held up his empty right arm—his left was still curled around the baby. The two-year-old was yanking the rope at his waist. "I fight for you!" he cried. "I've saved your neighbor's children! Put out the fire—I'll guard you!"

The women hesitated a moment. Then the one who had not screamed dropped her flail and pulled her companion to the fire. They stamped at it, beat it with a blanket, scraped earth over it from the floor. One of them grabbed a water jar and began sloshing.

Jokan put down the baby, barred the door,

pulled his sword out of the corpse, and took his
place as guard. He did not loose the two-year-old.
He might need to draw it close for a hostage if the
women turned on him after putting out the fire.

Had he joined his countryman, they could surely
have defeated the Ironsteaders. It would have been
two against two, and the men warriors, armed and
trained. But the other man had been wounded already. The fire would have spread beyond fighting;
they would have been forced into the streets again,
Jokan with a companion crippled by a leg wound,
a companion whom the animals would probably
attack, unshielded as he would be with Ironstead
children. Jokan could still hardly trust that charm
himself.

He saw with relief that the man he had killed was
not one he had known very well. One of Birn's survivors, who had joined Edrik's three hundred—
Jokan's three hundred—after a terrible defeat by
Senerthan's forest devils. He wondered what would
happen to him if his fellow westerners won tonight.
But he doubted they could win, not with the forest
itself fighting against them. He hoped the women
would accept him as a friend. The fire seemed to be
shrinking under their attack. He hoped they could
persuade their neighbors. Whoever won this battle,
he saw he would have to beg, plead, cringe for his
life. He shuddered and pressed closer to the door,
stared at the window, clenched and unclenched his
hand on his sword, trying not to look into the
future.

Tilis the Supple seemed to be comparatively safe
in a yard between two buildings, narrow enough to
stay dark in the shadow, wide enough to catch the

cool wind stirring from the south. Invaders had run past, animals after them, but none had tried to enter this area, blocked as it was by the body of one of their comrades.

But some scavengers—Tilis thought they looked like foxes—had already set to work on the man's corpse, and she began to fear they would try to come at Dob Tanner next. She thought he was still alive, but he lay so still . . . if they should start to gnaw at him before he was truly dead! Suppose one of these houses took fire? The flames were spreading . . . it must happen sooner or later. Dob's cat had run away somewhere . . . if people could find safe nooks so easily! If anywhere could be safe tonight, or ever again in the world.

She wanted to run and help some of her neighbors whom she heard screaming—she was not sure which ones they were, she thought once she heard Iama, her old teacher, but Iama should be in the forest—safe?—searching for young Yma. She wanted to run from the danger in town and find Iama, find any of them in the forest; she wished she had joined the search when old Sarn One-arm failed to bring the child back by twilight, instead of staying with Kal the Tireless. Tireless! He had fallen soon enough before those warmonsters. She didn't know who was attacking Ironstead, or why—the town had nothing to do with the war in the southwest, and though there were rumors that Gilmar the Old was forming armies again, what did Ironstead possess, or what had it done in the last generation, to bring the northern ruler against it? Was this some sort of practice, some training for warriors? And Kal's body, smashed to gobbets only an hour after . . . Who were these invaders, that the forest animals chased them like hunters?

She wanted to crouch here in safety forever, but she knew safety would not stay with her here for even another hour. She could not be safe anywhere for long, not even by the side of that stranger who had come and gone shouting for . . . which one of her neighbors?

The town was not large, and this yard was nearer its edge than its center. There was still a dark swathe, not yet fire-spotted, between Tilis and the woods, and neither invaders nor animals seemed to have come from that direction for several moments. Tilis began dragging Dob toward the forest, holding him with her left hand while keeping her grip on the handle of the stone-edged sword.

There was thunder in the distance, and dark clouds were moving towards the moon. Strange. There had been no signs of a coming storm all day, until now.

Edrik Short-shoulder had been among the first to connect the long-haired woman with the madness of the animals. Maybe Senerthan had found a way to train and enlist the forest creatures—these eastern devils seemed capable of anything in their own region, even those who did not claim to be the children of gods. Edrik was too active a captain to ponder the mystery any deeper at this moment, or to give way to terror at the thought that his people might really be fighting against gods. The hunters' moon god was at the fulness of his strength tonight, but all the more reason not to look up and tremble and lose one's own purpose. "Dulanis and the Cauldron!" Edrik shouted again. His dripping shoulder bound around hastily with an Ironstead sheet, both comrades and townsmen lying dead and Tilis the Supple's house fired behind him, he plunged back into the street, intent not on the woman who had managed to finish Yrn Broadjaw, but on the one who had led the animals into his line of warriors.

He rallied three men to him on the way. Several others were too far gone in fear or battlelust to answer his call. These he cursed. Others were already corpses or too riddled with wounds to follow. These he left without pause or promise. The first man who joined him, Gellan Pinchnostril, fell in a skirmish with two Ironsteaders and several animals, but Orn Wheytooth came in time to help Edrik and Gort Broadmiddle (whose face was masked with blood) fight clear.

They found her at last, standing in a doorway and keening in a sorrow that had nothing to do with the destruction around her. Edrik and his men did not know that she was called Wildraith or that the doorway she stood in had once been Ylsa the Widow's and Wildraith wailed at finding the place empty and deserted, Ylsa's last, uneaten meal of cheese crusts and bean porridge growing mold in its dish. They guessed only that to kill her might be their one hope of breaking the wild creatures' attack.

Orn had a spear, and Edrik commanded him to throw it. It went a little wide, and in an instant the beasts were springing in to protect Wildraith. She looked at the spear, picked it up, and threw it back, so clumsily one could not have said whether she threw it at Orn, or to him. He was even then going down beneath a wildcat, but Gort cleaved the animal with his axe and Orn escaped with a badly chewed right forearm, in time to regain his spear.

One by one, other westerners gathered to Edrik's shouts. Birn was among the first to come, and both leaders together mustered a strong effort.

Thick clouds covered the moon, but only those who, like Tilis the Supple, were escaping from town missed its white light. Those who fought on in the flickering glare did not. Nor did Ethaan and Arileth, since they were aiming into the fireglow.

Arileth's first arrow took Edrik Short-shoulder in the throat.

As he fell, a stoat sprang up over his corpse and jumped at Birn, fastening its teeth in his forearm. To Birn it seemed as if Edrik's soul had spurted out and turned on him. His courage broke and he fled. Orn Wheytooth and Annis Drymouth, one of the few women among the invaders, tried to rally their comrades again, but arrows were coming from the sky, as it seemed—three more men fell with shafts through neck or brains, Gort Broadmiddle caught two in the flesh and fat about his waist, and when Orn himself saw one in his own upper right arm and turned from the attack, Annis and the other survivors broke and fled as well, the animals chasing hard behind them.

Wildraith leaned back against the wall and stared at blood flowing from a long gash in her left arm. She felt it, winced, and felt it again, as if intrigued by the sensation.

Many Ironsteaders owed their lives to the animals that night. Many others owed theirs to having been away in the search for One-Arm and Yma. Almost all owed what buildings and property survived to the sudden rain blown to them by weather gods whom they called variously Oriloth, Rathelis, Murn, and Kildrais.

Goran Red-nose was among the first drawn back to town by the turmoil, persuading his companion Iama the Impartial that if her daughter and Sarn One-arm had returned or been brought home before this began, they would now be in more danger than if they were still in the woods.

Goran's outbuildings were largely consumed, but his tavern itself escaped the flames. The invaders had drunk much of his home brew, but a few barrels of beer and wine remained whole, as did the small, buried supply of twice-distilled cordials and rich drink brought in by northern traders. Nevertheless, the damage ate into that measure of prosperity Goran enjoyed, and he would have been reduced to the level of his neighbors had they not suffered even greater losses. But for once he willingly levelled himself yet further. He opened his tavern as an infirmary for the wounded and his upper floor as a council room for those survivors judged able to plan recovery; and he shared out his remaining liquors without counting the charge, where need seemed sharpest.

When the western warriors had fled, most of the wild animals pursued them through the rain, leaving only the dead and wounded in the streets. A crowd of Ironsteaders replaced Birn's and Edrik's men around Wildraith, staring at her over the ring of corpses as the downpour washed blood from their skins and fire from their houses. The stranger looked up, saw Iama the Impartial among the onlookers, and said to her, "Your daughter is safe. We will bring her back before lightfall." Then she smiled. "You will keep peace with all creatures tonight."

An hour later, the stag brought Yma the Young to Goran's door, left her there and bounded away to the forest again. This insured Wildraith's right to sit in Goran's upper room with those who met as leaders, either because of their previous importance in the town, or because of their behavior in the crisis, or because they were unwounded and comparatively clear minded. As a group, they remained nervous of the stranger, who would tell them nothing about herself but her fixed-name, who used weapons and human speech so clumsily, and who yet seemed to command all wild creatures and assume a command—though choosing for the most part not to assert it—over humans as well. There was some unvoiced suspicion that she was a were-creature. But they would have felt more nervous to have her wandering out of their sight than sitting quietly among them—especially as Ethaan and Arileth the Free Hunters, who also sat with the council in Goran's loft, made it no secret that they, like the animals, had joined the battle to protect this stranger.

Goran's upper room was a loft that extended over three quarters of his floor space below and boasted a rail at its edge and a permanent stairway instead of a ladder. The rail was shoulder high to Goran, but it was open cross-work. In normal times he hung it with woven cloths, but the cloths were now in use as blankets, so the bare rail did not completely block the view between loft and one end of the lower floor. Tilis the Supple was among the women and men who moved around the tavern trying to help Ydissa the Skillful patch the injured. So were the two women whose door Jokan Greenstick had guarded whilst they fought their fire.

Jokan, by decision of Goran, Tark Crook-finger, Indreth the Old, and the two women he had helped, sat bound near the loft's edge, where part of the rail had been smashed by his looting comrades so that little remained to keep him from toppling ten feet to the floor if he made a false move. He dared not complain. He was the only invader left alive in Ironstead, and gods knew whether those of his companions who had escaped the settlers, once the battle was lost, had not met an even worse death in the forest.

Goran climbed up and down the stairs, dividing his efforts between those who planned, those who patched, and those who came to the tavern with further reports of damage. Water ran down one far back corner, where the rain, still falling heavily, came through the burned thatch. Iama sat in the other back corner, comforting her own child Yma and a ring of tiny ones, including Jokan's two, whose parents had been lost. Onar and Ydissa had found the body of Yma's father, along with that of a headless westerner; but it was unlikely that Iama the Impartial would wither and die like a widowed spouse, for she had never been married to Wem the Old or anyone else, and she had already demanded care of the orphans.

Wildraith leaned against the wall, about midway between the watery corner and Jokan Greenstick, and stroked a wolf with a bandaged foreleg and a badger with a bandaged neck. The wounded wild creatures were being carried in and tended like the wounded townsfolk. Wildraith had not spoken of this, but the Ironsteaders felt it was both grateful and prudent.

"We could be worse off," said Goran, climbing to the upper room again with a pitcher of beer and another report for the council. "Onar says the crops are sound enough, except for a few places where some of the warmonsters crashed through on their way in. Whether we'll have enough to brew beer this winter . . . But we'll have the food, bar bad weather and late-season blight."

"And the stores were low at this time of year anyway," said Tark Crook-finger.

"All the less in those storerooms that were spared to fill the loss of those that were burned," said Indreth the Old.

Goran wiped his forearm across his mouth. "If I can share out my last liquor, those of us who still have storerooms can share with their neighbors."

"Fewer stomachs to fill, at least," said Rol Furchest.

"And fewer arms to gather in the harvest," said Indreth.

"A lot of rebuilding to do before the cold weather, too," said Tark.

"Be thankful you don't live farther south," said Ethaan. He and Arileth had once been as far south as the Great Curve where the Copper River looped into the Long Forest, and they had spoken with hunters and traders who had wintered in the foothills of the Whitepeak Mountains. "Most of our northern winters can be survived in a leafless thicket, at need."

"This is like to be a hard winter," said Indreth, "and we are house dwellers, Ethaan, not hunters with the living skins tanned like leather over our bones. And even at best our meals will be thin between now and harvest."

Goran took a drink of beer. "A lot of heavy work for hungry bodies."

"Your town is full of slain animals." Arileth spoke to the Ironsteaders, but looked at Wildraith as if asking her a question. "You would be wise to smoke their meat and use their pelts."

Wildraith nodded. "And slain humans. You would be wise to smoke their meat, too."

Iama and the children had not heard, but the others stared at Wildraith. Tark, Rol, and Ylith the Short drank beer from mugs that shook in their hands. Jokan shuddered, even at risk of overbalancing himself.

Wildraith returned their gaze, and after a few breaths the puzzlement cleared from her face. "Ah! You do not do that. Not here. Not now. Forgive me, I forget. My body is hungry and I thought of your hunger."

"Who are you?" whispered Arileth. It was the first time any of them had dared ask since the stranger told them her fixed-name. "Where have you come from?"

Wildraith shrugged. "From a far . . . place."

Ethaan took Arileth's hand and added his question to hers. "Do you have trait-names in that place?"

Wildraith smiled. "Trait-names. Yes, I need a trait-name, too. What would you give me?"

"Wildraith of the Animals," said Ethaan.

Seeing that his boldness seemed to please her, some of the others began to suggest trait-names.

"Wildraith the Prudent," said Indreth the Old.

"Wildraith of the Long Forest," said Goran Red-nose.

Tilis the Supple had climbed up to ask Goran if he could spare more brandy for Dob Tanner's head wound. "Wildraith Dark-eyes," she said, pausing on the top steps and leaving her question about the brandy unasked. She had noticed what few of the others except Arileth and Ethaan had ventured to notice, that there seemed to be no circle of color between the sightpoints and the whites of Wildraith's eyes, even when she gazed into a flame.

"Wildraith Straight-limb," said Tark Crook-finger.

This time Iama the Impartial heard enough of the talk to gather its purpose, and from her corner she supplied, "Wildraith the Preserver."

"Wildraith of the Far Woodlands," Arileth said softly.

Jokan Greenstick swallowed hard, craned his head to look up at the stranger as if hoping he might resemble a pleading hare, and suggested, "Wildraith the Kind."

Wildraith laughed. "Wildraith of the Many Names." She turned her head, studied Jokan Greenstick, and laughed again. "I will take this boy."

Jokan caught his breath and almost fell off the edge of the loft. For a moment no one spoke.

Then Goran said, "Curse us for fools, you asked for food a while ago, and we forgot. I'll bring you something right away."

"Wildraith the Hungry?" she replied, watching Goran squeeze down past Tilis, who still stood poised on the stairway. "Find food for all," Wildraith called after the tavernkeeper. "It is Ironstead the Hungry."

Tark Crook-finger got to his feet, hauled Jokan a few paces away from the edge, and scowled down at him. "Aye, take this one and welcome. It'd be kill him or watch him all the time, and his work wouldn't be worth the food he'd take out of our bowls."

Wildraith grinned at Tark and the other Ironsteaders. "You think I will eat him. No. I have this sword, and with it I am Wildraith the Clumsy." She kneaded her bandaged arm, and a few stains of

fresh blood seeped through the cloth beneath her
fingers. "He will show me how to lose this trait-
name. Then not so many animals will die to preserve me."

Jokan released a long sigh.

Arileth rose, crossed the floor, and crouched a
few paces from Wildraith. "We can teach you to
use bow and arrow, spear and knife. Take us, too.
I will never hunt my meat again, if you forbid it."

Ethaan came up behind Arileth and stood with
his hand on her shoulder, both of them gazing at
Wildraith.

She nodded. "Yes. Come. The hunting meat . . .
we will talk of it when we are hungry."

"Wildraith of the Many Names," said Tilis.
"You came looking for—Ylsa the Widow? Ylsa
Tender-face?"

"Ylsa of the Many Names," said Wildraith.
"Now she is not here."

"I can help you find her."

"You know where she is now?"

"No," Tilis confessed, "but I know her by
sight."

"And I do not?" said Wildraith.

"I—for a moment you thought—I thought you
mistook me for her—when you broke in to warn
us. And we're not alike . . ."

"No." Wildraith smiled again. "So you will
come with me, too, Tilis the Supple. We are five."

Chapter 5.

For the second time that summer, Birn Nine-toes faced the work of gathering survivors after a lost battle.

The Ironstead fighting had been even more disastrous than that earlier conflict with Senerthan's hunters; and while in fact the birds and animals pursued the westerners six or seven bowshots beyond town and then formed a ring of defense to prevent any invaders from returning, to the fugitives it seemed that every rustle in the rainy forest meant some creature about to spring at them from the bushes. For the rest of the night, a rabbit starting across a westerner's path or a grasshopper striking his leg in its half-flight was enough to send him running again. By daylight, however, a few warriors were beginning to find one another.

The first comrade Birn met, in the before-dawn darkness well out of sight of the smoldering town, was Annis Drymouth. Unmotherly, unsympathetic, sharp-tongued, she was yet a comfort, allowing him to hold her for some moments before she spoke.

"Is that you, Birn Nine-toes, coward? We might have killed the were-thing despite all, if our last leader had led us."

"And died like your first leader? Our deaths don't serve the Butter-hair when the fight's lost anyhow."

Annis grunted and slipped away from his arms to continue her walk through the forest, using her sword for a staff to probe the wet, wooded night. "We'll have rust enough to clean away by morning," she said.

Birn moved with her, keeping hold of her left arm to avoid separation. "I'm the sole leader now. There will be no more arguments between captains."

"You as well as another. Only one course for us now anyway. Back across the river."

"If it had been my choice, we wouldn't have gone against that double-damned town."

Annis snorted. "Who's left to deny that? Pray we find someone else for you to command, youngster, because I won't follow you mindless if we're the only two."

For the rest of the night they could not tell what direction they were going, but hoped it was away from Ironstead. Daylight came at last through clouds so thick they could not locate the sunrise. But they heard groans, and followed the sound to Gort Broadmiddle, who lay heaving in a mire of forest floor, rainwater, blood, and other fluids.

"Are you still alive, you old ram?" said Annis. She rolled him until she found the wounds. One arrow had pinched him in the left side and he had pulled it through himself. The other had stuck and broken off, leaving its head and maybe a knuckle's length of shaft inside. "It's all the wool you wear under your hide that's saved you so far," said Annis. "That and the angles they hit. Well, we made a hell-forge out of that damned town last night for a while, and today it'd take the fire god himself to give us a flame."

But they found an old fallen tree that the rain had not soaked through. They managed to weave a half-tent out of branches (shaking off the water as best they could) and the leathers that, folded, served them as unsatisfactory armor and, unfolded, as even less satisfactory makeshift bedding. Birn still had the small tinder box of hammered copper, one emblem of leadership, which he had taken from Ulkan Lack-tooth's corpse, while Annis had her iron, flint, and little pouch of dry stuff, some of which was still dry. Eventually they got a fire started by hollowing a place for it in the dead tree trunk and feeding it with the decaying wood. The surrounding, all-prevailing wetness forestalled any danger of a high blaze.

They dragged Gort to the partial shelter, where Annis dug out the remaining arrowhead and cauterized the arrow wounds, as well as all the animal bites she found in his rump and elsewhere. She and Birn scorched each other's minor injuries, after which all three of them slept. They felt safer from the animals now, since Gort had been left alone so long, helpless as he was; but Annis and Birn propped his large body at the edge of the cramped shelter, making him a barrier between themselves and the woods.

Another westerner, Utran Long-legs, found them before they woke. He had so far conquered last night's horror that, finding a wounded squirrel trying to drag itself up a tree, he had finished it off and carried it along. He now squatted near the shelter and ate the squirrel raw while his comrades were still sleeping. He flung its skin and bones as far as he could to hide the fact that he had not waited to share the meat. Then he too slept, rolling close enough to enjoy Gort's body heat.

Gort survived. Annis continued to credit his luck and his fat, and also the rainfall that helped cool his fever through the delirium that began late in the afternoon and lasted much of the night. The rain changed to a drizzle, which had become a light fog by the second morning, but this time they thought they made out a redder dawn glow in one part of the sky than elsewhere, and started away from it, Birn notching trees to keep their path straight while Annis and Utran pulled Gort along, his dragging feet leaving an additional trail, though it soon oozed away in the sodden ground.

The high trees and an echo reflection on the other side of true sunrise had deceived them, and for two days, the overcast, showers, and drizzle continuing that long, they moved east, deeper into the Long Forest. They found four more comrades. Two were already corpses, and one claimed he was not badly hurt but fell and died within an hour. They found he had suffered a long thrust from something like a spear, called it a wonder he had survived so long, and left him behind them. The fourth they found towards evening of the second day. Since they would soon need to stop for the night, they made camp around him (little as they had to make it with) and tried to patch him as they had Gort, but his wounds were festered beyond easy searing, and by dawn he, too, was dead.

That day the clouds broke and Birn's party saw their mistake. They turned back, and about mid-afternoon found a corpse lying across their trail that had not been there before. Utran Long-legs recognized the body, by its left hand, as Gund Eight-fingers. Gund had a couple of small, cauterized and healing wounds, probably from the attack on Ironstead, and one fresh hole in his head, where they guessed an arrow had been shot and pulled out again.

"Ironsteaders this far?" said Gort.

Annis grunted. "Senerthan's devils, more likely."

"We'll strike south," said Birn.

"Your command, Nine-toes," said Annis. "Senerthan's hunters run these whole bloody woods, length and breadth, of course." But this was the only comment any of them cast on Birn's decision.

So they turned southeast. It was harder to keep their direction since they no longer dared gash trees or leave any other marks to keep themselves going straight. Instead, after finding unmistakable evidence that they were walking in circles, by coming upon Gund Eight-fingers lying as they had left him, they devised a method of stringing out to hold their course. Birn went ahead; Gort, still leaning on Utran's shoulder, came next; and Annis kept up the rear. They would separate as far as they could without losing sight of each other. Then, at an arm signal, Annis would move up to Birn's place, and he would forge another length ahead. It was slow progress, especially when the forest was thick, and they learned that even using themselves as trail markers, they were wisest not to travel at all when clouds hid the sun and all shadows everywhere merged together.

They made fires only rarely, when they felt a desperate need for extra warmth—all of them were now suffering colds from their long exposure—and when they could find wood dry enough not to smoke much. They never had a fire at night. No

Wendy Adrian Shultz

animal or bird had attacked them since the fighting at Ironstead, so that their horror of the creatures had worn off. But their fear of Senerthan's hunters had not.

Ylsa the Widow was better acquainted with the forest and hunters' tricks of finding direction therein. But she had nowhere to run, except away from her old life—no motive to keep herself alive, save the instincts of her body. It did not matter to her if she went in circles, as long as the circles did not bring her back to Ironstead. So she wandered, sometimes dropping down exhausted in the day, sometimes awakening at night and running in the darkness from her memories, mindlessly killing and eating when small creatures or edible plants came within her reach and her stomach told her hand to catch and thrust them into her mouth, drinking when the rain fell on her and when she fell into streams or pools. She might have made the conscious effort and killed herself, but in these days and nights she blocked out human thought with such success that death and survival became equally indifferent to her.

The night came when, running from another nightmare in the darkness between moonset and sunrise, she fell over a human body. It was not dead, but asleep.

The sleeper woke, turned, shouted and thrashed out. Other forms moved into play, taking the shape only of noises—shouts and grunts, breathing and slapping sounds. There was a long struggle, half wrestling and fighting, half exploratory groping, filled with human voices that Ylsa's mind still would not sort into words and meanings. At last the confusion resolved itself into bonds around her arms, legs, and face, and into a panting, muttering wait for daylight.

As she lay there in the dark, half stifled by the damp and smelly gag poking up against her nose, unable for the first time to run from her thoughts, her madness rose, swelled, twisted tight upon itself and finally broke, shattered and drained away. She began to think again.

Dawn came slowly through the trees. Bit by bit, the shapes that had bound her and melted again into sounds resolved into visible shadows, then shadowy people. Twisting her head, she counted four.

She was used to dirt. In the work press of summer and the cold of winter, only people like Iama and her apprentice Tilis made time to wash regularly; for the others, a bath was a rare enjoyment. But these four people were dirty beyond the labor of harvest. Their stench was not so offensive to her, muffled as it was by the cloth of the gag and accustomed as she was to the smell of her own race. Indeed, after running alone so long, she found a hominess in the odor. But their dirt made it impossible to tell who they were. The morning light, though it came from a clear sky, only turned them from black shapes to smudged brown ones.

She did not think they were hunters, because hunters strove for a greater measure of cleanliness. It made their scent less obvious to the game. She assumed they were some of her neighbors from Ironstead. She must be as unrecognizably filthy as they, body and clothing, but if they had known her when there was no light to confuse their eyes, she could understand why they had bound her, in all friendship. She had been a madwoman. She thought she had been making ugly sounds. The gag would be a favor to their own ears.

Reason had returned, but caring had not. She felt little besides exhaustion. She dozed while waiting for them. When she woke, one of them was saying, ". . . and have to bury it."

"Too much time, Drymouth," said another.

"Nothing to dig with," said a third.

"We've got eight hands," said the first. "I suppose Broadmiddle's arms should be fit for a little work, if his horn's so ready. We've got our blades and all the bloody branches we want, and the ground's still mud. Wouldn't take any more time than this clever idea of yours about horning it."

"Damn you, Drymouth." The voices were so harsh and hoarse that Ylsa had trouble telling them apart, but she did not recognize them as belonging to any of her neighbors, and they spoke, between hawks and coughs, with a drawl more like her husband Forn's, who had come northeast from the Copper River settlements, than like any native Ironsteader's.

"It's a female. I felt her well enough getting a grip on her last night."

"You'd feel female parts in a he-bear, Utran Long-legs, if he was squeezing you tight enough."

"Female or male, Annis Drymouth, I say we use it while we can. Gods know when we'll get another chance."

"Aye, and you might as well be a dead treestump, Drymouth."

"Use a dead treestump, then," said Annis Drymouth. "You'll serve the Butter-hair as well one way as the other."

"Kill her and leave her," said a fourth, with a

slightly higher or slightly clearer voice.

"Aye, but first use her," said Broadmiddle or Long-legs.

"Leave her to show where we've been, Nine-toes?" said Annis Drymouth. "That's your leader's wit?"

"One more body, what bloody difference?" said the higher, clearer voice. "We'll untie it."

"The others were our own, Nine-toes," said Drymouth. "This one might be a forest devil of Senerthan's."

"Or another one of ours."

Drymouth gave out a barking sound that ended in a cough. "Clever captain! Telling us to kill someone who might be one of our own. No, Nine-toes, maybe you never learned all Edrik Short-shoulder's people, or even all of the Lack-tooth's, but I knew them. If this is a woman, she's not Tana Greyhair or Nellis One-breast, or Durana Scarmiddle from Lack-tooth's three hundred, and we were the only women. She's either a forest spy or an Ironsteader."

There was a murmur of assent from two throats, but Nine-toes insisted, "Would any of us know the others, Annis Drymouth? Now?"

Drymouth grunted and stepped over to Ylsa. "Awake, nightcomer?" Half untying and half tearing the ragged cloth, catching countless of Ylsa's hairs in the process, she got the gag off.

I was beautiful, thought Ylsa. Beautiful enough to have apprenticed myself to Iama the Impartial. If I had needed her.

"Unh," said Drymouth. "Well, she hasn't shouted. One of Senerthan's spies would probably have shouted."

"Unless she knew none of Senerthan's hunters

were close enough to hear," said Ylsa.

Her defiance seemed to please Drymouth, whose tone twisted in banter. "Or unless she understood a shout would've brought my fingers down around her throat. They're bony old fingers, nightcomer. I can think of more comfortable ways to be strangled. Who are you?"

"Ylsa of Ironstead."

"Female," said Drymouth. "Fertile?"

"I've borne."

"And maybe could again? Age?"

"Seven winters," Ylsa said bitterly.

"Not your brat's. Yours."

Ylsa could not remember that at once, nor did she see much reason to calculate it for the benefit of Annis Drymouth. "Near thirty."

Drymouth got to her feet and stood over Ylsa. "Between you and Lack-tooth and Short-shoulder, Birn Nine-toes, you've lost near six hundred this summer. Might as well take one back to the Butter-hair for breeding replacements."

"If we can get her back without her putting a blade through our spines," Nine-toes said in a surly voice.

"We've led prisoners back before," said one of the other men.

"When we were a fighting force, Broadmiddle," said Nine-toes. "Not when we were four snotty, flea-ridden stragglers."

Drymouth snorted. "So you finally admit it, Nine-toes. You're nothing but the captain of a miserable pack of lost fugitives, and not likely to pick up any more able-bodied members for your command until we're back across the river, if then. Think the Butter-hair will give you another three hundred if you don't bring her anything to show for this year's march except a barren old blade-slinger and a couple of scrabby survivors?"

Ylsa pushed and contorted herself to a sitting position. "I'm a free Ironsteader. I'm damned if I'll grow any children for your worm-eaten war."

"Near thirty," said Nine-toes. "Should still have ten or twelve bratlings in her, maybe more. Males to fight, females to breed—"

Drymouth cackled. "You think the Butter-hair's a god? Better tell her this one's a boy-breeder."

"Almost thirty now, and only one brat to show for it," said the one who, by his girth, must be Broadmiddle.

"Na, seven, wasn't it?" said Long-legs.

"One," said Ylsa. "One with the strength of seven. One with so much joy and beauty the forest god herself was jealous, curse her."

Drymouth hacked and blew her nose in a leaf. "Boy or girl?"

"Son. My Horj Brown-eyes."

"Boy-breeder," said Drymouth. "Good. Dulanis Butter-hair must be about forty by now. She wouldn't get much use out of this one's daughters."

"Dulanis Butter-hair is ever young, ever beautiful, ever gracious," said Nine-toes.

Drymouth coughed again and spat. "So is Senerthan of the Long Forest, eh? They'd both still better pray their little war's done with before they need any sons from the newest crop of daughters. Or before Gilmar the Ever-old, Ever-ugly, and Ever-mean comes down on us all."

Ylsa saw that unless these western herders decided to take her back for a stock cow, she would die. She guessed she could throw away her life by telling them that for two years before and seven following her son's birth she had tried to conceive again, by a score of males who had proved their fertility elsewhere. But she was too proud to throw her life, soured as it was, to these filthy, snivelling brutes. Or to plead with them. "I had one child," she said. "So fine a child I did not wish more. All the fertility of seven years went into the fusing of that one child."

"Would've been a warrior among warriors, eh?" said Annis Drymouth. "Think you can put your next seven years' worth into another hero, Ironsteader? Not that you'll find many of our men willing to put all theirs into one shot every seventh year," she added with a laugh.

Ylsa looked around at the three males and shrugged. "I'll do better than breed your Butter-hair a warrior. I'll make her one out of myself."

"You?" said Long-legs.

"Maybe." Drymouth put a violet blossom on her tongue and sucked at it. "The Ironsteaders had enough fight in them six nights ago."

"Only because of that bloody were-thing," said Nine-toes.

Ylsa gathered that the westerners had made an attack on Ironstead and been beaten off. She judged it best not to show her ignorance. "Aye," she said. "There's a were-beast waiting to be wakened in most of us Ironsteaders. Loose me and I'll fight the best of you."

"Likely enough." Drymouth chewed her violet. "Beside us, you're fresh and healthy."

"You've been running how long in the woods?" said Ylsa. "Six nights? I've been running twice that long, or more." She realized that she had confessed her absence at their attack on Ironstead, but she would not try to explain it away. She sat upright and scowled at them.

"Maybe she's the were-beast herself," said Nine-toes.

"Better loose me and fight while it's still day," Ylsa replied, wondering what they had seen at Ironstead.

Broadmiddle rose and stamped around the little glade, leaning heavily on a thick branch, to leer down at Ylsa. "Barehanded?"

"Bare hands, bare claws, bare fangs. Against all your metal, if you like."

Broadmiddle grinned. "If I win, I take you."

"Unh," said Ylsa. Broadmiddle might well win, but only by leaving not enough of her to be conscious of his horn.

"And if she is the were-thing. . ." said Nine-toes.

"She's not. We would've known it by now." Annis Drymouth hunched down and got Ylsa untied. They had used their belts and boot lacings, leather and sheep's wool, for ropes. Drymouth tossed them back to her comrades, then stood out of the way, wiping her nose on her own wool belt before putting it back around her tunic.

Broadmiddle, meanwhile, had got his weapons in hand, a long sword that he used instead of the tree branch to prop himself up while he waited, and a short axe. He was still grinning, but Ylsa noticed he had moved several paces away.

She did not get to her feet at once, gambling that he would not rush until she stood, and thinking to make as much as she could from his uncertainty that she might change into some forest animal. She tensed and loosened her muscles several times, working out the stiffness. Her health, like theirs, was going. She felt the aches beginning from within, the ugliness in her throat. But she would have enough strength for this fight.

She glanced around. The glade was small, the ground uneven; a tangle of green, twiggy growth, chiefly bramble and birdbane, began five paces to her right, spreading out between the trees. Somewhere beyond the thicket she heard a stream purling. Broadmiddle's companions had weapons, and were either clutching them tight or wearing them close in their harness.

But Broadmiddle had let his tree branch fall between him and Ylsa, a little to her left. Either he was slow witted, or too much the herder to think of anything as a weapon that had not been forged for the purpose.

Slowly she hunched up to a squatting position. He raised his axe. She lunged for the branch. He started forward. She hissed at him, catlike. He paused, and in that moment she swung the branch at his knees.

It connected with a loud crack. Broadmiddle howled and fell.

Ylsa stood. Broadmiddle had caught himself against a lime tree, but he was panting and grimacing. Ylsa took a step forward. Before she could take another, she felt an arm around her neck and a body pressing up to her back. One of Broadmiddle's comrades had jumped her from behind, and the other two stood watching, enjoying it or maybe waiting their turns. She felt a sharp edge at her right side.

Broadmiddle grinned and pushed away from the tree. Ylsa swung her branch again. This time it broke against his waist. He squealed, sobbed, and clutched his elbow to the bruised fat, but did not

fall. His friend jerked up and back on Ylsa's jaw
and sawed his sword through the coarse cloth of
her tunic and the upper skin. There was not much
else than skin between his blade and her ribs.

A few strands of white fiber still held the two
ends of her branch together. She swung once more.
The longer end finally snapped and went flying—it
glanced off Broadmiddle's sword arm. Ylsa threw
her left arm up and back and dug the end she still
held at her captor's face. The splintered cross-sec-
tion hit hard. He screamed and loosed her. His
sword bit at her ribs as he fell back, but not deeply
enough to cripple her.

Broadmiddle was coming at her with axe and
sword. She ducked and thrust the stub of her
branch into the area of his navel, hitting at his
groin with her other hand. One of his blades grazed
her shoulder as he flopped over her. He landed on
his back and lay there howling, his companion
partially caught beneath him.

Pressing her arm to her own bleeding right side,
Ylsa glanced around. Nine-toes was standing with
legs wide and weapons—sword and dagger—lifted.
Drymouth was leaning on an oak, laughing and
coughing, spear held loosely, sword and dagger
still sheathed.

Ylsa leaped at Drymouth and wrested away the
spear before Drymouth recovered from surprise.
The two women grappled, Ylsa to keep the spear
and get the sword, Drymouth to get back the one
and keep the other. Nine-toes advanced. Ylsa
jabbed the spear at him. He got closer. She kept
jabbing the spear. A couple of times she struck
him, but not deeply or vitally. She managed to
keep Drymouth between them most of the time,
and that was her main protection. Drymouth was

shouting at Nine-toes and the other men.

Ylsa threw the spear and used both hands to go for the sword. She had a grip on its hilt and kept it tight while Drymouth beat her arms with hard fists, first biting, then numbing nerves and making the scabbard jolt up and down on their legs. Drymouth reached for the dagger that was sheathed at the side of her waist, and Ylsa clamped down and caught that hand beneath her elbow.

Ylsa almost relaxed, then put everything into one jerk. Something snapped at the top of the scabbard—a leather guard-strap—and the sword slid partway out. Its double edges shirred Drymouth's side, raised blood. Drymouth pulled away and Ylsa got the sword completely out and jumped back, letting Drymouth avoid the blade however she could.

Ylsa got her back against a tree and panted for a moment. Drymouth was getting up and drawing her dagger. Nine-toes was coming around, carrying his weapons ready. Long-legs had pulled out from beneath Broadmiddle and was advancing behind Nine-toes, armed with sword and short spear. Even Broadmiddle seemed to be partly recovered; he was sitting up hefting his axe as if he knew how to use it as a throwing weapon.

Ylsa had not gone into this fight with any clear thoughts of an afterwards. Now she made the conscious decision to die at once rather than be raped and left wounded and festering. She shouted and hurtled herself towards Broadmiddle, presenting her back to Nine-toes and Long-legs, her side to Drymouth as she dashed past.

Broadmiddle shrieked and threw his axe. It went wide. Drymouth tackled Ylsa round the legs and brought her to the ground. Ylsa twisted halfway up

and swung her sword now at the woman who held
down her legs, now at Nine-toes. Some part of her
mind was thinking that she should not kill them
before they killed her, but she must not give them
the chance to disarm her before she was dead. Another part of her was feeling: *Kill them all and survive.*

"Enough!" shouted Drymouth. "Hold off, all
you slime-spawn."

The men fell back. Ylsa swung once more at the
other woman. Dodging beneath the swing,
Drymouth slid up and grabbed Ylsa by the throat
and one shoulder.

"Listen, free Ironsteader," Drymouth hacked at
Ylsa's face, squeezing her throat beneath the jaw,
"you handle that sword like a soupbone, but
you've got the blood for fighting. I'll make a warrior out of you, if you'll guide us out of this stink-
ing forest."

Ylsa did not respond. They sat for a moment like
stew seething in a kettle, Ylsa unable to breathe
and Drymouth apparently waiting for her to nod.
Ylsa saw Drymouth's dagger lying on the ground
where she must have dropped it in order to use her
fingers. Ylsa lifted the sword and let it fall from her
hand. Drymouth grunted and nodded but did not
loose her hold. Ylsa seized the dagger and brought
the knob of its hilt down hard on Drymouth's
stranglehold. Drymouth cried out and pulled away
her hand.

"I'll fight for Dulanis Butter-hair," said Ylsa,
"but only if she pays."

"She'll pay," said Drymouth. "But only if you
show her you can use weapons. The way they were
made to be used. Will you get us out of this forest?"

"For pay."

"Aye," said Nine-toes. "The Butter-hair will reward you well."

Drymouth found another leaf and honked her nose into it. "For what? You think Dulanis will be overjoyed to get us four back after this summer? We'll pay you ourselves for guiding us out, Ylsa Bare-hands. A weapon and two sheep from each of us, the weapons when we get to the Copper River, the sheep when we get back to our own lands. Meanwhile, share alike in food and shelter, and we'll start your training once we're across the river."

"You'll start training me tomorrow," said Ylsa. "An hour a day, before we move on. To prove your good faith. Share alike in food and shelter's no pay. I'll probably find you more than you find me." She looked around at the men. "And I don't couple unless I choose. I keep this dagger now." As Broadmiddle and Long-legs started growling protests, she added, "Use dry tree stumps."

"No coupling until you choose," Nine-toes agreed. "But no dagger. Not yet."

"Let her keep it," said Drymouth. "She's right. I wouldn't trust you bullhorns either. And I'd rather risk getting my own blade in my back some night than rot in these damn woods."

Ylsa coughed and nodded. Her throat was so raw she could have drunk blood in order to get something hot down it. "We'll start tomorrow. Today we shelter up, make a fire, kill some meat, seethe some leaves and berries, get some rest."

In fact, they spent two days there before moving on to the west and a little to the south.

Chapter 6.

The first of the Middle Wells had been dug by the legendary Harnath Woolskin, father of the earliest Keepers of the Cauldron of the Ancient Hearth. When his blood heirs died out, Lanis Deepbosom dug the second of the Wells and earned the Cauldron. Her son dying young and childless, the man sometimes called Ytran and sometimes Yglan of Simple Words dug the third well, but his mother had come from the eastern forest, and his family held the Cauldron for only three generations before Dulanis Butter-hair's great-great-grandparents dug the fourth and latest of the Middle Wells.

From the time of Harnath to that of Dulanis, the Wells were little more than a favorite tenting place for the Ancient Hearth. Then Dulanis entered her war with Senerthan and made Middle Wells her first town. She paced out enough land for three hundred sheep, cows and goats, and the fodder to feed them through half a year, and had this area enclosed with a thick, high wall of earthwork and stone. The trees her predecessors had cherished for their shade reminded Dulanis of Senerthan's forest, so she had them cut down, for both symbolic and practical purposes, and fashioned into strong gates for her wall; she spared only the short, gnarled fruit trees and the oldest, largest poplar, which grew between the first and second wells and which she used as a central post for her chief tent.

This much work took more than one year, and when it was done she increased the protected area each winter by adding new semicircles to the wall. Inside, she and her people went on living in tents, much as they had on the open plains. The tents were now made with thicker posts, more deeply planted, and heavier layers of hide and cloth; and the animals' pens were of a more permanent construction than in earlier ages, and eventually a few inner shelters, principally storage sheds and a house for children and new mothers, were of earthwork construction.

One late summer afternoon in the sixteenth year of her war with the moon god's son, Dulanis sat on many cushions in her chief tent, drinking cold water from her great-great-grandparents' well and listening to Tanris of Everywhere, the newsbearer and storyteller. All the tent's rolling panels were open to the breeze, now and then the smell of roasting beef mingled with the live-animal odors brushed in by the soft winds, and as the newsbearer spoke, Dulanis pictured the tale in a town much like Middle Wells. The towns of Senerthan's territory were in fact much different, but Tanris suspected her listener's thoughts and in some measure played to them. Tanris was a spy for Gilmar the Old, but she was also a conscientious storyteller.

This is the tale she told Dulanis Butter-hair that afternoon. In outline and certain details, it resembles rather closely what had taken place twenty days before in Senerthan's woodland town New Crescent, in the depth of the eastern woodlands:

The Five came out of the forest and stood before the great oak-log gates of New Crescent. Two tall hunters, one slender girl with the grace and beauty of a harlot, one boy in the sheepskin of the western pasturelands, and the fifth a dark woman with blue-black hair and a long, straight sword as her only weapon.

They stood before the gates and the small harlot hailed Senerthan's guard. "Have any strangers come this way?"

The guard said to his young companion in the gatetower, "None stranger than these, and that tall woman in their midst the strangest." Then he called down to the Five, "Have you come to trade, to fight, or to join the forces of the moon god's son?"

The tall, dark woman smiled, but the harlot replied, "None of those. We're looking for Ylsa Tender-face, the Widow of Ironstead."

The guard looked at the two hunters, grinned at the harlot, and said a few words to his young companion, who slipped down from the tower and ran to Senerthan's high-roofed bower in the heart of town. The guard opened the gates to the strangers.

("How did he open the gates?" said Dulanis.

"By means of a pulley and wheels operated from the gatetower, First of Herders," said Tanris.

"You'll make a model for me later," said Dulanis.

"I will, at least, draw a picture," the other promised before continuing her tale.)

Senerthan himself was in New Crescent at that time, to choose from among the older children those boys best suited to join his forces young, as scouts and archers. The town was crowded: its own three hundred women, their children, the forty men assigned there this summer, as well as Senerthan's personal command of three hundred, and the three hundred of his young cousin Meleth. Senerthan's bodyguard, sixty of his best warriors, were gathered with him in the high-roofed bower. Ten of them, the best of the best, sat around him sharing talk and wine.

("Are there any women in Senerthan's personal command?" said Dulanis.

"A few in his command of three hundred. None in his bodyguard of sixty."

"It's true, is it, that he never mixes his own seed into his new stock of forest devils?"

"As true as it is that you keep yourself, First of Herders, though some of his people blame him for it. It's said he has not looked at another in that way since he looked at Dulanis the Keeper of the Ancient Cauldron."

Dulanis smiled and nodded for Tanris to resume the narrative.)

When the Five came before him, Senerthan the First of Hunters hardly glanced at the small harlot, though she was lovely, nor at the dark woman, though she it was who had drawn most attention from his people. To the youth in sheep's wool he said, "Are you a spy for Dulanis the First of Herders?" And when the youth replied that he was not, "Then you should be," said the moon god's son, "for once to have been the Butter-hair's is to be bound to her forever in eternal loyalty."

Then he looked at the pair of hunters, and he looked at them the longest. "I do not remember," he said at last, "having seen you among my warriors."

"We are free hunters from the far north," said the man. "Had we chosen to give our allegiance to any but one another, we might as rightfully have given it to Gilmar the Old."

"All the Long Forest is mine," said the moon

Wendy Adrian Shultz

god's son, "even that part of it that lies on the land Gilmar claims. Just as all herdlands between the northern ocean and the southern mountains belong to Dulanis of the West."

Some say that the dark woman smiled at that.

But Senerthan was still gazing at the two hunters. "You will remain here in New Crescent," he told the woman. "And you," he said to the man, "will make the sixty-first of my own bodyguard."

"We two are Of One Another," said the huntswoman.

"We do not march for three nights yet," said Senerthan. "If he implants you, you need not couple with anyone else."

"I will not be penned away to bear children for Dulanis Butter-hair's warriors to kill," said the huntswoman.

The huntsman said, "Tell us what you can of the Widow of Ironstead, and we leave as we come."

"We know nothing of the Widow of Ironstead," Senerthan told them. "Your three companions may leave us as they came."

The small harlot said, "We will leave again all five."

"As a special grace," Senerthan told the hunters, "you may both march with me. But only among my three hundred, not among my sixty."

"We need them more than you!" said the boy in sheepskin.

"They are hunters," said Senerthan. "You are dregs, and I am the moon god's only son. I argue with no one. Go or I give you to my young would-be warriors as targets to prove their worth upon."

Then the dark woman opened her mouth for the first time. "You are the moon god's son?" she said, and she laughed until the tears splashed from her dark eyes.

The First of Hunters stood and drew his sword,
long, light, and strong. That sword had withstood
the death throes of bear, boar and stag. It had
flashed all but unseen between many a human
enemy's ribs. But the dark woman drew her own
sword, that rippled like a thread of clear oil, and
shattered Senerthan's blade with one blow.

The First of Hunters loosed upon them all his
bodyguard, who had held back only until he
should give them the command, as if they were arrows waiting the snap of his bowstring. But the
Five—the two free hunters, the small harlot, the
boy in sheepskin, and the dark woman—grouped
together in a close knot and cut their way from the
high-roofed bower, through the enclosure, out of
the walled town, and through the half-hidden en-
campment of Senerthan's personal command.
They left behind not one of their own fingers, but
more than four hundred of Senerthan's people
dead and dying, forty-eight of his bodyguard, all
but one of the town's forty men, twenty-eight of
its women and three of the oldest boys, one hundred and thirteen of Senerthan's personal command and two hundred of Meleth's, besides at
least fifty who may not survive the wounds they
took that day.

The moon god's son has declared them outlaws,
and promised a quarter-godhood and a fistful of
gems to anyone, hunter or enemy, merchant or
northerner, who brings him one of their heads, a
double fistful of gems to anyone who brings one of
them alive for a death of Senerthan's devising. But
although the woodlands belong to Senerthan and
his hunters, the Five have disappeared so deeply
into the Long Forest that not even Senerthan's best
scouts have yet been able to track them.

* * *

When the teller had finished her tale, Dulanis sighed. "But Senerthan himself escaped uninjured?"

"They say that the moon god protects his son," Tanris replied.

Dulanis crooked her finger. "I do not believe in Senerthan's half godhood, any more than that dark woman did. Such a man as the First of Hunters needs no divine protection. But whom he has outlawed, I will outlaw. Instead of gems, I will give a sheep for every stone in a fistful of pebbles, as well as half Senerthan's reward when I send him the outlaws or their heads. But not the boy in sheep's wool," she added. "If he is indeed a renegade from my own people, I will punish him myself. Who is this Tender-face the Widow of Old Ironstead?"

Tanris shrugged. "No one knows, First of Herders, except the five who search for her."

"Has Senerthan outlawed her, too?"

"No."

"Then neither will I. They may be searching for her as their enemy. But we'll try to take them alive and learn the truth from them. Four hundred and thirty-one people he lost, you say?"

"Besides at least fifty who may not survive their wounds."

"I will caution my people not to attempt taking any of these five unless they can do it with trickery." Dulanis had been writing numbers with a bone stylus on a bit of bare earth between her rugs and cushions. "That would leave Senerthan little more than five hundred to keep New Crescent."

"If he is still in that town, First of Herders. It's one of his principal places of refuge and breeding, well hidden in the Long Forest though near the western edge."

"Well, you're neither herder nor hunter, Tanris of Everywhere. I will not ask you to guide us."

Tanris crossed her arms in a display of gratitude. "You are as gracious as your gods, First of Herders. I would merit outlawry myself if I sided with any people. But I'll give you what directions I can so that you may find New Crescent."

Dulanis smiled and ordered water drawn from her great-great-grandparents' well to refresh the newsbearer.

In fact, Wildraith and her companions had left fewer than twenty killed and wounded in New Crescent. Tanris had not increased the number as a mere embellishment. Twelve nights after leaving Middle Wells, she sat with Gilmar and told him that Dulanis Butter-hair was probably even now on the point of losing half a thousand warriors in an attack on a forest town she believed weaker than it was. Gilmar agreed that even if Dulanis made allowances for a storyteller's exaggeration, the fighting at New Crescent and in the surrounding woodlands was likely to prove the clinching circumstance he had awaited.

As for the Five, they were as much a riddle to Gilmar as to Senerthan and Dulanis. He, however, saw no reason to outlaw them. Like rains and mud, heat and dust, gadflies and disease, he regarded them as coincidental facts of nature that helped or hindered, sometimes at random chance and sometimes according to the way a crafty leader understood how to make them work more to his enemies' disadvantage than to his own.

Chapter 7.

Irinore of the New Growth had been born to hunters, the third child of six who survived to adolescence. Slow and deliberate in her movements, clumsy with bow and spear, she had left the Long Forest in about her twentieth year and made a small farmstead for herself on the eastern bank of the Copper River Valley. The fifth spring that she worked her land, Diran of the Small Curve came north from his grandparents' farmstead and joined Irinore on hers.

All this had been before Dulanis Butter-hair and Senerthan the moon god's son quarrelled over their game of chess. Now in the sixteenth summer of the conflict Irinore and Diran had nine living children, the oldest nineteen years of age and the youngest four. They lived close enough to Gilmar's frontier that the fighting had not broken into their lives, and they had enlarged their fields until they cultivated most of the land within Irinore's little curve of the river. Their three oldest children, Diran the Younger, Orineth, and Rivan, now spent each summer in a small house on the eastern edge of the farmstead to be nearer the outlying fields.

When Birn Nine-toes, Annis Drymouth, Gort

Broadmiddle, Utran Long-legs, and Ylsa Bare-
hands came out of the forest at last, staggered
across half a day's march of rolling grassland and
saw the small wooden house on the edge of an ex-
panse of waving wheat, barley and rye, Gort's first
suggestion was to seize the place by force.

"Force!" Drymouth snorted. "There's not
enough of you left to roll up for a ram and batter
the door down with, Broadmiddle."

"We can't beg them for food and shelter," said
Birn Nine-toes. "They may be enemies."

"So you want to attack them the way you attacked Old Ironstead?" By now Ylsa had learned
the story from her companions. "If you'd brought
your people to us as friends, Nine-toes, we might
not have been able to feed and house the lot of you,
but what we could spare would've been yours for
the honest trading."

"What do you want us to offer them in trade,
Bare-hands?" said Utran.

Annis Drymouth rubbed a corner of her thickly
grimed tunic between her thickly grimed fingers.
"We can pretend we're still warriors, and trade
them a truce for some decent food, a bath, and a
dry place to sleep."

So they went down to the house with their palms
spread out in peace. They found Rivan alone inside, cooking barley porridge for the evening meal.
He was eager enough to accept their trade of truce
for food, even to give them the whole pot of hot
porridge and open access to the small larder with
its bread, cheese, and smoked meat. While they
were sampling the skins and bottles of liquid to
find one that held wine, he slipped out the door.

Utran Long-legs discovered Rivan's absence and

a skin of cooking oil at the same time. He spat out his mouthful of the greasy stuff and said, "Damn kid's gone."

"So would you if you were hosting us," said Drymouth.

"Let him go," said Ylsa. "Unless you want to get lost in the grain fields looking for him."

"We could fire the crops," said Birn Nine-toes.

Ylsa snorted. "Hunters think if it can be grown in a single summer it's not worth saving. I'd expect more sense from herders."

"I'll watch the door." Drymouth grinned ironically. "If there's treachery, we can trade our lives dear and give the storytellers another tale to sell for their dinners."

"At least we'll die with full bellies." Gort Broadmiddle went on stuffing sausage into his mouth.

They had found one small bottle of wine—the three young people's summer supply for special occasions—shared it out and finished moistening their throats with beer and fermented milk by the time Rivan brought back his older siblings. They approached the house cautiously, but, reassured that the strangers were only interested in getting across the river to the western herdlands, let them gorge their fill, heated water for them to bathe, and found enough cloth to blanket them for the night. Diran the Younger did what he could to scrape their leather clean while Orineth and Rivan washed the rest of their clothes as best they could in the bath water.

Annis and Ylsa had enough strength of will to eat and drink sparingly, and Birn was able to stop before his stomach swelled too tightly, but Utran and Gort further strained the farmers' hospitality by being sick as colicked horses in the night.

At dawn the boy Rivan climbed to the roof, eager for an hour in fresh air away from the visitors. From the roof he could see beyond the tall grain to his parents' farmhouse, some fallow fields and still uncultivated land, the small steading of Soram the Mottled—their only neighbor within half a day's walk—and part of the Copper River. When he climbed down again, he went straight to his older brother and sister and said, "There's a boatful of people coming up the river from the north, and another lot coming along beside them on the land. I think there's a bunch on the west shore, too."

Diran the Younger went in to the five strangers and said, "If you're sincere in repaying us with peace, can you turn your fellow warriors away from our land?"

They came outside. Annis, Birn, and Ylsa, who were in better condition than Gort and Utran, climbed to the roof with Diran and squinted at the bodies of fighters moving southward by water and land. They were still too distant to see details of face, clothing, or harness, but Annis Drymouth frowned and struck her upper arm. "If those are either hunters or herders, I'll swallow my toenails. My guess is that Old Gilmar the Crafty's making his move at last."

"They're not your people?" said Diran.

"If they're our people," said Drymouth, "we'll join them and you'll be safe. If they're Senerthan's hunters, we'll leave them Broadmiddle and Longlegs while the rest of us try to outrun them, and you should still be safe, with a little storytelling. If they're Gilmar's people, we're all probably as good as dead."

"Gods of the Ancient Hearth!" Birn pointed to a group of warriors that had moved away from the main party and was setting fire to the few fields of Soram the Mottled.

"Don't ask the gods to do anything about it," said Ylsa. "There's no kindness in any gods."

Drymouth struck her own thigh. "Trust Gilmar the Old."

"What are they doing?" cried Diran.

"Burning their way down the river valley," said Drymouth. "He'll make sure the Butter-hair and the moon god's son can't change their minds and join forces against him."

This latter part of the summer had been wet, and the grain was not yet ripe. It took fire slowly and with much smoke, but the warriors were persistent.

"We're not part of the war!" said Diran.

"Neither was Gilmar until now." Drymouth started down the ladder. "I wonder how the Butter-hair would like playing chess with *him.*"

They kept none of the news from those who waited below.

"Only because we've helped you?" asked Rivan. "They'll burn everything in our curve of the river valley, only because we've helped you?"

"He doesn't know we're here," said Drymouth.

"But it's got to be Gilmar," said Birn. "Senerthan's a devil, but he wouldn't have any reason to do this. Neither would Dulanis Butter-hair."

"Any more than you had at Old Ironstead." Ylsa looked at the unclouded sky. "I don't think the rain god's going to aim his piss in the direction of this fire."

"Oh, gods!" said Orineth. "Our animals!"

"He'll roast them on the hoof, most likely, for

his people's dinner." Drymouth licked her lips.

The smoke from Soram's fields was visible now above the heads of Irinore's grain. Rivan began to sob.

"There's one hope, such as it is," Drymouth went on. "Gilmar's going to leave this valley a scorched waste, cut the whole south in half with no food for any army that tries to cross the river, but he might not care whether or not you settlers die in the burning."

"We might as well burn as starve," said Diran.

"Save your fleeces now and get back to the forest when Gilmar's past," said Drymouth. "If we can get to the river, maybe we can hide in the water near the bank."

"And hope they don't moor their damn boat on top of our heads," said Utran Long-legs.

"There's a cave," Rivan cried, but Orineth stopped him.

"They might not care about us farmers," she said, "but you're fighters—enemy fighters, if you're right and Gilmar's making war on Dulanis and Senerthan both."

Rivan turned and ran away into the swaying wheat.

"You can't leave us!" Birn shouted. "We'll be lost—"

Drymouth caught Diran's neck in the crook of her arm. "Go on, you," she told Orineth. "Go chase the little one. We only need one to guide us through your damn fields."

"Let my brother go," said Orineth. "I'll guide you."

"Orineth—" Diran half choked.

"Don't be a fool," she answered. "We've got to tell the rest of the family, and your legs are longer than mine. Maybe Gilmar's people won't bother with any of us unless we get in their way."

Drymouth nodded at Orineth and released Diran. He looked at his sister. She embraced him and whispered a few words. He shuddered, glanced at her face, gave her shoulders one last press and ran after the boy.

"Keep up with us or fry in what's left of your fat," said Annis Drymouth to her companions.

Orineth waved for them to follow and turned into the wheat at a different angle from that taken by her brothers.

"Hey!" said Ylsa suspiciously.

"Where are you going?" Birn demanded at the same time.

"I thought you wanted to go the quickest way to the river," said Orineth. "Would you rather risk being burned in my parents' house? I won't take you there."

"The river!" said Gort Broadmiddle with something like a squeak in his voice.

They passed into the wheat.

It bent before them, pressed in around them, clotted under their feet, brushed with stubborn, feathery resistance against their progress. They pushed and threaded through two fields at a slant. Gilmar's main land party was nearing Irinore's land. Utran Long-legs cursed and Birn ordered him to silence. They shushed on through the grain after Orineth, never quite sure that she would not dash away and leave them floundering alone. Now and then she paused until Drymouth drove her on by asking if she was lost in her family's own crops. Smoke started curling into view from the edge of Irinore's fields. The drafts of summer air seemed warmer already with the smell and distant crackles of burning. Annis Drymouth drew her sword and gave Ylsa her spear. Birn and Gort likewise went with their spears unslung and ready, Utran with sword drawn.

At last Orineth brought them out into a fallow field. They were still surrounded on three sides by tall grain, but the fourth side was open and exposed, and at each corner of this view some of Gilmar's warriors were firing the grainfields that pocketed them in.

Ylsa seized Orineth as Drymouth had earlier seized her brother.

"The Butter-hair! The Butter-hair!" screamed Orineth before Ylsa could choke her speech.

Gilmar's people saw them and shouted. Spears and arrows flew at once. Their aim was good. Birn threw his spear and staggered as an arrow caught him in the thigh. Another arrow appeared in Utran Long-legs' chest and a third in Orineth's upper arm.

Gort Broadmiddle, who had been farthest in the rear, gave one shriek and fled back into the grain.

"Damn!" cried Birn Nine-toes, hitting at the shaft in his leg. Then he straightened and drew his sword ready for the warriors who were rushing towards them. "Go on!" he shouted to his comrades. "I'll hold them off."

Annis Drymouth grinned. "You'll fall on your face, boy. You heard him," she added to Ylsa. "Kill the sneak if you like, but don't stick around." Then Drymouth walked to Birn and put her back against his. "You might have made a leader after all, Nine-toes," was the last thing either of them said before the enemy came within reach of their two swords.

Ylsa threw her spear at the foremost enemy, but she was no born westerner to stay and die. She dragged Orineth back into the wheat, loosed her neck but held fast to the arm with the arrow in it, and drew her knife. "To the river this time." She wrenched the young woman's arm. "No more shouts or sneaks."

Orineth bit her lip and glared at Ylsa, then started to run deeper into the wheat as if determined to pull her arm free or leave it disjointed in Ylsa's grip. Ylsa kept with her. Gilmar's people did not follow. They continued to fire the grain and let the flames chase the fugitives. Ylsa suspected Orineth was running purposelessly now, but so long as they headed away from the smoke and crackling, they could outrun the fire.

Until they circled somehow into a field that had already been blackened and found a charred body trying to hunch its way through the stubble.

Orineth screamed. Ylsa let go her wrist and she ran sobbing to the burned man, but at her touch he jerked.

Ylsa came closer and looked at him. "Diran? You won't live."

He groaned and reached for his sister's hand, regardless of the pain. Ylsa waited until their hands were joined before she drove her knife into his back. She had butchered animals in her life at Old Ironstead, and more recently taken lessons in warfare from Annis Drymouth and Birn Nine-toes, so she only needed one blow.

Orineth freed her hand, stared at the pieces of her brother's flesh that stuck to it, screamed again and brought her fist down on the arrow in her arm, breaking its shaft and driving its head to a new angle. Fresh blood spurted.

"I'm sorry," said Ylsa. "There's no justice in gods or humans. You wanted to save him. Do you want to go on living now?"

Orineth rose and ran into the burning edge of a barley field. Ylsa followed. They tore through this and other layers of flame, through still unburned crops and across one more area of smoking stubble, careless of being seen but this time keeping to a straight line. Finally they came, not to the river bank, but to Irinore's farmhouse.

It was ablaze.

Orineth shrieked. Ylsa caught her, turned her round, and held her face to breast. It might have become something like an embrace of comfort. But a group of invaders was killing the family's chickens and geese in the poultry yard beyond the burning house, and at Orineth's scream a couple of the men looked up.

Again Ylsa seized the young woman's arm, but this time Ylsa ran in the lead, leaving it to Orineth to keep pace. Now she could glimpse the river herself, between outbuildings and across burned fields. She skirted the side of the house away from the poultry yard, barely glanced at another group of invaders who were noisily trying to drive the cows and one old horse into a fired shed, and ran with her knife ready in her right hand and her left stretched tight pulling Orineth behind her.

The warriors already on land seemed too busy with their burning and slaughtering to give chase. Maybe they would have, had they realized these

were women, but women were not easy to tell from
men when they were dirty and distant. A few arrows flew at them, but mostly the invaders were
content to leave these two for fire, hunger, or the
men in the boat to finish off.

The boat was coming in to shore, and its warriors were fresh and thirsty for some of the sport
their companions had been enjoying. They set up a
shout on catching sight of Ylsa and Orineth. Two
victims still remained, whether male or female, and
the oars began to churn faster.

The two women reached the riverbank, and now
it was Ylsa, inland-bred, who hesitated. Never until now had she seen a stream of water too wide to
be bridged by a pair of logs, and swimming was to
her something people did in the tales of travelling
storytellers. But Orineth, breaking free, plunged in
at once among the reeds, and Ylsa followed. For a
moment her foot touched bottom—then she
slipped down into a drop-off and thrashed about
choking until she found how to use water resistance and handfuls of slimy water plants to pull
herself back to the place where it was chest deep.

Orineth's head was appearing and disappearing,
the reeds shaking near it. At first Ylsa thought she
too was struggling out of a deep spot. But she was
trying to break reeds near the base of their stems.
Ylsa worked nearer, snatched Orineth's shoulder,
pointed to the approaching boat.

"We—breathe through—these," Orineth panted. "And—"

"Bleed!" Ylsa splashed her arm into the area of
water that was reddening from Orineth's wound.

Orineth gave another awkward, furious tug at a
reed.

Ylsa looked at the boat. It was within easy

bowshot, but coming at the wrong angle. If it proceeded straight as it was going, it would pass them by a field's length—as Ironsteaders measured their forest-bound fields. The boat warriors seemed to have lost sight of their targets. They loosed no arrows, and their faces turned here and there as if scanning the reeds. Maybe Gilmar had ordered them to be careful of wasting their bolts. But Ylsa could see the teeth in their open mouths.

"The cave?" She squeezed Orineth's shoulder. "Your brother said—cave?"

Orineth nodded, turned in the water, and pointed toward the bank. Ylsa saw nothing except clay, reeds, water, and an overhang of turf. But she pushed Orineth in the direction she was pointing.

The young woman fell forward with a splash. Shouts went up from the boat, and a few arrows landed among the reeds near the women. Orineth ducked underwater, tugging her companion. Ylsa submerged, reluctantly but quickly. Water ticked at her nostrils and she kept her eyelids closed, groping through dark, weed-cut airlessness at the end of Orineth's arm. They had to break the surface twice for air, but now they moved without splashing, and the warriors in the boat must have lost sight of them again. Ylsa learned that she made faster progress with patience than with force.

She had not seen the cave because its mouth was almost entirely beneath water level after the recent rains. That was good; it meant Gilmar's people would have equal or greater trouble trying to find them. The floor of the riverbank cavern was underwater too, but the roof rose generously. Orineth and Ylsa stood, shivering but hidden, in water that rose to their armpits, and listened to the muffled noises of the boat and its warriors thrashing through the reeds outside. Orineth almost fainted and Ylsa held her up. They'll follow her damn blood and find us, thought the widow. And probably they would have, had the red trail been left on land, but in the water it must have spread too widely and dissolved too rapidly to guide them, for they did not find the hiding place, and eventually their noises faded away.

A small, crooked semi-circle of the entrance was still above water level. From outside, as Ylsa had seen, it was as good as invisible to eyes that did not know what to look for; but it let a little daylight into the cave. The women waited until the twilight faded almost to black before they ducked through the cave's mouth again and groped along the riverbank to a place where they could climb ashore.

Embers glowed in what had been the farmstead. A brighter glow about the southern horizon showed where Gilmar's army had found other farms to burn. Necessity forced the women to huddle over the hot ashes of a shed, drying themselves. Ylsa waited for Orineth to curse some god or gods.

Instead, a spot of bright fire flared up from the area where the dwelling had stood. They saw two figures bending over its light, one of them much smaller than the other. That any of Gilmar's warriors had been left behind was unlikely, so Orineth and Ylsa helped support each other to the place, and found the young woman's mother and youngest sibling feeding the new flames with bits of wood and dung that had somehow escaped burning until now.

That morning Irinore had taken her four-year-old son Mathan with her when she went to muck out the privy in one of the fallow fields. She was showing him how to work the human manure into the earth when the invaders came. Only the instinct to protect her youngest could hold Irinore from seeking the rest of her family. She hid with Mathan in the one hole available, and the northern warriors did not spend enough time on a fallow, apparently empty, field to find them.

Gort Broadmiddle, too, had survived, rolling in the soot of burned fields and cringing in whatever cover he could find. He staggered to the women in the middle of the night, dropped down on a charred beam, and asked only once whether there was anything to eat or drink.

"Nothing," said Irinore after several moments. "They bittered even the well."

"You can drink your fill from the river," said Ylsa, "but you'll have to get there on your own haunches. We haven't found a cup left whole."

Orineth whimpered with the pain of her arm.

"My waterskin," said Gort. "I still have my waterskin. It's empty."

"We'll fill it in the morning," said Ylsa. "Did you see what happened to Drymouth and Nine-toes?"

"Dead. Utran Long-legs, too. All dead, Barehands. All dead." He sat hunched and meek, saying no more but shuddering now and again, until Mathan crawled into his lap. Then he began to sob. He wept for a long time.

In the morning they made a more thorough search for any food the invaders might have left, and they found one more survivor. Midway between the family's dwelling and the outermost summer-house at the edge of the fields was an old root cellar where the outermost house had once stood when the farm was smaller. Rivan had crawled into this cellar. Two invaders had discovered him, one of them gray-bearded. They must have been kinder than their fellows, for they left him there with a piece of sausage, and no one else came. The boy had eaten all the sausage and thrown it up again in the night, and was now licking his own tears in his thirst.

"A graybeard," said Gort. "Half of them were smooth-chinned lads."

"Gilmar's first crop," said Ylsa. "Annis Drymouth said he was raising his own army and watching for his summer. She was right."

"No one can be crueller than the young!" said Irinore. It was the only time they heard her voice rise to something near a wail. She seemed calm when she insisted they search until they found remains that could be more or less equated with her husband and six other children. The sun was near setting when they found the last corpse, but they set off at once northward along the riverbank and walked for some hours, until they fell, so weary that they slept at once. They did not want to stay at the farmstead until the resemblance of charred human bodies to over-roasted meat became a temptation.

When morning came again they searched for edible weeds; the invaders had left the wild growth between farms to burn or not as the flames carried or died. Then Ylsa, Irinore, Orineth, and Rivan searched the river's edge for driftwood to make a raft, while Gort Broadmiddle sat on the bank with

Mathan and fished, using his old knotted cord, old rusty hook, and bright green grass for bait. Counting the broken man and the small boy as one, Ylsa reckoned they were leaving the farmstead the same number they had come, five strong.

Orineth's arm was infected and useless, and they would probably have to cut it off. But she worked one-handed. "I ask nothing else," she said, "but to grow children for the Butter-hair's army."

"We could go back to the forest and find Senerthan," said Ylsa. "Gilmar's fighting him, too."

"How many days did you straggle through the forest and meet no hunters?" said Irinore. "We would have to wait for Senerthan to find us. We have one guide to bring us to Dulanis Butter-hair's people."

"If enough of him holds together," said Ylsa. But because Senerthan was the son of a god, and because her own chance of fighting rather than being made to bear children seemed a little better with Dulanis, she worked on the raft.

Chapter 8.

Fighting and the movement of armies stopped between late autumn and early spring, but storytelling and the travel of lone newsbearers went on, rarely hindered by the mild northern snowfalls and freezing rains. That midwinter Tanris of Everywhere sat on old furs in one of Senerthan's favorite burrows and helped while away the long, lone hours of his night by telling him in fuller detail how Gilmar's advances along the Copper River Valley had been stopped last summer at the Middle Curve, south of the Island of the Chess Game:

The Five came across the wild grassland: Zokan of the Western Plains, Ethaan and Arlis the renegades from your own people, the small harlot whose name is yet unknown, and Wildrath, called of Nowhere, Veil-eyes, the Stranger, their First of Outlaws.

("Called 'the Heretic,' " said Senerthan.

"Wildrath the Heretic," Tanris agreed.)

They looked down at the river and its rich valley. The Middle Curve half-circled many farms, but they chose the smallest and northernmost, one narrow dwelling-house, two outbuildings, three fields, of which one lay untilled, and a pasture for a few goats and a cow. This was the steading of an old man, his widowed daughter and her only son, still a child. We do not know whether the Five treated them with force or kindness, whether they revealed their outlawry or begged shelter as simple wanderers. But they spent the night in the larger barn, and the old man's grandson stayed there with them.

In the morning Gilmar's armies spread across the north horizon, on this bank, on the western bank, on the river itself, coming toward the farmland of the Middle Curve, and the sky was clouded behind them with the smoke of burning.

The Five came out of the barn and took their stand in the untilled field, which lay by chance between the advancing army and the rest of the farm. They faced two thousand on this shore alone, not reckoning those in boats nor those on the western bank. The old farmer, his daughter and grandson brought rakes and scythes and came to join them. The boy, who was little taller than his mother's waist, carried a flail. But the Five sent them back, telling them to run south and rally their neighbors, saying that eight could not succeed where five must fail.

So numerous were Gilmar's warriors that to right and left the first row split into thin flanks and carried their torches around the Five to reach the growing grain. But those in the middle who paused to crush these few defenders like a hill of stubborn ants went no farther, and many of them will never go back. Each one of the Five fought well and ably, but Wildrath's long bright sword took the most.

(When telling the tale to other listeners, Tanris

would speak of a high barricade of corpses, hundreds dead and writhing, Gilmar forced to bring more attackers from the boats and the western bank. But Senerthan knew exactly how many of his own warriors the Five had killed at New Crescent, so Tanris curbed her exaggeration. The truth was sufficiently impressive.)

The right and left flanks turned in to take these defenders from behind, but the Five formed a circle and fought on. The northerners slipped in their fallen comrades' blood and stumbled over their comrades' thrashing limbs as fresh warriors tried to get at the outlaws. The direction of a shrewd captain could have brought the entire two thousand in a surge that must have ended it at once, but Wildrath had killed Gilmar's oldest captain in the first onset. The other leaders were young, for this campaign should have brought them experience rather than called upon it. Most of the warriors behind them were confused, unable to see why their march had slowed, shouting, pushing, even trampling one another in their attempts to keep up their forward pace. Without shrewd direction, perhaps even with it by now, a massed charge would have cost more northern lives than the Five were taking.

Far beyond, the bravest farmers were gathering with their rakes, axes, scythes and hoes and flails. The Five must finally die, but they were buying the free people of the Middle Curve time to prepare a resistance more determined than Gilmar's army had yet encountered in its southward drive.

Gilmar himself was in the leading boat. When he saw the confusion in the untilled field and the settlers closing their ranks between the first and second farms, he made his people row him ashore. He did not wait for the boat to touch land, but mounted his silver-gray stallion, that he always keeps near him, even on the water, and cleared the last few spearlengths to the beach with a leap.

Gilmar rode at a gallop to the untilled field, and when he came near enough he raised his gold-inlaid sword and turned it point down, shouting an order that his people stop fighting and fall back.

When Gilmar's army obeyed, the Five stopped fighting also, for they had no enemy left within reach of sword or thrusting spear, their arrows were spent, and to break their circle and rush at the northerners would be to die uselessly. So both sides waited in uncertain truce while Gilmar rode his silver-gray stallion to a point just beyond the reach of Wildrath's sword, that gleamed now with blood. The old First Man of the North recognized as if by instinct which of the Five was their leader.

"Join my army," he said. "Each one of you may be captain over three hundred, or if you prefer not to separate, together you may lead a thousand."

"Are you also the son of some god," said Wildrath to Gilmar the Old, "to destroy farmers' work with less mercy than drought and flood, rot or small, hungry creatures?"

"The needs of war," he replied. "This summer I burn and destroy so that in summers to come folk may live united, happier and more secure."

(Senerthan snorted. Tanris reminded herself that this was not an audience before whom she ought to present Gilmar's arguments.)

"Now I understand why your kind seeks what you call power," said Wildrath, "for I would use it to stop your destruction and send you back harmless to your own fields."

Then she lifted her sword in both hands, holding

its blade lengthwise, and the last film of blood slid off until the silvery metal shone like clean, clear oil.

Huge swarms of flies and stinging gnats rose from the river and muffled Gilmar's army like a smothering fog. Grasshoppers and beetles hurtled against their legs, wasps and bees drove their barbs into any uncovered flesh. Birds swooped at them like larger insects, aiming their small sharp beaks and claws at eyes, ears, the tongues in shouting mouths. Frogs by the thousand hopped up the banks, followed by lumbering turtles—they died beneath the northerner's feet, but even in death made their slayers slip and stumble and fall.

And while the creatures attacked, the sky darkened. The river churned higher than its banks, capsizing all of Gilmar's boats. The clouds threw down their rain, hard as arrows, quenching in a moment the torches and what fires had already been started in the grain. Wind and lightning played with Gilmar's people, both on the eastern and the western bank, but left the distant farmers untouched. The Five stood, sodden with rain but avoided by creatures and lightning, and watched as Gilmar's proud army became a rout, each warrior turning to scrabble north as best he could. Gilmar was the last to turn, but he did not attempt to rally his people and continue his southward push. He gathered as many as he could, once the wind and rain had stopped, and sent them home in small groups, foraging for food along the edges of the land they had burned.

So he winters in his own northern towns, and he has joined the moon god's son and the first daughter of the herdlands in naming Wildrath the Heretic and her companions outlaws.

*   *   *

Wendy Adrian Shultz

"She could not have called up the creatures, winds, and storm," Senerthan objected. "Only the child of a god could do such things, and a god's daughter would have recognized a god's son."

Tanris laid one hand over the other in token of acquiescence. "I usually tell my tales to common folk, First of Hunters. I may have forgot to prune away such exaggerations as the common folk love. No doubt the storm arose by chance, and the creatures went wild in sensing its approach. Nevertheless, Gilmar was turned back at the Middle Curve."

"So all the southern part of the river valley remains unharmed," said Senerthan. "At least for this year. I had begun prayers to my father and his siblings when first my scouts brought me word of Gilmar's march. My prayers were answered."

Tanris said, very meekly, "It is unfortunate your divine father did not destroy the outlaws at the same time."

"The gods are kind. They must intend some favored mortal to enjoy the reward for capturing this Wildrath the Heretic and her companions. So Dulanis Butter-hair has outlawed them, too? What have they done to her?"

"Nothing yet, that I have heard, First of Hunters. Dulanis Butter-hair added her reward to yours immediately on learning of their insult to you. If her people should take them, she will send them to you, keeping only Zokan, since he is a renegade from her own people."

"She may keep the small harlot as well," said Senerthan. "Indeed, if my people take them first, I'll send Zokan and the harlot as gifts to Dulanis, provided I keep the two renegade hunters. And Wildrath the Heretic."

"You are wise, First of Hunters," said Tanris (the spy). "This Wildrath may be a greater menace to you than Gilmar and the Butter-hair together. They say she respects nothing and no one."

"Between Gilmar and this Wildrath," said Senerthan, "Dulanis Butter-hair may be in worse danger than ever she was from me."

In that mild winter many people from the Copper River Valley south of Middle Curve, fearing that Gilmar would renew his attack in the spring, left their farmsteads to settle deeper in the southeast or southwest, or even to make their way north and seek safety within Gilmar's borders. The small family that had sheltered the Five the night before the battle was the first to travel north.

Others left their farms and joined Wildraith. The Five became fifty, then eighty-three. Wildraith accepted them with a shrug and left them to the marshalling of Ethaan and Arileth, Tilis the Supple and Jokan Greenstick. The only thing she herself requested of all these new followers was to ask wherever they went—and they could rarely eat well when all kept together—if anyone had news about Ylsa the Widow of Old Ironstead.

Part II

Chapter 9

Once across the river, Ylsa and her companions had followed Gort Broadmiddle in a wandering westward path until they met a family of twenty-three members in four generations, still living in tents as all herders had before the war. These people helped them cut off Orineth's festered arm. While she lay recovering, a group of western warriors came by, making their way back from the battle at New Crescent to the Butter-hair's stronghold at Middle Wells.

Shrewdly, Dulanis had not trusted Tanris of Everywhere's final figures, but had sent nineteen hundred warriors to defeat the thousand her enemy had with him at the beginning of the tale. She lost four hundred and ninety-four at New Crescent, and a hundred and sixteen more to skirmishers and unseen archers as the army went and returned through the unfamiliar forest. As nearly as her captains could reckon, the moon god's son lost enough at New Crescent to have made the campaign worth its cost, for the westerners succeeded in killing or scattering most of the children and fertile women in the breeding community.

But when the Butter-hair's army came back to

the place a little north of the Island of the Chess Game, where they had forded the river on their way east, they found a wide, bare, and blackened desert where before had been fields of grain and cattle for the taking. They had stayed in a body long enough to cross the water, but once on the western bank they broke into small groups and spread out to forage their separate ways home. Many of these small groups were caught in the retreat of Gilmar's army. The northerners might be a fleeing rout, but they were wild in their desperation.

The group that stumbled across Ylsa and her companions were still strong enough to ignore the great-grandmother's plea that she had already given a son and two grandchildren for Dulanis Butter-hair's army and to force seven more of the herding family to come with them: two grandsons aged fifteen and eighteen, a granddaughter aged twenty-three, her husband, and their three small sons. They also took several goats to help provision them for the remaining distance to Middle Wells. They were not sorry to find willing comrades in Irinore, her two sons, her daughter Orineth who was so eager to produce new warriors for Dulanis that she began coupling with the strongest western men at once despite the pain in the stump of her arm, and in Ylsa Bare-hands. They took Ylsa for another farmer from the river valley, and she did not correct them.

From the beginning of the war, Dulanis had made it her custom to see and speak with each new member of her armies, whether for fighting or child-bearing. But after sixteen years the meetings tended to brevity in the most relaxed times, and it was not a relaxed time when Ylsa's group reached

Middle Wells. Others were straggling back daily to their ruler's chief stronghold. Dulanis spent most of her waking hours listening to grim reports or laying new plans around Gilmar's entry into her and Senerthan's war, and her waking hours lasted longer than the summer daylight.

The young herders newly brought from their family's tents she bound to her service almost without hearing them speak. They were westerners and therefore hers to command. Indeed, only the woman made any protest: "Could we not breed children as well beneath our own roofskins?"

"I need other work from you besides," said Dulanis, "and I am Keeper of the Ancient Cauldron." But she ordered that until this woman's husband, according to the old traditions, was killed, she need couple with no one else.

She accepted Irinore and Orineth with a few questions, a nod, and a smile. She held their hands a moment to fix their loyalty to herself, and touched her palm to their waists to bless their fertility. She consecrated Rivan and four-year-old Mathan to her army by holding their hands and touching their heads before she assigned Rivan to the training grounds and returned Mathan to his mother for several more years.

"And you?" she said to the last of the new women.

"Ylsa Bare-hands, trained by your captains Annis Drymouth and Birn Nine-toes, who died fighting Gilmar's northerners."

Dulanis held Ylsa's hands between her own, then reached for her waist. Ylsa jumped back.

"I swore to Drymouth and Nine-toes I'd give you a fighter now, not children for the future, and they accepted that oath. I am barren, Dulanis Butter-hair, and if you try to fold me into your breeding-pens, I'll rip open my own womb and die."

"My women train on the practice ground when they are not big with child," said Dulanis.

"And the man who tries to couple with me I'll gut or geld."

Dulanis looked at the captain of the group that had brought Ylsa. He confirmed that she was already fierce enough with several weapons to endanger anyone who tried to test her infertility.

"Fight for me, then," said Dulanis. "But if your claim proves false, you will be folded with my other childbearers." She touched Ylsa's head and assigned her to the practice grounds. She did not connect this Ylsa Bare-hands with Tender-face the Widow of Ironstead in Tanris of Everywhere's tale of the Five at New Crescent. Ylsa's face was no longer tender.

Gort Broadmiddle could tell Dulanis nothing. What scattered details he remembered of the summer had merged into incoherence. He lived on more than forty years. He saw the end of this round of warfare and all the lands from northern ocean to southern mountains united under a single pair of rulers. Or he would have seen all this, had all his wits been with him. From the summer of Gilmar's first invasion he lived mostly in dreams and nightmares, with some clear-minded periods when he could help train the seven- and eight-year-olds. He never regained more than half the bulk that had earned him his original trait-name, and folk called him Gort Scarbelly or Gort Wanderbrain instead, but as the seasons went by his hours of peaceful dozing in the sun grew longer and his fits of screaming more infrequent. Orineth's grandchildren came to love him.

Meanwhile Dulanis, Senerthan, and Gilmar the Old licked their wounds and laid their plans. Orineth and hundreds of other women in the West, East, and North kept breeding a new generation for their rulers, two of whom were aging but generally considered ageless, the third aged but generally considered preserved by his years, like a well-cured piece of meat.

Irinore had one more daughter before she turned too old to breed; then she joined Ylsa on campaign and became a captain of three hundred. Gathering as many as she could of the women available for fighting, she made her command one of the fiercest in the Butter-hair's armies.

Ylsa's hair began to silver, and her womb never again swelled. She earned new trait-names: Ylsa Tightmouth, Ylsa Quicksword, and Ylsa the Unflinching.

Tales about Wildraith began to include the fixed-name of her quarry, but it was a common name in the north and not uncommon elsewhere. Had Dulanis suspected, she might have tried to use Bare-hands to bait a trap for Wildraith, but the ruler was more inclined to believe that Ylsa Tender-face was a storyteller's everyname. As for Ylsa Bare-hands, Quicksword, the Unflinching, she gave only passing attention to the tales that were sung and told.

On the first march south, Gilmar's army had supplied itself from the farms before destroying them. The following summer they would not have had that resource to draw on until they reached

Middle Curve, and even from that point takings would have been thinner, because so many settlers had left their farms. With Dulanis, Senerthan, and the remaining valley farmers alerted, Gilmar did not care to depend on a finely-stretched supply line.

The common folk whispered that Gilmar feared Wildraith most of all. His answer was to double the reward for any of her companions and treble it for herself. This only fed the whispers, so after a few years he withdrew all offers of reward and said only that whoever captured outlaws earned the pleasure of dealing them death and keeping their possessions. Thus he helped ensure that anyone who could capture them would probably deliver them to Senerthan or Dulanis, these rulers never withdrawing their offered rewards, not even when the increase in the outlaws' numbers threatened to impoverish them if anyone should succeed in bringing them Wildraith's entire band. But most of the common folk delighted in the tales and to any dreams of rulers' rewards they preferred the chance that Wildraith would be near when they needed protection. Many prayed for Wildraith. Some prayed to her. She seemed neither to encourage nor discourage it, though some of her followers had strong views on the matter. As all three rulers made warriors out of unwilling common folk, the armies themselves were infected with secret affection for the outlaw band.

For a full year after his initial attempt on the Copper River Valley, Gilmar kept to his own lands, devising strenuous new training for his warriors. He had begun his breeding encouragements long enough ago that he could now harvest a good number of lads to freshen his army each season.

The first children of his enemies, breeding programs would not be ready in any number for two or three years yet, although some of the largest and best developed were being taken into the armies young. All that first summer after Gilmar's attack, Dulanis and Senerthan ordered no armies into each other's lands, but sent their warriors up and down the river, watching for a new invasion from the North. Easterners and westerners skirmished when they met on the same side of the water or at a place where it could easily be crossed, but there were no major battles and comparatively light losses. Both armies gathered new members, more often with force than persuasion, in the southern part of the valley and wherever else they found common folk. But sometimes this recruiting was prevented by the sudden interference of Wildraith's outlaws.

When the second spring came, Gilmar seeded the northern part of the river valley with his own people, households of farmers to plant crops and warriors to protect them and their cattle. His idea was to repeat his attempt to waste the whole valley to the southern foothills, this time stocking the first half of the march from fields planted for no other purpose. He would leave these farms intact on his southward march, to resupply his warriors when they returned from burning the free farms in the southern part of the valley. On the return, each household loyal to Gilmar would fire its own fields once they had served their intended purpose, and join the northern army on its way home. Gilmar thought the plan even better than that for his earlier invasion.

Senerthan and Dulanis were clever enough to order their people to destroy the new settlements, but that was why Gilmar provided warriors to guard each farm, and why he sent two companies of three hundred patrolling the riverbanks from North Twist to Middle Curve (though they usually turned back a comfortable distance from that place of evil memories). Dulanis and Senerthan succeeded in destroying a few farmsteads, but did not yet trust one another enough to attempt even a temporary alliance or a concerted drive from both sides, so the Butter-hair's people and those of the moon god's son continued skirmishing with each other more often than they attacked the new northern enemy. And Wildraith's outlaws showed their impartiality by appearing now and then to protect some house of the northerners from overwhelming odds.

That winter Dulanis and Senerthan began making use of the storytellers and newsbearers to send messages to one another.

For as long as tradition remembered, there had been nine principal storytellers between the ocean and the mountains. Since the storytellers themselves remembered the tradition most diligently, the constancy of this number since the time of Ondaris the Second (before whose adulthood all history was chaos) might have been questioned. But it was a convenient number, allowing for three principals each from the north, the east, and the west. There had always been disagreement about the birthlands of many legendary storytellers, however, and in the last several generations some great ones had come from the far south. It was this, perhaps, that had inspired the modification of allowing for two principals from each of the longer-settled regions and three called "of Everywhere."

During most of the War of the Chess Game, the

nine principal storytellers considered themselves to be Tanris, Gornith, and Attaran of Everywhere; Ornar and Ylith of the North; Loris and Derek of the West; and Othan and Derileth of the East. Many listeners thought Dathan of the South better than several of the Nine, and he might have been recognized instead of Gornith, Loris, or Attaran, all of whom were younger than he, if he had not clung to his original trait-name 'of the South.'

A few hundred lesser newsbringers roamed the area at the beginning of the war. Their numbers increased as the fighting spread, since in the time of the northern wars to be a storyteller had been to enjoy safety from the armies. But eventually the number of storytellers grew so large that first Gilmar, then Dulanis and Senerthan started pressing into their service any minor newsbringer who could not demonstrate a clear talent for singing or storytelling, and the number of wandering news-bringers settled back to nine principal and a few hundred lesser ones.

Each ruler realized that some of these true storytellers were also spies, for each ruler had the allegiance of some of the spies. Tanris, Ylith, and eleven lesser storytellers had pledged their secret loyalty to Gilmar; Loris, Gornith, and seven lesser ones to Dulanis; Derek and ten lesser ones to Sene-rthan; Derileth to both Dulanis and Senerthan; At-taran to all three; Dathan of the South to none of them; and so on. Nevertheless, the rulers allowed all talented storytellers to wander freely, as long as their spying did not become too blatant. To have tortured or gutted a storyteller, especially one of the Nine, would have been to rouse the anger of all the others, for the storytellers' bonds to one anoth-er and their craft went deeper than their allegiances

to any ruler. And though they did not fight, they
did help shape opinions among the common folk;
also, the remaining spies might secretly change loyalties in their outrage. Moreover, storytellers, even
when suspected of spying, were too useful to a ruler
to be destroyed lightly. Their news balanced and
supplemented the scouts' reports, and both Gilmar
and Dulanis, and even Senerthan to some extent,
delighted in priming suspected spies with such information as they chose to send their adversaries.

But Dulanis and Senerthan were very careful in
their choice of message-bearers that winter, using
only Loris, Attaran, and two lesser but more
trusted talents. Senerthan would have used Derek,
but he was travelling in the north, or Dathan, but
he refused and turned back to the cold winter of his
native south rather than enter this game of spying
and warfare.

Attaran, he who spied for all three rulers, had
been so skillful that each believed his loyalty undivided. In fact, it became undivided that year. Attaran had already felt strange new stirrings in his
own mind, and after helping carry messages back
and forth between the First of Hunters and the
First of Herders until spring, instead of turning
north to bring all this news to Gilmar, he chuckled
deeply to himself and slipped south along the river
until he found and joined Wildraith's outlaws.

When Gilmar marched his army south the third
summer, Wildraith Veil-eyes again stood in his
way, this time with more than a hundred outlaws at
North Twist. Gilmar routed them, killing three and
capturing two but losing a hundred and thirteen of
his own men. That night some of the outlaws,
Wildraith with Ethaan and Arileth according to
some storytellers, with Jokan and Tilis according

to others, with Rada the Cautious and himself according to Attaran of Everywhere, crept in and freed the prisoners. Gilmar whipped the men of the North Twist farms for allowing Wildraith's people to gather, gutted two farmers in place of the escaped outlaws, and took the rest into his army at once.

Next day Gilmar saw smoke to the south. Reaching its origin, he found that Dulanis Butter-hair had burned his own people's farms. He forced his army on, even as he sent mounted scouts to learn the limits of the destruction. The fields were blackened only for a two days' march, many of the routed farmers and warriors having been able to make a stand at Small Curve, so the northerners suffered mild hunger, not starvation. But near the Island of the Chess Game they met an attack by Senerthan's warriors, who thinned their ranks with arrows and then disappeared into the island trees and a network of underground burrows on each bank. Gilmar began to suspect the temporary alliance against him.

At Middle Curve, the northern army met the outlaws again, and this time four of Gilmar's remaining captains, three of them veterans of the earlier rout, laid their weapons flat on the ground and sat on them at first sight of Wildraith the Stranger leaning on her famous sword, with her people behind her. Some of the common warriors, their minds haggered by the earlier encounters with outlaws, and remembering that this was where the storm had turned them back three years ago, panicked at once. Rumors spread that the armies of Dulanis Butter-hair and Senerthan the moon god's son waited beyond the outlaws, all three leaders allied, and more northerners panicked. Gilmar shouted at his rebellious captains. He finally bullied one into rising and striking sword against shield in a signal of attack, but the other three sat unmoving. Many of their men followed their example, and this revolt caused still more panic.

Then Wildraith laughed and raised her sword, and the panic became a second rout, the northerners trampling their own comrades. Gilmar hurled his spear and several curses at Wildraith before riding to regroup his people as best he could. He did not succeed until the next day, when he judged it wisest to abandon this particular plan until Wildraith could be captured and new discontent sown between Dulanis and Senerthan.

The outlaws had killed nobody this time at Middle Curve. In fact, they bore away and nursed about twenty of the trampled. Several died, including two of the captains who had sat down in rebellion. The rest, among them the third rebel captain, joined the outlaws. The fourth of these captains, he who had finally stood up at Gilmar's command, had escaped with the routed army, to have his nose slit as a traitor and then he was hung by the ankles and left to die on the western bank across from the Island of the Chess Game. This did not prevent many of the farmers and warriors whom Gilmar himself had planted in the northern part of the valley from deserting either to Dulanis, Senerthan, or Wildraith. Also, the number of free settlers began to increase in the valley once more, and trade between regions, which had died out as the merchants' wagons and pack animals were likely to be seized by whichever ruler's warriors found them first, picked up again along the Copper River.

Chapter 10.

The winter following Gilmar's second attempt to burn the river valley, the storytellers travelled again between east and west, with the result that one day when a late, wet snow was falling, Dulanis Butter-hair and Senerthan of the Long Forest sat in one another's presence for the second time in their lives.

The Island of the Chess Game would have been the most convenient middle ground, but they had avoided it because of its sharp memories.

Not far from the foothills of the Whitepeak Mountains, the Copper River divided at the Upper Fork into the two branches called the Great Curve and the Short Flow. These ran together again at the Lower Fork to continue their course to the northern ocean, but between the forks lay more fertile land than folk could think of as another island. Here Adrak the Discontent had brought his family and herds during the years when Ytran Simple-words' descendants kept the Cauldron of the Ancient Hearth. His herds and crops prospered despite the short growing season, and his grandson married Adrith, a hunter from that part of the Long Forest that brushed the foothills. Nevertheless, except for a few scattered hunters and for the shy race of mountain dwellers called the Tangletongues because of their incomprehensible speech, Adrak's successors had long remained almost the only people south of Laniscleft, the long, narrow eastward bend in the river that was recognized as the boundary of the herdlands.

The fixed-name Adrak had come to be repeated in each generation. The present Adrak, trait-named the Slow, had agreed to host a meeting between Butter-hair and the moon god's son provided neither they nor their attendants brought any weapon across the water into her land, not even a short knife to cut their meat. (Some of Adrak's own people, however, carried weapons, particularly those who watched the bridges and the ferry.)

This long War of the Chess Game had begun to make the free southerners feel that for their own safety they should unite under one ruler, as had the northern farmers, the western herders, and now at last even the eastern hunters. Adrak the Slow was most likely to become First of the South, not only because of her heritage but also because she had earned her trait-name by her caution, deliberation, and fair-mindedness, always made to serve peace and the smoothing of quarrels.

Senerthan and Dulanis had been discreet in laying their plans, but when they set out for Adrak's Stead, each ruler accompanied by nine personal attendants and three hundred warriors, complete secrecy was no longer possible. Tanris of Everywhere came to Middle Wells a day after Dulanis had left. No one remaining in town (nor anyone with the Butter-hair except herself and two attendants) knew her destination, but the direction she took had been plain. Tanris hurried southwest between the Butter-hair's line of travel and the river until, just south of Middle Curve, she heard rumors that a large party of hunters, thought to be led by Senerthan himself, was moving southwest out of the forest. Tanris traded three pearls for a horse and cantered him across the triangle of river valley known as East-Tongue that cut into Laniscleft. Travel being part of her craft, she arrived at the Lower Fork before either Dulanis or Senerthan. She could not be sure that Adrak's Stead was their goal, but it was the oldest and most famous settlement of the south and would be the best place to learn further news, so she crossed Eastfork Bridge and continued to the ancient round structure, mounded over with thick layers of dirt against the southern cold, that was Adrak's winter dwelling.

Although Adrak had no hard reason to believe the storyteller's coming other than coincidence, she was not entirely pleased. She sent two of her people to find and bring back Dathan of the South, who was a kinsman of hers by marriage. She must have wanted a second storyteller at hand, one of whose impartiality she could be as confident as of her own. Unfortunately, Dathan was climbing mountain trails and trading story material with the Tangletongues (he had learned their language as nearly as possible for one not of their race), and he could not be found until late spring.

Senerthan arrived a day after Tanris, and the Butter-hair half a day after Senerthan. The moon god's son brought his nine personal attendants across by the Farpoint Ferry, while Dulanis and her nine came over the Southfork Bridge, surrendering all weapons as Adrak had enjoined them. They left their small armies of three hundred on the banks, far separated from one another's sight by both branches of the river and part of Adrak's land, but keeping their weapons.

Adrak's people built their winter barrows small, for added warmth, and the southern landkeeper permitted Senerthan and Dulanis a single attendant apiece inside her dwelling. She hoped they would bring advisors as calm-headed as her own husband and daughter, who sat flanking her at the far end of the room, facing the only door. Senerthan brought his young cousin Erthan of the Subtle Mind, who had charge of questioning all prisoners, while Dulanis brought her uncle Ytran Crook-tooth, who had invented the great bows and other war devices.

The southerners had set up two large chairs of polished pine, with high backs and carved armrests, facing one another across the hearth at right angles with the door and Adrak's family. The moon god's son and the Keeper of the Cauldron took their places in silence, their attendants sitting on cushions alongside. Adrak's fire jumped brightly between them.

"Man, First of Hunters," Dulanis said at last.

"Woman, First of Herders."

They sat for some moments longer, saying nothing more, until the probable First of the South cleared her throat.

Then the First of Hunters said, "The years burn away in this fire between us."

"They pass," said the First of Herders. "Is it true that the moon god's seed may never spread into a new generation?"

"My father's seed awaits a worthy vessel."

"And my cauldron, a worthy spoon to stir in the spice."

They gazed at each other again, until Erthan, Ytran, and the three southerners shifted for comfort on their cushions and chairs. Many storytellers later sang that the fire blazed of itself almost to the smokehole during this time. The truth was that at last Adrak the Slow rose and added more cow chips to the flames. Before returning to her chair, she told the two rulers, "Together, you could keep both your lands safe from Gilmar in this generation."

Dulanis nodded. "Gilmar is old. At his death, we could join the North to the West and the East."

"A fitting heritage for the grandchildren of a god," Senerthan agreed.

Adrak returned to her chair and sat thoughtfully, gazing at both her guests.

Tanris whispered a few words to Adrak's husband, who smiled, turned to his wife, and murmured, "She may be too old."

Dulanis may have overheard. Never shifting her gaze from Senerthan, she said, "Nor am I yet too old."

"The moon god preserves the only woman in this generation worthy to mother his grandchildren," the First of Hunters replied.

The First of Herders frowned a little, but went on, "I have not brought the Cauldron of the Ancient Hearth, but there is still time before sunset for the daylight ceremony of my people."

"And night will soon brighten the moon for the ancient ceremony of the Long Forest," said the moon god's son.

Tanris spoke aloud. "Where is Jokan Round-face? Will the moon god restore his arm as a wedding gift to his son's bride?"

The Butter-hair's face hardened and her fingernails dug into the arms of her chair at this reminder of how Senerthan's arrow had cost her favorite uncle an arm in the aftermath of the chess game; but she sat unmoving. Senerthan, however, seized a piece of burning dung from the fire and hurled it at Tanris. It caught her in the chest, but fell off at once and hurt her less than it had Senerthan's hand.

Adrak the Slow stood again. "Tanris of Everywhere," she pronounced, "you have broken storytellers' ancient privilege of witnessing in silence. Leave this chamber. Nevertheless, Senerthan of the Long Forest, you also have broken my conditions, and you will promise each of us here a blanket of good furs, Tanris to name which animals hers shall be made from—"

"I'll give you three blankets, Adrak of the South," said the moon god's son, "to show that I freely forgive your words. And I'll give Dulanis of the West ten blankets of the finest black and white mottled skunk fur. But to Tanris, not so much as a mangy hareskin to warm her hands!"

"Save your mottled skins," said Dulanis. "I'll wear the wool of my own plains. And I take Tanris of Everywhere under my protection."

"First of Herders—" he began, turning to her.

She stood. "The First of Hunters has shown his nature. Would the moon god Ormrathe protect me from his son's next rage?"

Senerthan stared at her, clutched his slightly scorched right hand into a fist, and strode from the barrow. His cousin Erthan of the Subtle Mind leered at Tanris before following him out. Tanris closed her eyes at Erthan's gaze, for young as he was his ingenuity in questioning Senerthan's prisoners was already famous. Storytellers had been favored until now, but Senerthan had just proved the power of his rage over storytellers' safety, and sooner or later someone would realize the possibilities of accident or unexplained disappearance. From that time Tanris avoided the deep forest and Senerthan's strongholds. It limited her usefulness, but Gilmar paid her well for that day's work notwithstanding.

Nor was Adrak the Slow entirely sorry. The hint had been strong that an alliance and marriage between Senerthan and Dulanis might threaten the free south as well as Gilmar's north. So Adrak permitted Tanris to remain with her several days longer.

Tanris chose this course rather than the Butterhair's protection because she suspected what did in fact happen when both Dulanis and Senerthan rejoined their small armies on the other side of the water. Coming into sight of each other at the Lower Fork, they followed the river downstream until they reached a place where it could be forded, and then drove together in the Battle of the Rocky Shallows. Storytellers sang that Dulanis and Senerthan both carried sword and spear into this battle, and that the two leaders met more than once in nearly fatal combat before nightfall stopped the fighting. Ytran Crook-tooth died there, along with more than four hundred others, the loss being about equal on both sides. In the morning, Dulanis and the remnant of her army had disappeared from the western bank, so Senerthan led his surviving warriors back to the Long Forest with no more loss of time, leaving the southerners to burn or bury such corpses as the cold river current had not carried away.

Meanwhile, Adrak had the Eastfork and Southfork Bridges destroyed, cut the ferry ropes, and grounded all boats and rafts on her own side of the water, leaving only the small Narrows Bridge, which was on the southernmost side of the Great Curve and could be easily guarded and quickly burned. Her precautions were prudent but unnecessary since the war did not again dip south of Laniscleft.

Chapter 11.

All the next summer Senerthan stayed in the Long Forest looking for and training new fighters. Dulanis, however, posted scouts along the river and the northern frontier, reckoned how many warriors she could spare for each of her strongholds, chose four hundred and fifty of the best riders and ordered them to be ready to ride anywhere attack might threaten, and took four companies of three hundred north to Gilmar's land. She had never gone with her army into Senerthan's woods, nor had he himself come west into her grasslands. But Gilmar had done them both the honor of leading his warriors in person, and Dulanis meant to repay it.

Irinore's company was one of the four. It was still two-thirds male, though already including more women than any other company. Ylsa, whom nobody remembered as being of Old Ironstead because she was Tightmouth about her past, Quicksword or Unflinching in battle, was Irinore's fourth in command. The second was a man eight or nine years younger, named Bitran Hardfoot.

Bringing a herd along through its accustomed wild pasture, Dulanis and her army gained the frontier with no problems of a supply line. But where Gilmar had simply followed the largest river known outside wanderers' tales, Dulanis had only the reports of scouts and storytellers to guide her course.

She turned northeast, aiming for Waterstead, the chief and oldest town of the north. She did not burn the farms along her way, except for a few that resisted her people's demands. Remembering Gilmar's campaigns in the river valley, Dulanis preferred not to leave a waste that her army might need to recross, nor to rouse the farmlands at her back. Most of the people left on these northern farms were those whom Gilmar had not wanted as warriors and those who had hidden because they did not want to fight, but if sufficiently angered they might gather into a troublesome force.

"And she's afraid of Wildraith," Irinore said one evening as she and some women of her company sat around their fire on the edge of a farm, eating the northerners' geese and chickens, which made a change from their own goats and cows.

"Wildraith's never been reported this far north," said Caris Crookbrow.

"She's never been needed this far north," said Ondreth of Laniscleft, who admired the outlaws. "Gods know what she'll do if we burn another farmstead like that one yesterday."

"The gods don't know." Ylsa threw a chicken bone into the fire and lay down as if to sleep. "Or don't care. And neither does Wildraith."

"Then how do you explain the people she's saved?" said Ondreth. "Farmers, merchants, children—"

"Tales. Storytellers' cheap pay for their supper

and bed. Have you ever seen an outlaw scout?"

"Like it or not, Ylsa Tightmouth," said Caris, "the outlaws had a hand in turning those northern devils back. Twice."

Ylsa grunted. "All right, the outlaws are like the gods. If by chance they're nearby and watching, and if it pleases them, maybe they'll help you. But don't pray for it." She closed her eyes.

"I don't like burning farms myself," said Irinore. "If the Butter-hair wants to burn another one, maybe someone should remind her of the outlaws."

Caris shook her head. "Or maybe not. She might start burning to try and draw them here. She might decide she'd rather send Wildraith Heretic to the moon god's son as a peace offering than trap Gilmar in Waterstead."

"She'll never make it up with Senerthan," said Irinore. "Not now."

"I'm not sure," said Caris.

"If the outlaws do come," said Ondreth, "I'll join them sooner than burn another farm."

Irinore yawned. "If you say anything like that again before looking around, I'll kill you myself before someone else reports you."

Ylsa snored.

Wildraith and her outlaws did not appear, and Dulanis had to burn only one more farm before she and her army came in sight of Waterstead.

As the Copper River flowed into the far north, a ridge of bony rocks and waterfalls combed it out into the several branches of the Longstraits. As they reached the fine sand of the delta, some of the Longstraits muddled together again to form a wide

mouth emptying into the ocean. According to dim
legends, the earliest people had built Waterstead
with the timber from their huge ships when they
could navigate no further upstream, raising their
houses above the straits on tall wooden platforms.
The middle part of the town still stood high above
the water, though some pieces of scaffolding were
replaced each year. An ancient splinter preserved
in the ceremonial scabbard Gilmar's grandfather
had captured from Sorum during the northern
wars was said to be the last wood from the original
ships left in existence.

To east and west the town had winged onto the
shore. Many of the outermost houses, resting on
more solid ground, were built of rock and clay. The
newest part of Waterstead lay outside the fortified
walls raised in the time of Gilmar's grandfather
and restored by Gilmar as if he had suspected a
new attack.

Dulanis first saw Waterstead in midafternoon
sunlight. She would have preferred to arrive early
in the day when her army was fresh, or after dark
when they could camp at a little distance without
fires and hope not to be sighted. But circumstances
had failed her. Her scouts' reports had conflicted
or misled, the terrain proved sometimes easier and
sometimes more difficult than expected, the warriors were restive so deep in Gilmar's territory and
would have been hard to hold back. Dulanis decided not to hold them back now. She sat poised
for a few moments on her dark red horse, until
about a third of her army had gathered behind her
on the rocky ridge. Then she led them at a run
across the plain toward the western wing of Waterstead, leaving the rest of her warriors to follow as

they came up to the ridge in their turn.

Circumstances had failed Gilmar also. Hearing Tanris of Everywhere's report of the meeting at Adrak's Stead, he had expected Dulanis and Senerthan to claw at each other's flanks all summer, and so he had felt free to chase a rumor that Wildraith's outlaws were busy in the woods on the eastern border of his land. He himself was several days' march away in Forestedge, once the favorite stronghold of his grandfather's rival, Ilsa the Crafty. The advisor he had left to govern Waterstead, Narum the Fringe-pate, was no more than half competent. Gilmar did not allow anyone who showed overmuch ability to attain a place of high power. Unwed, the last of his immediate family, he mistrusted capable leaders more and more as the years went by. Unlike Dulanis and Senerthan, Gilmar had been generous with his seed, but any son or daughter who tried to play upon the relationship met some accident or sudden sickness or rough brawling drunkard with a steady knife. Gilmar's younger siblings, his uncle and aunt, and many of their children by marriage had met similar deaths. In the last few years, his remaining kinsfolk and most ambitious captains and advisors had been put in the foremost ranks of battle or sent alone to scout in dangerous places. Tanris of Everywhere was a cousin of Gilmar's who had sworn to him she would always remain a storyteller and never bear a child.

So Narum Fringe-pate, having survived in Gilmar's service for years by accepting orders without thought or question, was unsure how to give them. When a few farm people had brought rumors of invasion from the west, Narum sat in the ruler's house on the highest scaffolding in town, held his bald head in both hands and wondered how dangerously competent it might appear to send messengers to Gilmar at once, while the people of Waterstead chewed their own versions of the rumor. Some who lived outside the wall began moving inside with their possessions. Narum sent out an order that there was to be no panic. It did not inspire confidence. Confusion developed at the west gate when someone's overladen cart lost a wheel and blocked the way. The wall captain had the gate closed. Receiving a garbled account of this, the captain on the other side had the east gate closed also. Rather than directing some better organizing at the gates, Narum approved their being closed, thus turning what the west wall captain had meant for a temporary measure into a permanent one. For the best part of two days, the townspeople outside the wall shouted and fermented among their buildings.

Then Dulanis and her army appeared on the ridge, with the westering sun at their backs, and made their charge. The people of the unprotected western wing stormed their own town's wall, trying to get inside. Dulanis had told her warriors to be as merciless as Gilmar's had been in the Copper River Valley, and there was slaughter when they reached the buildings. The west wall captain risked Narum's displeasure by opening the gate, but the mob blocked it again almost at once, crushing and trampling one another until the invaders were upon them. Northern and western warriors struggled to fight each other, both sides slicing through unarmed townspeople in their way, while the wall captain tried to muster enough hands to reclose the west gate, and Narum finally sent messengers through the east gate to find Gilmar.

Both gates were closed at last. About thirty western warriors, finding themselves trapped inside the town, did so much further damage that the northerners killed them however they could, with no thought of taking any alive. Dulanis lost about eighty more in the fighting outside the wall, but the town's losses went much higher. Virtually everyone who had lived in the west wing, except those who had come behind the walls at the first rumors, died in that attack. The people of the eastern wing were luckier; most of them got through their gate before any of the Butter-hair's army reached that side of town.

Dulanis made her people tear down all outside wooden buildings that had not been fired in the attack and pile the wood against the gates. She lost some warriors to the arrows, spears, and rocks aimed from the wall, but the mounds of splintered timber, brush, and bedding blazed up bright beside the wooden gates. It would have worked, except for the west wall captain. He managed to form his fellows into lines for passing up buckets of water to douse the flames and loads of rubble and mud to block the charred holes. The fires struggled on into the night, but the wall remained a barrier.

Dulanis drew back her army, made camp on the ridge, and consulted with her captains. They could retreat to the border of their own land and make ready for Gilmar's retaliation. They could continue east after the riders who had been seen leaving town just as the east gate was closed, and try to meet Gilmar between Waterstead and the forest. They could push south along the river and spend

the rest of the season harrying Senerthan, trusting
the forces Dulanis had left in the west to protect
her land from Gilmar. Or they could settle in
around Waterstead.

Irinore, who had been a captain of three hundred for two years, was the only one of the four to
prefer a retreat to their own border, and she
changed her opinion when it became obvious that
this plan must include wasting as much countryside
as possible to weaken Gilmar's supply line. Neither
Dulanis nor her captains thought it prudent to turn
southeast and strike at Senerthan. Horth Long-
thumbs, who was the most experienced captain,
pointed out that there might also be danger in leaving the fortified town between themselves and their
own land while they went in search of Gilmar. So
they settled in around Waterstead.

Of the twelve hundred warriors she had brought
north, Dulanis had more than a thousand left. She
did not like to spend them in skirmishes or attempts to undermine the wall when she did not
know how large a force Gilmar might bring. She
had all available corpses spread in the water of the
Longstraits just upstream from town. Then, to
further choke the northerners' water supply and to
occupy her army during its wait, she put it to work
damming two adjacent branches of the river.

This was hard work for warriors from the
western plains, and Dulanis hardly expected much
use to come of it aside from giving her people
something besides Gilmar to fill their minds. But
her army did include some, like Irinore, who had
lived a good part of their lives near the river. With
these to direct, and five hundred warriors at a time
working to their orders, the streams were dammed

and their water mingling in a reservoir below the falls by the time scouts brought Dulanis word that Gilmar was less than one day's march from her with an army of between two and three thousand at his back.

She had not realized she would be so far outnumbered. She should have taken into account that, despite his losses in the Copper River Valley, in his own lands Gilmar would still have reserves to draw upon; that, all breeding encouragements aside, the farming North was more heavily populated than the herding West and hunting East. For an hour she thought of retreat. But would her warriors have time to scorch the land thoroughly behind them? Even if she tried to buy a margin for escape by trading the time needed to destroy the countless wooden bridges over the Longstraits for the time Gilmar would need to get his army across by other measures.

Then she considered her dam, with a high basin of water swirling into it from the heavy falls.

Five major and six minor branches formed the Longstraits. Where two of the major ones had flowed several days ago, sluggish streambeds of mud and reeds now lay drying in some areas, partially watered in others by marshy cross-channels that connected them with the neighbor streams. Dulanis burned all bridges over the easternmost of the emptied streambeds and two-thirds of the bridges over the westernmost. She spread half her army along the ground between the two streambeds. The other half she kept in reserve on the solid land west of the straits.

Irinore and her third in command, Utran Quickarm, watched with twenty men of their company

hidden at the dam. Irinore's second, Britran Hardfoot, and a hundred more of her company were
with Dulanis among the reserves. The rest of
Irinore's three hundred stood between the dry
streambeds close under the dam, supposedly looking to Ylsa Quicksword but in reality so thin-
stretched and spread out that, like all the other
warriors in the long line, they must depend more
on the Butter-hair's instructions beforehand than
on any battle-leader's cries during the action.
Irinore was not pleased to see her company split,
but Dulanis believed her warriors' loyalty to the
Keeper of the Cauldron should outweigh their loyalty to immediate comrades, and with a few excep-
tions she had put those she considered weaker between the streambeds and saved those she considered stronger for her reserves.

Standing above and between the lines of muck
and rotting fish, looking to left and right at warriors who would probably not be able to hear her
commands, Ylsa the Unflinching thought: We're
bait. A lot of us, maybe all of us, are going to die
with the northerners even if the Butter-hair's idea
works, and a precious flood of tears she'll drop for
us. Dulanis Butter-hair would make a fitting wife
for a god's son, true enough. How many of us understand we're going to die this afternoon for a
woman who looks at us as the gods look at blades
of grass? But here we stand and wait.

As for herself, Ylsa did not greatly care how
much longer she went on living. She had cared
when she was very young. A number of young men
and one young woman stood with her among the
bait. The woman was Etaris Pinchbirth, who had
borne two stillborn babies and a deformed creature

that lived half a day. It was not hard to guess why
Etaris would be willing to die. Ylsa supposed the
men had somehow learned early to see the stupid
ugliness of things.

The enemy appeared. Gilmar was easy to pick
out, riding his silver-gray stallion. His army
spearheaded behind him, a line of warriors at least
thirty across, the flying birds knew how many
deep. All the old conniver had to do was keep his
army in its spearhead and drive through the
stretched line of westerners at one place in the
streambed, to hit the Butter-hair and her bunched
reserves on the far bank.

But Dulanis had not left the gamble solely to
Gilmar's choice and to the fact that the Longstraits
bridges must comb the northern army to some extent, as the rocky ridge combed the Copper River.
For years Dulanis had required her fighters to mas-
ter as many weapons as they could. Almost everyone in her army had bow and arrows. Now, as
the northerners began to squeeze over a select few
bridges and draw near the dry streambeds, Ylsa
and the other battle-leaders gave their shout. In the
comparative silence before the armies came together, it passed from mouth to mouth along the line;
western bows went up, and the first round of arrows took down a score of the enemy.

If I were Gilmar, thought Ylsa, I'd aim to keep
my army as close as possible, thicken the ranks
when I could, and charge in a spearhead anyway.

But Dulanis was spreading her reserves to
present a less concentrated target, and Gilmar
might see the chance of the Longstraits line curving
around at his back. And he had two or three times

Wendy Adrian Shultz

as many warriors as Dulanis, besides reserves in the town. He began to spread his army out for a charge along the length of the straits.

According to their earlier instructions, the streambed warriors conserved their arrows, but volleys loosed now and again demonstrated that the more Gilmar's people spread out, the more of them came into range and the farther they must continue spreading if they meant to take the entire streambed line at once rather than leave their own ends exposed to a closing of the enemy line's edges.

Now at least half the northern army seemed to have reached the next ridge of higher ground to that on which the westerners waited. Only the dry streambed separated them. Had a single bridge been left between, Gilmar might even this late have pulled his army back into a long, narrow spearhead. Ylsa expected him to do so anyway, now that he could be left in no doubt as to the destruction of all bridges over this branch of the straits. But he thickened his ranks north to south facing the western line. The northerners were three or four deep when at last they charged into the muddy streambed.

The westerners shot arrows quickly now, until their supply was gone. They thinned Gilmar's ranks, but it was still two or more to one along most of the streambed when the northerners gained the near side and started scrambling up.

Irinore, Utran Quickarm, and their twenty were pulling away a pair of large boulders near the base of the dam. But some of the northerners were gaining the top of the dry bed. The westerners, loyal to Dulanis' instructions, began descending to keep Gilmar's people down, slipping in the muck, growing unrecognizable in the reddening ooze.

Plunging down, Ylsa sent her spear through one attacker's middle and used her sword to lay bare a second one's lungs, but this marked her as dangerous and almost at once she had another couple to hold off in the streambed. It did not prevent her hearing the grinding and rushing to her right. She gave the three short whoops that signalled the westerners to retreat—but not so fast their enemies could get out with them.

That last direction was hardly needed. The steep streambed was so slippery that they needed luck and chance to get out. At every step they slid on a fish or a clot of blood-slick slime or somebody's intestines. Every clump of muddy plantlife they grabbed to help pull them up came out in their hands. Every time they stooped to crawl up on hands and knees, or bent to drive in one of their weapons for a ladderhold, they risked someone else's blade through their backs. Ylsa chopped, saw her nearest attacker spurt crimson and clutch himself, turned and got half a pace up the side of the streambed, turned again and cut at another attacker.

But the boulders were out of the dam and the flood was coming. The warriors nearest the dam were already engulfed. Here and there others were starting to forget their rulers' quarrel and let everyone scramble for safety unthreatened by any weapon but the water. In a few places warriors were even trying to help each other, careless of whether the mud coatings concealed comrade or enemy.

In other places the fighting went on in face of the water, and the carelessness was in whether the

fighters were trying to strike down enemy or comrade. Around Ylsa, they were still fighting—maybe
because she had been so fierce when she jumped
down a few moments ago. She sliced someone
lengthwise, saw the reddish mud go redder from
left shoulder to right hip, turned for another step
towards high ground.

The hole in the dam enlarged itself. Half the wall
of rocks and boulders burst outward with a noise
that turned most faces south for an instant.

In that instant, someone's blade drove through
Ylsa's left cheek.

She spun and struck. She heard a scream and
didn't see much because of the blood that sluiced
over her.

Then the water hit them.

Ylsa had never learned to swim. Broad, deep
stretches of water were not plentiful in the western
herdlands; what pools there were tended to be
quiet and placid, and finding time to swim in
them would not have helped her much against this
churning torrent. For a while she thought of giving
up and drowning—at least the flood was clean liquid. Then the clean liquid filled her nose, her neck
and lungs spasmed and her mind said: *Turn your
knife on yourself rather than strangle like this!* But
her knife and sword were lost, carried out of her
grasp by the force of the water before she had realized it. So at last she thrashed up to the surface,
caught a little air, and bumped on somebody who
seemed to be flailing successfully towards the bank.
She held onto this person's middle. He tried to
wrestle, but on finding the effort carried both of
them down he gave up and let her hold on while he
kept their heads above the surface most of the time

until the water had filled the streambed high enough that they could pull themselves over the remaining lip of overhang onto the ground between straits.

They were back on the stretch between the two branches of the Longstraits that had been dammed but were now rushing full again. Gilmar's northerners should have known how to swim, but a lot more of them had been trapped than had made it out of the flood. Likewise, more of the Butterhair's people had died than survived in that line. But those northerners who had reached the bank seemed for the most part to be leaving the western survivors alone.

Gilmar himself had somehow come through whole—doubtless jumped his famous silver-gray stallion up the streambed before the torrent came. Horse and man made a clear rallying point at one of the bridges Dulanis had left across the westernmost streambed. The old ruler was gathering his forces for a spearhead drive at last. But Dulanis had left those few bridges for her own warriors' retreat, and she was hurrying with a reserve company to prevent Gilmar's crossing.

It would be a very weak spearhead even if he assembled it. At least half his army, Ylsa estimated, was caught on the far side of the once-drained streambed. They had not reached it in time to be trapped and drowned, lucky for them. She saw a few trying to pull over bridges from the eastern straits to make rafts, but she doubted very many of them would cross the bridgeless torrent within the next hour, even if they sincerely wanted to.

Nevertheless, Gilmar could afford to ignore the few draggled westerners who had reached high ground, coughing, shaking, for the most part weaponless, wanting only to roll in the comparatively dry and solid earth.

Ylsa turned to the man who had brought her out of the flood. "If you're one of Gilmar's, swim back to the army there, and I won't say anything." She pointed to the eastern bank and the warriors assembling rafts.

Whether he had not seen or chose to pretend he had not seen Gilmar at the bridge, the man dived back into the water and swam for the opposite bank. Ylsa lost sight of him. Afterwards, when the pain of her face wound caught up with the time she had to be aware of it, she thought she must have spoken only in her mind.

Meanwhile, the Butter-hair's warriors were trying to set fire to the bridge Gilmar was urging his warriors across, and the next bridges to right and left. The bridge nearest the dam had gone with that heavy burst of water. Ylsa spotted a bridge still standing about midway between the dam and Gilmar, and made for it. Other westerners joined her, calling exhausted, water-mazed comrades to come while there was one safe bridge. Seven in all crossed there, three being carried and dragged by the others. Irinore and most of her small force of dam-breakers—less Utran Quickarm and four others who had been too close when the boulders broke free—met them at the bridge.

"Ylsa?" said Irinore. "Gods!"

They waited on the safe side of the bridge until they could be reasonably sure no more of their own would reach it. Then Irinore fired it. Dulanis and her reserves had soon quashed Gilmar's attempts to cross farther downstream, and were destroying all remaining bridges. Gilmar stayed on his bridge until the last moment, and even with the west end about to fall he seemed half inclined to leap his stallion through the flames to the Butter-hair's bank and fight her hand to hand, but just as the planking started to give way he turned back to the land between the straits.

Gilmar sat on his silver-gray horse and Dulanis on her dark red, and shouted threats at each other until the rest of the bridges were consumed between the falls and Waterstead. But the fighting was over for that day. Half Gilmar's army was still stopped on the far side of the first reflooded stream, the rest dead or trapped with their ruler between two unbridged branches of the Long-straits. Some of the Butter-hair's people were trapped there also, and the enraged Gilmar had his warriors make long work of most of them, though here and there a few northerners preferred to pretend in the confusion that an enemy was one of their own comrades.

Ylsa's group discovered they had brought a wounded northerner over the bridge with them; some wanted to push him into the Longstraits, but Ylsa and Irinore forebade it. He died in the march when Dulanis began her retreat that evening.

Gilmar got his army to Waterstead. The west wall captain, not knowing if he would be praised or gutted for his generally successful efforts to save the town, had chosen to disguise himself and disappear into the crowd. He took his first good opportunity to slip away southeast and eventually found and joined Wildraith's outlaws. Gilmar hung Narum Fringe-pate head down from the high scaffolding of the ruler's house, left one of his army captains in command of the town, and set off the second day in pursuit of Dulanis.

She eluded him. Instead of marking her trail with a line of burned farms, she moved as quickly and secretly as possible, and when the wounded died, she had small companies drag their bodies some distance away, creating false trails. Soon her army was separated, but most of the little quarter-companies reached their own herdlands in safety, to regroup at Gandreth's Wells near the northern border.

As in all battles, friend had sometimes killed friend during the blur and press. Ylsa never knew whether her left cheek had been taken away by a northerner or a westerner. She guessed the weapon had been either a knife or a spear. She could not speak clearly again until winter, and she devised a mask to cover the scar. She made herself meditate on her good fortune in not having lost her teeth or jaw. She had one more trait-name now: Maimed-face. It was not an uncommon name after a generation of warfare. Nevertheless, few used it in her hearing.

Chapter 12.

Irinore's former second in command, Britran Hardfoot, had died at the bridge keeping Gilmar from crossing. Ylsa became Irinore's second, Caris Crookbrow her third, and Etaris Pinchbirth, who had survived Longstraits with a lost finger, her fourth. Irinore's was turning into a company predominantly of women.

Dulanis left most of Irinore's depleted company at Darkpool, about a day southwest of Gandreth's Wells, to spend the winter healing their wounds. Only the four first in command knew they were also posted to help keep watch in case Gilmar broke ancient practice and attempted a winter campaign. When alone, the commanders sometimes discussed who would prove the shrewder, Gilmar to try it or Dulanis to have forethought it of him. Etaris Pinchbirth called the mere idea of winter warfare impious, even in the mild north. Caris Crookbrow called it impious but clever. Irinore called it no worse than burning a peaceable river valley, and Ylsa Maimed-face said that whatever worked was good warfare.

That season Ander of Everywhere visited Darkpool. He was a minor storyteller and would never

be named one of the principal Nine, but he had
learned the wisdom to be grateful he possessed
enough talent to keep him out of anyone's army.
He was not a spy. He did not much enjoy performing for rulers since, though they had the means to
pay well, they also heard so many newsbringers
that they could judge whose skill deserved the best
pay.

One evening Ylsa and a few others were eating
stew and hull-crackling bread when Ander came in
to gather his audience in this particular earthwork
round-room. Instead of finding another place, Ylsa
retired to the wall, where she sat against an old
piece of dyed sheepskin, polished her new sword,
endured the lingering pain in her cheek, enjoyed
the body warmth of a fewscore comrades, and half-
listened a little more closely than usual. This is the
first song Ander sang:

Wildraith comes where north meets east,
And looks toward Forestedge,
And sees a trader coming light,
With but one wagon and one beast,
So there she makes her wedge.
  There's Wildraith standing forefront,
  Her hunters left and right,
  Then Hardstick and the pretty runt,
  What trader dares to fight?

(When singing this song to an audience not com-
posed of warriors, Ander made that line, "Against
whom none dare fight." And when his listeners
were mostly male, he used another word than
"runt" for the small harlot. Even with his present
modifications, someone snickered. Ylsa yawned

and muttered, "Bones and blood like everyone
else." But Ander knew how to ignore a little restlessness, and sang on.)

> He glanced around, he glanced behind,
> He held his donkey's head,
> "I am a merchant poor in goods,
> With little in my cart to find,
> And weak for war," he said.
>> "We do not plan to weapon you
>> Or rob you of your goods.
>> I only ask for answers true.
>> I'm Wildraith of the Woods.

> "Now tell us, trader, where you've been
> And tell us, have you heard
> Or met that woman whom I seek?"
> "Oh, is she thick or is she thin
> And is she soft or hard?
>> "And is she enemy or friend,
>> And do you wish to speak,
>> Or slay, or all your fortunes blend?
>> And will you pay the weak?"

> "She's tall and beautiful and red.
> Our reasons we don't tell.
> She's Ylsa of the Iron Back.
> We have not seen her face," they said,
> "But we'll repay you well."
>> "An Ylsa of that kind," he cried,
>> "I met along the track,
>> And she had comrades, too," he lied,
>> "And I will bring them back."

> He hurried back into the town,

And there found scoundrels five.
"Now one of you will Ylsa play.
When we have Wildraith's payment down,
We'll take the group alive.
  "You are five big and brawny men,
  And we'll have double pay."
  "We five can easily fight ten,
  But which will Ylsa play?"

They squabbled there an hour or more,
For none of them was fair.
At last they took the reddest one,
And borrowed clothing from a whore,
And shaved his facial hair.
  But he was lumpy as a knee,
  His skin all brown and dun.
  They wrapped his face and said that he
  Was blistered by the sun.

So back they went to Wildraith there,
All wrangling on the way:
"Will we take them to Gilmar old,
Or to Dulanis Butter-hair,
Or Senerthan Moon's-ray?
  "Gilmar is nearest, Butter-hair
  May give the richest gold.
  The god's son has the sharpest care
  To catch this outlaw bold."

They came where Wildraith waited still
With her companions four.
"Come forward, Ylsa Iron-back,
For I've searched river, field, and hill,
But I need search no more!"
  "But my reward!" the trader said,

And opened wide his sack.
"All wild animals," she said,
"Will help protect your track.

"No more you'll fear the wolves at night
Or slap flies in the day.
If any robber chances near,
For you the animals will fight,
And this shall be your pay.
    "But now, red Ylsa, come to me,
    And whisper with me here."
He stepped across, while secretly
He loosed his knife and spear.

"Now why this bandage on your face?"
"Sun-blistering," he lied.
"And why the caution of your pace?"
"I know no reason for your chase,
I'm doubtful," he replied.
    The little harlot stepped in place
    Close by Wildraith's side.
    She stared at body and at face:
    "This is a man!" she cried.

That trader's big and brawny five
Might easily fight ten.
But Wildraith and her supple four
Could twenty fight and stay alive
And fresh to fight again.
    The creatures came from wood and field,
    And ringed them by the score.
    The outlaws made those five to yield,
    And yet were hardly sore.

"How shall we punish rogues and liars?"

Jokan Hardstick said.
"My beasts are eager," she replied.
"I'll let them chase them through the briars
And nip them bare to bed."
    The rascals clutched their wounds and fled,
The creatures at their side.
    Before they came bare-rumped to bed
    That night, they'd pelted wide.

"And this false merchant cowering here?
Good Wildraith, you're too mild.
He'll make a target for our bows,"
Her hunters said. "We'll teach him fear."
But Wildraith only smiled.
"Wolf howls will rob his sleep at night
And every wind that blows
Will bring the flies and midges light
Around him where he goes."

And so that trader goes his way,
Regretting much his greed.
If he had spoken with her true,
At least, so many poor folk say,
She'd help him in his need.
    And where will Wildraith next appear?
    I know no more than you,
    But you and I need have no fear,
    If all our words are true.

Ylsa snorted. "All true! Damn silly claim for a storyteller."

"I don't see why it shouldn't be true," said Ondreth of Laniscleft.

"Maybe." Ylsa shrugged. "So now we know what Wildraith the Great was doing last summer about the time we were dying in the Longstraits. Well, at least it was a little different from the usual Wildraith-saves-somebody tale."

She rolled her blanket around her, with her face to the wall, and took no part in the discussion of why Wildraith might be looking for this Ylsa Iron-back.

Chapter 13.

Gilmar did not move down in the deep of winter, but he came well before false spring. He struck Gandreth's Wells one sleety midnight. The earthworks were high, the gates triple-layered wood, yet the attack came so suddenly and so hard that the town was ablaze within a few hours of dawn, and not one of the Butter-hair's people escaped. When Dulanis heard of it, she said that Gilmar must have had a spy or two inside the wall, some storyteller or trader or corrupted westerner, to open the gate for him; but if so the spy or spies were the town's only survivors, and he, she, or they never confessed to having been there that night.

Meanwhile, a herding family about midway to Darkpool saw the smoke against the white morning clouds. They mounted the oldest grand-daughter on their one fast pony and sent her to Darkpool with the news, while the rest of them rolled up one tent and hurried from between the two settlements, driving as many of their animals as they could in their haste. Gilmar's army found the remaining tents and herds about noon, spent a few minutes plundering the tents and a few hours roasting selected livestock for their meal. The family escaped, except for the oldest granddaughter who, upon reaching Darkpool and telling Irinore of the smoke, insisted on staying to fight rather than attempting to dodge the invaders alone across the plains.

Irinore sent three messengers of her own, all fertile townswomen. Then she paced the earthworks, making sure everything was prepared. Darkpool would not fall open so easily as Gandreth's Wells apparently had.

Ylsa joined her, looking toward the north. "They say Gilmar's army follows him like a herd because he pays better than Dulanis."

"At least Dulanis is fighting to protect her land," said Irinore.

"What was Gilmar doing last summer?"

Irinore ground a small clump of brown winter sod between her fingers. "We spared as many northern farms as we could. Gilmar spared no one five years ago in the Copper River Valley."

"Then why is Dulanis fighting the moon god's son, too?" said Ylsa. "Rulers and gods. They don't even think of us as creatures."

"Maybe not." Irinore stooped to examine a split place in the wood around one of the gate hinges. "Should we stop fighting and let them kill us?"

Ylsa started giving her sword a little extra sharpening on her whetstone. "That's what I've said all along. We should fight for ourselves and choose our sides for our own advantage, not theirs."

Irinore shouted for the blacksmith to come and reinforce the hingeplate, and Ylsa walked away, still honing her blade.

Gilmar's army came in sight close to sunset, cast-

ing long shadows to their left, driving stolen herd
animals with them clumsily, like farmers, but sufficiently. They camped just out of bowshot, slaughtered sheep and goats, roasted them whole, made a
coarse show of wasting the hides and wool, sang
warriors' songs and settled down for a feast and a
night's rest.

Gilmar himself rode his silver-gray stallion up to
the gate. In one hand he held his standard, the
gilded grapes of the united North. In the other he
carried his ceremonial scabbard, upside-down and
empty to show he came unarmed. But both he and
his horse glittered red in the last sunlight with
metal body-pieces to turn spears and arrows, and
nine thin warriors rode around him, likewise weaponless, but bringing large wooden shields to in-
terpose at need.

"Herdsfolk!" Gilmar shouted. "Your little village that was on my border lies black and smoking.
Its earthworks are salted, its wood has gone into
the fire, its people are dead to the last baby
scooped unformed out of the womb. Some of them
died slowly. That village was larger than yours, its
wall higher."

Irinore shot an arrow into the ground halfway
between the gate and Gilmar's knot of men. It was
as if she had spat to show she was not listening.
The old ruler ignored it.

"You can die like your fellow westerners," he
went on. "Or you can open your gate and join my
own people for a long, free and happy life."

As he described the benefits of fighting in his armies or raising babies for the same and tilling his
warm northern farmlands, Ylsa muttered to
Irinore, "Let me answer him."

"He deserves no answer." Irinore notched another arrow.

"Let me answer him anyway." Pushing down Irinore's hand, Ylsa hoisted herself to the top of the earthwork. "First of the North! How do we know you won't just slaughter us when we open up our gate and come out to you, all trusting?"

He lifted his scabbard and standard a little higher. "I do not claim to be a god's son or the purest flower of five generations, but my promise is firmer than either Senerthan's or the Butter-hair's, firm as the prayer granted by a god."

Ylsa aimed quickly and hurled her spear at Gilmar's unprotected face.

The men around him were equally quick and thrust their shields in its way. It caught and thrummed in the foremost triangle of wood. Gilmar laughed as he turned his stallion and led his escort back to camp.

"He came in truce," said Irinore.

"All the better target," Ylsa replied. "If I'd been successful, we'd have won this campaign at its start, saved the Butter-hair's lands, and got one enemy out of the war. It would've been worth a broken short-truce."

"Now the gods will fight for him against us," whispered Etaris Pinchbirth.

"Sacrifice me," said Ylsa. "At least half our own people won't be fighting for him against us. They'll know better than to trust his promises and risk opening up now I've angered him."

Irinore nodded.

All the next day Gilmar's army kept to its camp. "Maybe he intends to starve us out," said Caris

Crookbrow as the smell of roasting meat came over the earthwork.

"It'd be better to open the gate and die fighting," said Etaris Pinchbirth. "Now, before we lose strength."

Irinore slapped her arm. "We won't lose strength. He may be trying to tease us out in restlessness, but he won't try to starve us. Not at this time of year with our winter supplies at the level they should be, and Dulanis sure to come before we run low." She gave a young town lad orders to start stewing the dried meat for their own meal, neither more nor less than they would have prepared had Gilmar not been camped before their gate.

"Dulanis may come," said Ylsa, "if your riders get through, and if she doesn't decide to give Darkpool up like a chess arrow." (Most westerners called the least powerful chess pieces 'words,' but Ylsa had never lost the eastern habit of calling them 'arrows.')

"She won't," said Irinore. "She'll have to meet Gilmar sooner or later. Best sooner, before he's too far south, and now while she can concentrate all her fighters without worrying about Senerthan."

"Yes," Etaris agreed. "The moon god's son wouldn't risk any impiety of a winter campaign."

"Hunh," said Ylsa. "Dulanis won't know whether it's Gilmar or Senerthan. Or with how many warriors. We couldn't be sure ourselves yesterday when we sent the riders."

"Should we try sending another messenger?" said Caris.

"No," said Irinoire. Today Gilmar had a line of guards posted around Darkpool. "The Butter-hair

Wendy Adrian Shultz

can guess which one it is by where the attack's come from, and she'll bring up too many rather than too few. She'll want to crush him as fine as she can."

Ylsa stood. "It's been as good fighting with you as with anyone. I'm going to get some sleep while we have the chance. They might try us tonight."

"They didn't last night," said Caris.

"They chose to rest last night," Irinore replied. "I'd have done the same after burning a town and putting in a day's march."

Ylsa had already left them.

Irinore divided her warriors into six groups and kept two groups on watch at all times, staggering their turns so that half the watchers would never be more than a few hours' tired. Gilmar's first attack came shortly after midnight, when Caris Crookbrow and a man named Lon Widemouth were leading the watch. Gilmar's people must have edged close under cover of darkness and silence. Several score flaming arrows suddenly struck the wooden gate.

Lon Widemouth shouted an order and the defenders began tilting water down the outside of the gate. They lost three people to enemy arrows. The watchers hardly needed to call the sleepers; the tumult woke most of them.

As the last flames fell from the gate, the northern army seemed to draw back into darkness.

"Is he giving up for the night?" said Lon Widemouth.

"Or leaving us to worry," Caris replied.

"He's broken our rest," said Irinore. "Maybe that's all he wanted for now." She announced that everyone who could sleep again should do so. More accustomed to fighting in the open, with at least some chance of retreat, most of them were wakeful and nervous. She kept them busy picking at the frosty ground and piling up the earth behind the weakened gate. Ylsa went and slept, and she did not, like others who tried it, come out again in an hour to join the earthworking.

Hours later, near dawn, Gilmar threw his army against Darkpool again. They began with a battering wedge at the gate, but this seemed to be mostly ruse, for when the defenders gathered on the gateside, more northerners in greater numbers rushed in from the other direction to thrust notched poles up against the earthwall and climb.

Irinore's company was well enough disciplined that most of those whom she had earlier ordered to keep watch on the far periphery had resisted running to help defend the gate. Their shouts brought others back, and for a time they managed to strike down climbing poles and northerners.

But Gilmar had brought more than a thousand. Irinore's three hundred of last summer were now two hundred and twelve, some of them not yet completely healed and some newly chosen this winter from the Darkpool people, nearly-grown youngsters and women past childbearing. Besides the warriors, trained, wounded, and new, there were three hundred and twenty townsfolk, half of them children, and more than half of them frightened beyond the measure of fear that strengthens. And the earthworks were scarcely three warrior-lengths high.

Soon, here and there, some northerners were gaining the wall's top, running along to strike at defenders or finding the treadholds to descend in groups and wedge against the townspeople. Still, for a time, the defenders were able to kill most of the penetrators, but the more of them who got inside, the more divided work there was for the small and decreasing number of westerners. Some of Irinore's warriors choked until they became easy targets when they found their feet slipping on dismembered limbs of children they had known since birth or for more than half a winter.

Then Gilmar's battering-wedge crashed through the gate, and northerners chipped away at the wood edges until they could begin pressing in over the new shoulder-high earthwork thrown up that night.

As dawnshed filled the settlement, Irinore looked around and saw no townsfolk and only a few score warriors left standing among the buildings, besides the thirteen or ten with her trying to stop the flow at the broken gate. Etaris Pinchbirth was in her group, Lon lay dead nearby with his mouth split still wider by an enemy blade, she thought she glimpsed Caris Crookbrow and Ondreth of Laniscleft fighting back to back between gate and farther wall. She had not seen Ylsa since shortly after the start of Gilmar's second attack. Many of Darkpool's rooms were dug into the earth, but almost all the roofs above ground were in flames.

Irinore gave the three close-strung whoops that signalled her warriors to retreat—with her group if they could reach it, otherwise any way they could find. She fought on at the gate a few moments longer, losing two more companions but gaining almost a score who managed to push through to her, among them Caris and Ondreth. She did not attempt to lead them out the gate, blocked as it was by the last of Gilmar's army pressing to get inside, but up to the watchtower and down a nearby climbing-stick that the northerners had deserted when the gate broke. Several jumped rather than wait their turn to climb. One jumper injured herself too badly to move and had to be left.

The few trailing northerners still outside saw the escape and made for the little band. Fortunately, when Irinore removed her last plug of defenders, most of the press had hurried on through. Irinore lost three more fighters, including Caris Crookbrow, but the rest cut free and gained open field.

They huddled down in the stiff brown grass on the far side of a rise and took a few moments to rest. They were twenty-three: Irinore, Etaris, nineteen of their warriors and two townspeople, one a balding fellow on the downslope of his prime, the other a girl in her early teens. Fifteen women and eight men in all. The townsgirl and five warriors were wounded and took this time to bind up the bleeding as well as they could.

They were on the eastern side of Darkpool and south of Gilmar's camp. Halfway to the limit of their vision was one of the rare stands of trees, chiefly poplars, that dotted the plains, marking water sources. Irinore gave her survivors little longer than enough time to steady their breathing before they started for the trees. The townsman tried to argue it would be the first place the northerners searched, but Irinore cut him short. If Gilmar decided to make a wide sweep, they would have small chance wherever they retreated, but meanwhile they needed water and the hope, elusive or not, of shelter.

They were a third of the way when they heard the sweep coming behind them. Irinore formed her people into a wedge facing town, herself at its point, and they waited. The rising sun cast their shadows long before them toward the northerners who appeared in a line, backed by the smoke of burning Darkpool. This was only a small part of Gilmar's army, perhaps a hundred, but it would be enough. It shouted again and formed for a charge.

But an answering shout came, not from Irinore's people who were saving their breath for the clash, but from behind them. They glanced back. Another line had appeared from the stand of trees. Maybe a score were mounted and galloping forward, the rest—two or three hundred—followed at a run.

The northerners faltered. Irinore considered telling her wedge to retreat toward the newcomers, in the hope they were friends, but that might be to invite quick attack from the closer line of known enemies, so she ordered the wedge to hold tight. Whoever led the northern command—it was not Gilmar—got back his wits and shouted for the charge, clearly hoping to reach Irinore's group first.

They did, but only moments before the riders. Foremost was a red horse carrying a woman with black hair plaited thick and shining round her head, and a sword that gleamed more like liquid than metal. More northern warriors dodged away and fled from that weapon than were struck down by it, but the immediate effect was much the same for Irinore's people. The other riders, chief among them a youth with the straw-colored hair most common among westerners, and a small woman whose size belied the force of her blows, swung their weapons with more determined aim. When arrows started arriving from the runners—striking only northerners, never westerners or riders, in spite of the confusion, the last of Gilmar's men gave up the attack and ran.

The black-haired woman stopped her horse in front of Irinore and Etaris.

"Wildraith?" said Ondreth of Laniscleft.

Wildraith nodded. "I've heard of an Ylsa Quicksword who fights for Dulanis Butter-hair, an Ylsa Closemouth who wintered in Darkpool with Irinore of the Copper Riverlands?"

"I'm Irinore," the captain replied. She was too tired to appreciate more than dimly the idea that it was her old companion whom Wildraith Veil-eyes had been searching for through all the tales and ballads. "Ylsa's not with us. I wish she was. I think she's dead in Darkpool."

Wildraith looked at the smoke. "You are all who survived?"

Irinore shrugged. "There may be a few others who got over the walls somewhere else. If Gilmar's people haven't cut them down yet."

Wildraith said, "My people will help you," turned her horse, and started galloping in a shallow curve to the south, followed by her score of riders. Some of the unmounted outlaws helped Irinore's group to the trees, fed them, blanketed them, saw to the wounded. Most of the outlaws went northwest, routed Gilmar's camp guards and followers and herds of unbutchered meat, set fire to the tents, and faded away before the warriors looting the town saw what was happening and began to hurry back.

Wildraith completed her circuit of town before midday. She and her riders brought back twenty-six more western warriors and three townspeople who had got over the wall, some of them without waiting for Irinore's signal. Ylsa Quicksword was not among them.

"She's dead, then." Irinore gulped the outlaws' sharp honey-wine. "Dead like Caris and Lon and the rest."

"Wildraith?" said the small horsewoman they now knew was called Tilis the Supple. "If she's dead . . . shall we stay and try to find the body? I might be able to recognize it, be sure . . ."

Wildraith shook her head. "If she is killed, then she was not Ylsa of Ironstead. If my Ylsa dies, I will know."

"So she wasn't your Ylsa." Too much of Irinore had died five years ago with her farm and most of her family for her eyes to water now, but she took another long drink from the wineskin. "She was a strong woman."

Ondreth was the only westerner who asked why Wildraith wanted Ylsa of Ironstead. Wildraith shook her head again and did not answer. Not even her first four, Tilis, Jokan, Ethaan and Arileth, had ever been told the answer to that question.

By midday, the outlaws were moving back toward the river, taking the Darkpool survivors with them in a southwest line.

Meanwhile, about the time Irinore was deciding on escape, some of Gilmar's men were finding six children guarded by one warrior in the wellroom. The warrior was Ylsa Quicksword.

The wellroom was three-quarters belowground, with stone-paved steps and a low, turf-covered roof. The settlement also had three shaft wells, but the wellroom source was generally considered the Darkpool itself. As long and wide as a short person, it filled half the chamber. Its edges and part of the surrounding floor had been lined with flagstones cross-hatched for better footing. Milk, fermented milk, ale, wine and cheeses were stored along the walls in jars of stone or wooden casks covered with wax and clay to take advantage of the cool without suffering from the damp.

Some time ago in the middle of town, Ylsa had stumbled on two children huddling against a wall, staring at the battle confusion and waiting to be killed like their playmates. She had pushed them down the nearest stairs, which happened to be those of the wellroom. The other four children were already there. Ylsa didn't like the place as a refuge. It had only the one way in and out, and it was sure to be looted sooner or later. But it would be hard to burn, and half the children were too small to be gotten over the town wall with the settlement full of northerners. So she shoved the children into a corner and crouched at the foot of the stairs.

When the invaders spotted the stairway and started down, she sprang up to meet them. Soon the narrow, semi-enclosed passage was plugged with bodies, and Ylsa retreated a little, not really expecting the clump of carnage to hide them until the battle outside was over, but using the time to rest.

The northerners cleared the stairs and started down again. Ylsa choked the passage a second time with dead and wounded. Once more they cleared the stairs and once more she blocked them. This time there was a much longer wait before the invaders began removing the bodies. Ylsa beckoned one of the older children to help tie up some shallow cuts on her limbs and torso. A couple of wounded enemies struggled in the mass on the stairs, making it hump feebly like one single dying creature. Noises of the rout came down to the well-room, and several children sobbed in their corner.

At last the invaders started dragging their comrades' bodies up out of the passage again. Ylsa came back to the foot of the stairs and waited. Eventually, as twice before, the passage was cleared, and she tensed for the next attack.

But this time no one came for some moments. When the first man did come, he sat on the top step, sword drawn and pointed downwards but otherwise seeming at ease.

"Herder!" he shouted. "They tell me you've killed twenty or thirty of my men here."

"Gilmar yourself," said Ylsa, looking at the length and breadth and gilding of his sword, and when he laughed she added, "And I'm just as ready to kill you."

He stood and descended three steps. She mounted three. They stood staring at each other across the remaining four or five steps. Ylsa's patch had long fallen from her scarred cheek. Gilmar squinted at it and laughed.

"Maimed-face," he said. "Are you the patched one who tried to spear me yesterday?"

She took a fresh grip on her sword—thin compared to his—and charged up.

He moved quickly despite his bulk, was at the

top again, and let a pair of his men close down in front of him.

Ylsa retreated a few steps. "No, I didn't think you'd stand one to one, old man of the North."

He laughed again. "You have a choice. Block these stairs with my men one more time, and we'll wall over the opening and leave you tombed with the bodies. Or come up in truce and take command of a company for me. I'll need at least one new captain thanks to you and your herders."

"They say you pay generously," said Ylsa.

"I'll pay you as much as any born northerner."

"I was born closer to your North than the Butter-hair's West." Ylsa measured the children's chances if she left them here hidden, and decided the invaders must have heard or glimpsed them by now. "What about these children?"

"How old are they?" said Gilmar.

"Seven, the oldest one." He was actually ten, but small for his age, and Ylsa guessed Gilmar's reason for asking. The older the children, the less likely that resettlement would change their first loyalty.

"We'll settle them on northern farms," said Gilmar.

"All right." It might be a trick, but death by betrayal would be faster than death by suffocation in a damp cellar with decaying corpses. "Come on, youngsters, we're selling out to the enemy."

Much as Gilmar mistrusted competence in anyone who might share his high work of rulership, he liked and looked for competence in the warriors and under-officers of his armies; otherwise, he could hardly have made a fighting force from his people. And something in this maimed-faced woman's hard practicality rang a perverse response in his sense of humor. He would have her watched closely, paid well, never raised above a captain of three hundred, but so long as she kept her part of the bargain, he would keep his. Besides, he could threaten to have the six children killed by their adoptive northern families if Ylsa betrayed him.

He never had to make this threat, however, for Ylsa felt no reason to betray him so long as he paid her and left her as much alone as a warrior could be left to do her work.

The destruction of his camp slowed Gilmar's invasion but did not stop it. He had a second thousand warriors, with their supplies and followers, coming five days behind the first, and a thousand, whose planned role would be to string out and guard the supply lines, coming behind the second.

He sat on his stallion between the burning town and the burning camp, cursed, looked in all directions and saw only plains, low hills, and an occasional stand of leafless trees, and cursed again. But his chief quarrel was with Dulanis Butter-hair, not Wildraith's gadflies. He sent two companies of a hundred each back north. If they found any outlaws in their path, they were to fight, kill, and capture. (They did not find any outlaws.) But their chief mission was to tell the two forces coming behind to hurry their march. The two hundred themselves were to return to Gilmar's lands, settle the six Darkpool children on six widely separated farms, and spend the rest of the season gathering and training more young warriors. (These orders they carried out successfully.)

Gilmar sent Ylsa Maimed-face north with these

two hundred, so she had no further part in the invasion that year.

He ordered the rest of his people at Darkpool to go after the scattered animals rather than the outlaws. With what beasts they could recover and what stores they could loot from the town, they did not starve, though they did suffer from a freezing rain that fell that night. Gilmar himself slept in a makeshift tent of plundered blankets and the skins of fresh-slaughtered sheep.

He had more than six hundred fighting men left after the Gandreth's Wells and Darkpool losses and the two hundred sent back north. When his second thousand arrived, he joined the two armies and proceeded south.

Dulanis had made her own plans for such an out-of-season attack. She began gathering her army the hour that the first of Irinore's messengers reached her from Darkpool. Though she did not know of the slight delay Wildraith's outlaws had occasioned Gilmar, it served her well enough. She met Gilmar between Darkpool and Middle Wells at the Old Mounds, twelve hundred westerners against sixteen hundred northerners. Many of the northerners were sick from their unsheltered time at Darkpool, and the westerners fought to protect their own home herdlands. It was one of the war's fiercest battles, bloodier than New Crescent or Rocky Shallows or even Longstraits. It provided the storytellers some of their best material, and they sang for generations of the Nine Moments during that battle when Dulanis and Gilmar came sword to sword. When it was over, more than eight hundred westerners and nine hundred northerners were dead and dying, not counting the northern camp helpers and followers who perished when Dulanis struck their camp about midday.

Gilmar's forces still outnumbered the Butter-hair's, and he might have been said to have won the battle. But he was deep in enemy land and she on her home ground. So he prudently began his retreat that same night. Dulanis harried him all the way. Her army was constantly swelling up again with companies that had not been able to come in time for the battle itself. They dashed in and out for skirmishes, suffering light losses while killing more than half the northern survivors of Old Mounds. Gilmar could only squeeze together the stretched supply guard of his third thousand.

They fought a second battle at Darkpool. This time the Butter-hair's people outnumbered the invaders and though the death count was much less on both sides than at the Old Mounds, Gilmar was finally driven back into his own lands.

So the great campaign of that year was fought before the fighting season, and all sides spent the summer watching one another, with an occasional border skirmish.

The outlaws, meanwhile, brought Irinore and her little group to within a day's march of Deepspring, one of the herders' easternmost walled towns, and there parted with them. Ondreth of Laniscleft decided to go with Wildraith. Had Irinore been a captain who inspired less loyalty, or had Wildraith herself made the least attempt to recruit them, more of the Darkpool survivors might well have turned outlaw. Even Ondreth had a long struggle in her mind. She did not announce her decision until Irinore and the rest were exchanging last thanks and farewells with their rescuers.

"I was afraid you'd do this," said Irinore. "It's your choice, Ondreth, but you could have had Ylsa's place in my command. And if the chance falls on us, I'll have to claim you as a deserter and loyalty-breaker."

"They saved us from the northerners," said Ondreth.

"They would have saved the northerners instead if we'd outnumbered them."

"Repeat that to Wildraith's own ears."

Irinore repeated it to Wildraith's own ears. The First of Outlaws merely smiled and nodded in agreement.

When at last Irinore reported her story to the Butter-hair, she did not include Ondreth's desertion but let her be counted as one of the many dead. Nor did she attempt to draw any line between the warriors who had waited for the signal to retreat and those who had escaped over the wall before it came. She did tell how Wildraith had come to their help at the last moment.

"She is still an outlaw," said Dulanis. "It does not change her heresy in the judgment of the moon god's son. And she could not have saved you had you not first brought your people out of the town."

Irinore was called a remarkable captain for having saved even forty-six of her command, besides herself and five townspeople. Her reputation now firm, Dulanis gave her freedom to fill up and train her company however she chose. Irinore filled it almost entirely with women and it became the force it was to remain for the rest of the war, perhaps the single band the storytellers celebrated most after Wildraith's. Irinore only regretted the loss of Ylsa the Unflinching, who should have remained her second in command.

At the beginning of her service to Gilmar, Ylsa had to demonstrate her aversion to serving as a drain for the lust of Gilmar's men, as she had had to demonstrate it to those of Dulanis Butter-hair. But when one northerner had lost a rib, another most of his teeth, and a third half of his appendage itself, her new comrades accepted her celibacy as her old ones had done, and she fit well into the northern army, except that she never again came as near to making a close friend as she had with Annis Drymouth, who was years dead, or with Irinore of the Copper River, whom she believed dead.

Chapter 14.

The Coldsilver River had its source in a deep forest spring and flowed southwest to join the Great Curve of the Copper River. Hunters had long considered the spring blessed because of its clarity, pure tastelessness, and the healing herbs that grew near it in abundance, as if an ancient herb cultivation had gone wild. Older generations had called the area around the spring Gods' Garden. Senerthan had declared it peculiarly sacred to his father Ormrathe and made it the site of Ormrathestead, his holiest stronghold. He also changed the name of the Coldsilver to Ormrathe's River.

Ormrathestead, like many of Senerthan's deep-forest settlements, had no all-encircling walls. Even now in the twenty-first winter of the war Senerthan had only enclosed certain strongholds at the edge of his forest with full walls on the western and northern plan. Otherwise, he depended on trees for watchtowers, preferred protective coloring and mobility of movement to restrictive defenses. Ormrathestead, moreover, was protected both by the god's consecration and by the many other settlements between it and the western and northern enemies.

One such settlement was Oldbowers, farther downstream, long a traditional place of courtship and marriage nights. Oldbowers had enlarged with Senerthan's breeding program, and he had provided it with a low tower of stones, wood, and mud where the young children could be guarded in case of attack, but for the most part the hunters still lived in natural or temporary woodland shelters, invisible to untrained eyes.

The eyes of Wildraith's outlaws were not untrained. The hunters who came to her taught the herders and farmers. Some outlaws thought it fine sport to penetrate Senerthan's unwalled breeding bowers by night and impregnate or be impregnated by any drowsy hunters who chanced to be sleeping alone.

Jokan Greenstick, now often called Hardstick, was the only one of the first Five to indulge in such adventures. Tilis the Supple had let her former talent rust and enjoyed celibacy since the half-burning of Old Ironstead, while Ethaan and Arileth were exclusively Of One Another. And Wildraith did not approve of the business. When forced to comment, she questioned the similarity of dreaming acquiescence to conscious consent and the wisdom of leaving Senerthan more children for his army or raising baby outlaws to face danger from all sides. She refused to warn any of her followers to take care when they went on these exploits or to give them sympathy if they returned with tales of near capture.

Nevertheless, Jokan seized every opportunity, and when Tilis tried to caution him, he replied that if she and certain other comrades were less diligent in following Wildraith's impossible pattern, he and

those like him might not have the inclination left
for Senerthan's hunters. This was no more than a
partial excuse, for Jokan did enjoy a number of
willing outlaws and they him. But he felt frustrated
with Tilis for refusing his love; and then, the very
danger added allurement to slipping in and out of
a sleepy hunter's embrace.

The second midwinter after Dulanis invaded
Gilmar's North, two nights after the full moon
(storytellers would later make it the actual night
when Ormrathe's circle was roundest and
brightest), Jokan paid another visit to Oldbowers.
The sky was heavily clouded when he came, but
sunny days and hunters' skates had left the frozen
Coldsilver clear of snow. Jokan followed it to a
shelter of dry branches, found two women sleeping
in one bed for warmth, and spent a pleasant hour
between them. One showed a little surprise, for
hunters seldom moved from bower to bower at
midnight, especially in the winter season when
more males shared the breeding settlements. But
Jokan persuaded her, as he had others, that he was
something between a dream and a were-beast in its
human form. Some outlaws pretended to be gods
in this game, and Senerthan might have had other
supposed divine offspring to threaten his unique
claim, except that the hunters thought afterwards
it had been a dream, or could not be sure which
man's seed had sprouted, or thought of
Senerthan's cousin Erthan Subtle-mind and
prudently kept silent. But Jokan knew Wildraith's
opinion closely enough to respect her scorn of
playing at godhood, even if he did not respect her
dislike of this impregnation game in its other
aspects.

When he emerged, filled with the usual mixture of satiation and naggling guilt, a little snow was falling and the clouds were thinned so that the moon now diffused its light through them. Five years as one of Wildraith's chief captains had taught Jokan much woodcraft, but even so his footprints seemed hardly noticeable to his own gaze, and he counted on the continued snowfall to cover them, or a wind to blow them away in drifts. Still, he walked upriver, away from his present outlaw camp, intending to use the rest of the long winter night doubling back and zig-zagging.

One of the Oldbowers children, a girl of about eight years, came outside to relieve herself and saw Jokan's trail. She woke her mother, who alerted the rest of the community. Jokan was taken and bound well before dawn by a group of eighteen skate-shod hunters, including the two women which whom he had recently coupled. One was outraged and wanted to stretch him out on Ormrathe's frozen river and see at once if all their brains together could not prove as subtle as Erthan's single ingenuity. The other was amused and pointed out that they owed the seducer no less reward than to be presented whole to the moon god's son. Most of the party agreed with the second woman, though probably thinking less of what honor might be due their captive than of how Senerthan would receive the news that an outlaw had been taken alive and not brought fresh to him when he was only a day's journey distant, less if travellers skated up Ormrathe's Rivers.

Jokan had killed one hunter and wounded five seriously in the struggle. Their companions cached them as comfortably as possible, sent one of the swiftest skaters back to Oldbowers with the news, put the dead man's skates on Jokan's feet and taught him this mode of travel perforce as they hastened to Ormrathestead.

Attaran of Everywhere had learned quickly and readily how to move through the forest, but being more attuned by nature to the skills of storytelling than of fighting, he was content to serve Wildraith as a scout. Even in the cold season when all warfare was quiescent the outlaws had to break into smallish bands and change their hiding places often in order to share the forest's bounty with Senerthan's people. Attaran was searching out new campsites when he saw eleven hunters skating upriver in the dawnlight with Jokan of the West bound in their midst. Attaran reckoned his chances of effecting Jokan's rescue, found them ludicrously slight, and hurried to Wildraith.

Those who had chosen outlaw life and loyalty to Wildraith now numbered three hundred nineteen, but she lived most of her time apart, rarely allowing more than four companions. She remained aware that the original outlawry had been laid upon them all because she laughed at this little forest chieftain's claim to be the moon god's physical offspring. The outlawry might have come later, from any of these rulers, for serious concerns of life and death, as humans counted life and death; but as the cord unwound it had come through her amusement. Thus, the greatest danger must be near her.

Twice or thrice she had tried to elude these followers completely. If they refused to disband when she was gone, if they persisted in making another side in the game of human warfare, then Ethaan, Arileth, Tilis, Jokan, Yrn Long-grin, Ilith the Rust-haired, Attaran of Everywhere and others could give them the leadership they desired. But Ethaan and Arileth always found her; Tilis, Attaran, and the others pleaded with her. So she stayed. However carefully they must move, they were a growing number to help her search for Ylsa of Ironstead. And was her great aim so much more important, after all, than their petty warring?

The few she allowed near her served as messengers to hold the outlaws together in a web of communication. They changed frequently, and the group with her today would not be the group near her tomorrow or yesterday. They also gave her companionship—more than she wished, but some measure of companionship was valuable. Being human now herself and bound by certain limitations of personality, she preferred some comrades to others. The four who came with her from Ironstead were dearest to her affections, even the weak and selfish Greenstick.

Tilis the Supple, Arria of the Northern Shore, and Yrn Long-grin were with her the morning that Attaran, the fourth, brought news of Jokan Greenstick's capture.

"His coupling sport again," said Tilis.

Humanity limited Wildraith's awareness, as it limited everything else. She had moved sensually deadened through the night of battle at Ironstead, understanding why so many of her sibling aspects chose the slower incarnation of growth from infancy. Later, learning some physical control of her brain material, she had drowned in a tiny particle of what she knew as pure spirit. With practice, she had regained, not native unity with her sibs, but assimilation of all creatures' awareness in her own guardianship of the woodlands. These were still her charge, would be unless she failed her errand and plunged into the painful cold climb through long, lone-torn timelessness. She could have known, even in this brain, all that the forest knew, but found it better for most of each day and night to leave her fellow creatures privacy of movement. Now she tuned her mind to the creaturely senses in this small part of one small woodland, and witnessed all the details seen and felt by birds, beasts, trees and dreaming, frozen moss. "His coupling sport again," she said. "My little Greenstick."

"We five could rescue him from eleven," said Yrn Long-grin, generously including Attaran's weapons.

The storyteller closed his fist in negation. "They were already too close to Ormrathestead. We couldn't reach them in time."

"They have already entered Senerthan's bower," said Wildraith.

"How many does the First of Hunters have with him in Ormrathestead?" said Arria. "About nine hundred, isn't it?"

"Closer to a thousand," said Attaran. "But half of them are children, younger than fifteen years. And no walls around the place. A fair enough fight, if we can gather all our people."

"Many of the children would fight with their parents," said Wildraith. "Many would die for Jokan Greenstick's silly game." She had learned something of how humans, despite their actions, valued these lives for their own sakes.

Tilis was weeping openly, but she said, "Let him die. He knew the risk."

"He'll suffer before he dies," said Attaran. "Erthan of the Subtle Mind is with Senerthan in Ormrathestead."

Arria of the Northern Shore closed her eyes in thought. "Couldn't we slip in tonight?"

"Tonight will be too late," said Tilis. "Senerthan and his cousin will have had the whole day with nothing to do but amuse themselves."

Attaran mused, fist to chin. "We probably wouldn't have time to gather our full strength in that case anyhow."

Wildraith stood. She had known since hearing Attaran's news what she would do, and she had let her captains exercise their brains long enough. "Come. We should have time to save most of Greenstick."

Yrn, Arria, and Attaran rose at once. But Tilis caught Wildraith's hand. "No! Wildraith, let him die!"

"You can best me with every weapon, Tilis Supple-arm," said Attaran. "But I am not afraid to follow our First of Outlaws."

Wildraith looked at them all. Three who could not think of a good plan but trusted her unthinkingly. One who could think of a plan, practical if unacceptable, and who used her mind to guess something of the truth. Wildraith sighed and moved her hands so that she was grasping Tilis rather than Tilis her. "You are not afraid to follow me, Attaran, because you believe I plan some wonder to save us all. Tilis does not stop thinking when I say, Come. Her fear is wiser than your trust that has no use for thought. Someday Tilis may be the greatest of you all." How clumsy human speech remained, even after five years. Wildraith turned to

Tilis and disengaged her hands. "But I think you fear more for me than for yourself, and this is less wise. Now come."

Attaran and Arria were watching the snow evaporate from the ground. Yrn Long-grin remained a little more bold. "You'll gather the animals, won't you? The animals, Wildraith?"

"Is it so much easier to gather animals than outlaws?" said Wildraith. That was not the full reason. Outlaws must be alerted by human messengers, while forest animals would come at the touch of an instant thought; and animals could travel faster. But Wildraith had learned other ideas. The weighing of this against that, which seemed to be what humans called honor and allegiance. And curiosity, intense curiosity. She had felt disappointment verging on despair, wounds, heat, hunger, cold, weariness, even some undeadly but annoying disease. What could Erthan of the Subtle Mind devise more painful than ordinary human life?

She summoned three wolves and a pair of hawks, and a porcupine with its own curiosity insisted on tagging along. As it turned out, she did not need their escort. Her group found a ten-year-old boy hunting near the settlement. He shot a few arrows at them, but they dodged easily. Tilis and Yrn soon disarmed him and covered his mouth. Wildraith checked with creatures in sight of Ormrathestead and learned that the boy's shouts had not been heard.

She knelt in the snow and looked into the boy's eyes. "Go to Senerthan of the Long Forest and tell him that Wildraith the Heretic offers a trade. If he would rather have me than the outlaw his people from Oldbowers brought to him this morning—"

The boy's eyelids opened wider; he had been at

his hunting game since before light and did not know of the captive, or he would have been in Ormrathestead trying for a glimpse. Yrn, Arria, and Attaran were protesting loudly.

"Tilis the Wise stands silent," Wildraith told them. "You trusted me to save our companion with a wonder. Let it be a wonder of my own choosing." They quieted reluctantly and she looked back at the child. "Senerthan must send his captured outlaw to the tall ash tree that lightning hit last summer, inside the rocks that some folk call ancient ruins. Senerthan may send as many hunters as he likes, but they must not bring bows or spears or any weapon that is thrown. They will free the outlaw and let him leave in peace, doing him no further injury. When he is gone from their sight, I will come and be Senerthan's captive. But remember this and repeat it clearly: the First of Hunters must understand that I give myself only for the rest of today and tonight, only until the first rim of morning sun appears above the horizon, whether visible or clouded." She picked up the boy's bow, spear, sword and hunting knife, and gestured for Yrn and Arria to release him.

He looked at the animals. "You're Wildraith?"

"Yes. Repeat the message."

He repeated it accurately. "But how do we know you'll come?"

"If I did not intend an honest trade, I would not tell him I will stay only until sunrise."

Seeing they did not plan to hurt him the boy swaggered in his role of important messenger. "I want my weapons back."

Wildraith smiled. "I'll bring them to the tall ash tree. Now stop delaying."

The boy ran towards Ormrathestead.

Yrn and Arria argued all the way to the ash tree.
Tilis was silent and seemed resigned, Attaran fell
silent and seemed to expect a miracle instead of a
trade. They arrived and found a hiding place behind the boulders that resembled ruins but were a
natural formation left by glaciers when this conti-
nent was in the northern hemisphere.

"They are coming," said Wildraith. "Some of
them have spears and arrows, but it may only be
that they fear betrayal. They are bringing Greenstick."

"Is he whole?" said Attaran.

"He has bloody hands and fingertips, but he
walks unaided."

"The fool!" Tilis blinked rapidly and gripped
her spear. "You should have let them keep him.
It's no fair trade, even if you let them hold you for
two heartbeats."

Wildraith drew her nameless sword, her gift
from the soldiers' god, forged and tempered—in a
sense—in hell, which was not so far from heaven in
the coexistence of planes. She would not need this
sword at present, and in so far as there was anything material about it, she did not want to risk its
falling into Senerthan's possession. She moved it
back and forth in the sunlight, watching the gleam
of its nearly translucent blade. She was like the
hunters' boy, jealous to keep her toys. She looked
at Tilis. "Do you plan to run out to them when
they come and tell them you are Wildraith?"

Tilis shuddered into herself, showing that
Wildraith's surmise was near the truth.

"An hour ago," the First of Outlaws went on, "I
thought you were my wisest companion. Perhaps
you are, after all. But I see I cannot entrust this to
you." She looked around at the others. Arria was

another woman and might be foolish enough to attempt what even Tilis had thought of. Yrn could be reckless. Wildraith turned to Attaran. "You are bearded, and use all weapons clumsily. Keep my sword until I return, and do not try to become a story for others to tell."

He took the sword and nodded.

She entrusted her knife to Yrn, her small axe to Arria, to Tilis her bone needle and the necklace of polished pebbles and braided cords that a child had given her in the Copper River valley. These were all of human manufacture and would not enable their keepers to claim her identity. She had neither spear nor arrows. Left alone, she would not have needed to hunt her food. The axe and the knife she used for cutting wood, fashioning garments, the many other small, everyday tasks. She had never learned to fight with any weapon but the sword.

"And if you don't come back to us?" Attaran whispered at last.

"I will come back." She did not like to think of the other possibility, of the timelessness apart, of universes burning and reforming unexperienced while she struggled back in darkness alone.

"But if you don't," said Arria. "The gods know what Erthan may do in a day and a night."

Wildraith smiled. "Very few of the gods know, I think. And very few would be curious to know. But if I don't come back . . . give my sword to Ylsa the Ironstead Widow."

"And if we never find her?" said Yrn.

Wildraith looked at Tilis, then Attaran. "If you cannot find her, give it to the one you think wants least to hold our outlaws together."

"How . . ." Yrn began, but choked his voice as they heard Senerthan's people approaching.

They came with a caution that suggested their bows and spears were indeed carried for self-protection. Senerthan had sent thirty hunters to see the exchange, but they might not realize there were no more outlaws waiting than those the boy had seen.

"Better odds than when you turned Gilmar back at Middle Curve," Yrn whispered. "Better than when you visited Senerthan in New Crescent." Yrn had not shared either fight.

"Do you think Greenstick is worth even thirty bodies?" Wildraith replied.

Three ropes bound Jokan, one holding his crossed wrists, one hobbling his ankles, one looped tightly round his arms and waist. When the hunters came to the tree, they argued with each other for a few moments in low voices before they cut the rope between Jokan's ankles and dropped the long ends of the one about his middle. He shook free, glancing at them. They stood aside to clear a path for him and he took it without waiting to see whether they would untie his hands. At first he walked. When he got a few paces from them, he broke into a run, stumbling on the small rocks that sprinkled the ground near the boulders. The hunters sent no weapon after him, and he ducked safely through a space in the rock formation some distance from where his friends waited.

Wildraith moved from the crevice where she had been watching. Tilis caught her arm.

"They have traded honestly," Wildraith told her. "Go find Jokan Greenstick and untie his hands."

Tilis let her go and turned toward the place where Jokan had entered shelter. Wildraith took the boy's weapons and went out to the hunters.

They looked at her as nervously as Greenstick had looked at them. She tossed the child's weapons to the snowy ground between them and herself. Seeing that these were small and she had no adult weapons of her own, they seized her and pulled her out of sight of the ash tree and boulders. They would have left the boy's things had she not reminded them in time. They glanced back often. When well away from the place, they stopped long enough to make hasty work of binding her as they had bound Jokan, except that, for speed, they did not hobble her ankles. From their conversation she learned that some of them had wanted to tie Jokan to the ash tree and not loose him until they had her, that others had planned to join the outlaws rather than return to Senerthan without a captive if this trade had been offered in bad faith. Wildraith mused on the bonds formed between leaders and followers.

As they neared the settlement, however, the captain of the thirty stopped them and cracked the irony of Wildraith's meditation. "You've acted in honor," he said. "We agreed that if we got this far without being attacked, we'd offer you a choice. We're willing to kill you quickly here and take our chance that the moon god's son will be content with your corpse."

Wildraith shook her head. "I will see tomorrow's dawn. But I rejoice that you do not borrow all your thoughts and courage from your ruler's commands."

The captain shrugged in seeming disappointment. But many of the others showed relief. So they had simply borrowed their temporary courage from an intermediate commander instead of the one they conceived—because most humans would not look deeply enough into themselves—was their highest chief.

They walked on and entered Ormrathestead. The moon god had not consecrated this place, but the hunters had made it clean and pleasant. They had even laid down stone paths from bower to bower, so confident were they that attack would never come here. By keeping to the paths they preserved as much land as possible for plantlife in the warmer seasons. It was less fragrant in winter, without the growing herbs and flowers; and what snow had not already been trampled was trampled now by the easterners pressing close to see Wildraith captured at last. Nor did they wash so often in cold weather. But Senerthan had sanitation plans that would do credit to more careful humans in more fastidious cultures, even if Senerthan's principal motive was only to preserve his supposed holy spring.

About a third of the Ormrathestead dwellings were underground burrows, although their openings were more decorated than disguised. The aboveground bowers were more permanent and visible than those of the middle forest. Skins and furs supplemented boughs and withies over the wooden frameworks, almost in the style of the western herders except that the skins came from hunted rather than domestic animals. Here and there a wall had been insulated with logs or stone and earth against the wind. Senerthan's own large bower, built over the source of the spring itself, was almost entirely stone and earth, layered so thick that plants grew on it in summer, a sort of burrow bulging up instead of tunnelling down. Its entrance-way was an arch of saplings thickly intertwined with fragrant green pine boughs.

Warm in his almost draftless dwelling, Senerthan sat at a small fire with Erthan of the Subtle Mind and Meleth of the Mossy Bower for his only companions during the wait. "You see," said Meleth when three of the thirty brought Wildraith in (leaving the other twenty-seven on guard at the pine bedecked entrance), "I said she would come."

"I am very pleased," said Erthan, "to acknowledge my mistake."

Senerthan looked at Wildraith. "First of Outlaws."

"Yes. In so far as I am called the First of Outlaws, you may be called the First of Hunters."

"It's not my only trait-name."

"Trait-names," said Wildraith, "are easy to give and lose."

"True," he said. "You have one you can easily lose: 'The Heretic.' I have one that can never be taken from me: the Moon God's Son."

Wildraith laughed. "You have no reason to be ashamed of your father, but he was not a god."

Senerthan had been playing chess with Meleth. He snapped one of the pieces. "Do you say that my mother Seneth of the Sure Bow lied?"

"Lies have many reasons," said Wildraith. "Unconsciousness of the truth may be one."

"You are unconscious of the truth—that the great moon god Ormrathe fathered me on Seneth Sure-bow of the True Speech!"

Erthan grinned and interlaced his fingers.

Wildraith said, "You limit your thoughts when you try to bind any god to a single name. And the moon god has parented no human."

Senerthan brought his fist down on the chessboard. It did not break, being squares of brown and black-dyed deerskin sewn together, but the pieces went scattering. "Even your own filthy outlaw owned me the god's son this morning!"

"Lies have many reasons," Wildraith said again.

"And he would soon have told us where to find you," Erthan added.

"Perhaps." Greenstick had not begged to follow Wildraith from Ironstead because he was strong. But she was happy he had held out even for a time against Senerthan's much-feared cousin.

"And you will acknowledge me before morning," Senerthan went on.

"Then or never," she agreed.

Meleth was gathering the chess pieces and replacing them apparently by memory (though Wildraith thought she was remembering the positions a little to her own advantage).

Erthan grinned again and began flexing his fingers one by one. "Don't hurry me, cousin of the Long Forest. Almost five years I've been preparing for this task."

"See you don't spend the next five years performing it!" Senerthan seized Erthan's shoulder, then pushed him away.

Erthan rose and brushed himself off. Meleth continued placing the chess pieces. Both of them were obviously accustomed to Senerthan's anger.

"We can finish this game without the runner you broke, cousin," said Meleth, "since you'd captured it already."

"I could spend nine days," Erthan boasted— keeping a prudent distance from Senerthan—"before even beginning to cripple."

"We know you could, cousin," Meleth said calmly and quickly, as if to forestall another refreshening of Senerthan's rage, "and it does not interest us."

Erthan stepped around the fire, displayed the length of his fingers before Wildraith, then closed his right hand on her upper arm, digging in with a force nicely calculated to stop just short of breaking his fingernails, which were also long.

"Senerthan," said Wildraith, "the boy made it clear to you that I will stay only until sunrise?"

Senerthan had caught his temper again, but was breathing hard to hold it. "The bargain, I understood, was that you would leave at sunrise, not that I must promise to let you free."

"The boy is a careful messenger," said Wildraith. "See that he has all his toy weapons back safely." Then she let Erthan lead her from Senerthan's bower.

He took her first to his own burrow, where, after feeding her meat broth, bread with honey, and wine, he wrapped her in a bed of thick furs and left her to rest. The wine was heavily herbed. Aware that Erthan's motive was to furbish her bodily strength, she relaxed and slept. Her sibling aspects, as usual, refrained from encroaching into the natural dreams of her brain, but from hour to hour certain of her creatures jostled for attention, making her aware to a drowsy degree of the precautions and preparations they watched outside. The porcupine who had followed her this morning was especially agitated, and a lone linden tree on the outskirts of Ormrathestead quivered even in its winter stillness.

So when Erthan returned to wake Wildraith and lead her out into the evening twilight, she was unsurprised at the crowd of hunter-warriors who waited at the burrow's mouth, likewise at the amphitheatre of packed snow which the Ormarathestead majority had rolled up around the lone linden where a chosen few men and women worked to Erthan's specifications.

Half a thousand voluntary laborers had raised their circular wall of white tiers more than three metres high and more than six thick at the base, with one passageway. Most of Ormrathestead's nine hundred women, men, and children occupied this improvised theatre, using furs and mats for the mutual insulation of their bodily warmth and their frozen benching material. A small fire burned to one side of the tree, and thirty torchbearers sat spaced along the top tier, while two more stood on the ground flanking the tree. The arena floor was neatly cluttered with inanimate creations large and small, so arranged as to block the onlookers' view as little as possible. Opposite the entranceway, in a line with the tree, the people had sculpted a throne of snow, but the First of Hunters was not in it. The assemblage seemed no less eager because of his absence.

Wildraith knew that in the forest beyond the amphitheatre, both animals and outlaws were also drawing in. They had been gathering all day, but softly and carefully, so that not even the hunters, generally so observant but now excited with their own activity, were aware of it. With the dark, Wildraith's people edged ever nearer. Ethaan and Arileth were there, the other hundred and thirteen hunters who had chosen allegiance to Wildraith over Senerthan, and the forty ex-herders and ex-farmers whom Ethaan and Arileth judged to have learned forest ways the best. Tilis was with them, and Jokan Greenstick although his hands were bandaged and he kept farther back than anyone else save Attaran of Everywhere. The animals and birds were numberless to any mind but a god's, and more came by the part of an hour. So far, they were only such creatures as normally remained abroad in the winter, but Wildraith felt the hibernators stirring in their dens. Limited by humanity, she found it tricksome to soothe the bears, chipmunks, and reptiles while at the same mortal time repeating her commands to the other beasts not to close prematurely. As for her human followers, she could only reach into a few of their minds very imperfectly, into most of them not at all; she had to rely on their respecting her promise and the animals' example.

Two hunters bound her to the reluctant linden tree, facing the empty throne. Erthan came forward, carrying several small instruments in an otterskin envelope, and explained their possible uses. While he spoke, one hunter gathered up three small children and left the amphitheatre. The rest of the audience pushed closer towards the throne, where the view would be best.

Wildraith realized that Erthan was trying to play upon her fear, but his present words blended with his boast that he could work nine days before starting to cripple, and she remained simply curious. Moreover, she was comforting the linden tree.

"You did not make such long preparation for my follower this morning," she remarked at last.

Erthan grinned. Having finished showing her the small instruments, chiefly metal, in his hands, he began pointing to the large shapes around them, which had been constructed fresh today of branches, stone, snow and ice. Five years ago he had had some permanent furniture in certain strategic forest burrows, but Wildraith had told her outlaws where these places were and they had dug in at every chance and destroyed the equipment, forcing Erthan to perfect his field system of travelling light and making shift with local and seasonal materials.

The moon was almost three-quarters full and unveiled, though clouds floated below it in the east. Still, much of the arena was dim and shadowed to human eyes. Eventually Wildraith interrupted Erthan to ask, "Is all this more fearsome when it is seen unclearly?"

He grinned again. "I thought you outlaws had night vision. Like owls and hunters."

Though Wildraith's physical vision was probably superlative for a human, she knew the difference between what she saw with her incarnate eyes and what she saw through the eyes of her nocturnal creatures. But all she said was, "Your audience grows restless. Do you trust their night vision, or do you plan to make them wait for daylight?"

Erthan stepped close and gently rubbed a file on the side of her throat. "People sometimes beg me to hurry on with my art. They usually seem to regret their haste."

"Already you've lost your day," she replied. "Remember sunrise." She felt the forest thrum. "Erthan Subtle-mind, you will earn your traitname if you are away from me at that hour."

She knew by his chuckle that he did not believe her. "You're right," he said. "Our audience is growing restless. They've come to hear Wildraith the Proud Heretic admit my cousin Senerthan's mother was loved by a god." He shrugged and pointed to the shapes he had not yet explained. "So as for those, wait and imagine."

He stepped forward to a torchbearer, opened his otterskin case and selected an instrument, held it high and flashed it through the firelight for the audience to see. He posed and postured until Wildraith guessed this might be the reason Senerthan chose to stay away. She yawned. Erthan was a showman, but he overpuffed his act.

With a last flourish, he beckoned the torchbearer to return with him and hold the torch beside Wildraith. Delicately he cut the sleeve away from her left shoulder and started making small incisions in her upper arm, stepping aside after the first few as if to let the audience see, even though there could be little for them to see except a bare shoulder and a little blood. He held the blade in the torchflame, stepped close, and resumed his scribepoint.

As long as interest continued her predominant emotion, she was not particularly bothered by the pain. But Erthan had already exhausted her intellectual interest in his methods; in bringing boredom, his preliminary explanations had had something like their desired effect. There remained all that the application of his instruments, like pointers, could teach her of anatomy, and this was a field of surprisingly vast inscapes. But concentrating on the same brought ever-quickening sympathy with the emotions of creatures who lacked knowledge of existence without flesh. And Erthan was clever. Thus she learned from him the potential false-eternity of time and the seeming solidity of fear.

Halfway to midnight, she gave her first scream. Erthan bowed and postured, the audience laughed and applauded. In the woods outside, Ethaan and Arileth started from their cover. Two wolves turned snarling and snapping to warn them back.

Animals and outlaws waited side by side in mute alliance, but Wildraith's animals had the greater command.

A few of Senerthan's hunters glanced up, as if sensing the outer noises beyond their comrades' applause. One man left. Perhaps it was coincidence. Some few of the audience slipped away quarter-hour by quarter-hour.

At midnight Erthan, who had worked all this time in silence and dumbshow, told the assembly, "Now is the hour when the blood is weakest and the will most feeble. Tonight the moon nears his highest at this hour, fit sign for the occasion. Send for Ormrathe's son to witness our triumph."

The torchbearers set out, and Erthan returned to Wildraith. "Now the navel," he murmured to her and himself. His relish was so obvious that she smiled a little.

He cut away her clothing to bare a strip of waist. He frowned and widened the opening, then widened it again. Wildraith had no navel.

The man who held the torch for Erthan let it shudder in his hand. Erthan took half a step back, rubbed his chin, and slowly grinned. He gripped his torchbearer's arm for a moment to steady it and nodded as if binding him to silence. No one else could have seen the unexpected. Erthan stood in front of Wildraith and stalled with menacing taps until Senerthan had arrived and climbed to the throne. Still keeping between victim and onlookers, Erthan made a long flourish and reverence to his supposedly semi-divine cousin. Then, with intense care, he began to carve out the missing depression.

She gave a second scream and part of her sensed

that one short, false acknowledgment of Senerthan's claim could scarcely disturb a quark in the vast weave of the universe. What would it be so much more than to speak in this human way of "sunrise"? But if she uttered the lie, he would no longer have his motive for prolonging her human life; and her reason remembered that dawn must come sooner than the end of the climb which waited for her if this body died without answering Ylsa Ironstead's curse. So she made only noises, no words, as Erthan treated the artificial navel as he might have a real one, with frequent cauterizings. And at last Senerthan rose, said: "Perhaps we should have waited until my father's circle was at full round," and left in apparent disgust.

Erthan rested a while, but as too many of the audience were following their leader away, he cut the intermission short and returned to his labors.

By three-quarters of the way to dawn, many humans would have found a measure of native anesthesia. But where their senses would have deadened with excess and exhaustion, Wildraith was still discovering new levels of material awareness. Erthan seemed to ascribe all evidence of this to his own subtlety, and showed no signs of weariness. His audience was very small now, but those who stayed on were the most appreciative.

The whole sky clouded under before dawn. Two or three snow flurries speckled the arena. The creatures grew more and more restless, angrier, and Wildraith's control was slipping from them as she needed what remained for herself; but her sibling aspects must have taken charge for her, though by now she could no longer sense them at all.

As the sky turned blue and murdled gray, some

Ormrathesteaders began returning to the amphitheatre. Senerthan was not among them, but Meleth of the Mossy Bower was, and the audience swelled again to about three hundred. As the linden tree became more visible, it showed its upper branches thick with owls and other birds. Some of the hunters whispered and pointed up, but most seemed to think it less interesting than Erthan's moves. Wildraith had long been removed from the tree in favor of Erthan's various makeshift frameworks.

Erthan had not spoken since midnight, except to give a few instructions to his torchbearers and two assistants. Now he chuckled at Wildraith and said, "Where's your sunrise?"

"My creatures feel it," she whispered.

He had her stretched this time on a bed of twisted branches and ice, only a few strips of clothing left on her body. He bent over her with a glowing needle, and at that moment her creatures felt the sunrise.

The owls swooped from the linden tree and swarmed down on Erthan. The mice and rats and small gnawing creatures who had been able to creep unnoticed into the arena shadows scrambled up Wildraith's framework to chew her free. One torchbearer and Erthan's two assistants started towards him, but more birds descended each instant to beat them off, while wolves, badgers, wildcats, boars, stags, beasts of every kind streamed in at the narrow entranceway and appeared atop the high snow wall. They did not strike the audience to kill, but to hurt and throw into confusion.

Weapon noises told of fighting outside. Outlaws began pushing into the amphitheatre with the animals. The hunters had not come unarmed to see

Erthan's performance, and those who could hold their wits tried to reach the human enemies. Others, especially mothers with children, seemed intent on simple escape.

Then the bears came, roused from their hibernation, huge shapes lumbering one by one through the narrow passage. More and more of the hunters chose the way out over the top of the amphitheatre. Meleth of the Mossy Bower managed to gather several torchbearers and others to set to work knocking down part of the hard-packed wall. Stories were later told that some of the animals had actually helped those hunters who were trying to get out.

The owls flapped away from Erthan of their own accord. He staggered up, blinked the blood from his eyes, held his hands up before his face, and shrieked. Arileth had an arrow notched, but shot it elsewhere when she saw why Erthan shrieked. All his fingers were torn away. Thoughts of human vengeance had gone through Wildraith's brain during the night, and her owls had filtered them up.

She took pity now and sent instructions to the nearest lynx to finish Erthan at once. Then, fainting, she let a dozen smaller creatures nudge her onto the back of the largest bear, and knew little more until evening, when she awoke in one of the outlaws' safest retreats.

She was alone with her first four and the curious porcupine, who curled beside her bedding, flattening its quills and feeling vaguely that it would be comfortable, sometimes, to have fur that human fingers might stroke. Wildraith stroked it with her mind and, very carefully, with one heavily bandaged hand.

"We lost Arria of the Northern Shore and young

Idran Broadnose," said Arileth. "Clean deaths. Senerthan lost at least ten, including Erthan."

"You should have let my creatures do it all," said Wildraith. "I did not want death this time."

"Not even Erthan of the Subtle Mind?" asked Jokan Greenstick.

Wildraith drank some of the broth that Tilis held to her mouth before answering. "Poor Erthan. Yes, maybe as well he died. He prepared so hard for me. The rest of his life's work would have been dull for him."

Senerthan refused to believe the torchbearer who was the only other witness besides Erthan to Wildraith's lack of a natural navel. Nevertheless, he gave him Erthan's former duties. This man did not enjoy the work, so it was as well that Senerthan had fewer prisoners questioned in the years that followed, and only when his need for military knowledge was keenest. Indeed, the First of Hunters came to be called the mildest of all three rulers in this respect.

Gilmar the Old expressed regret when he heard of Erthan's death. He had spoken sometimes of trying to hire the Subtle Mind away from Senerthan if the chance arose.

Chapter 15.

It seemed to Senerthan that Gilmar and Dulanis must have weakened each other's armies beyond quick repair when they fought that late-winter campaign. So he used the quiet year to group his own warriors, and, the spring following his cousin Erthan Subtle-mind's death, he divided them into two armies. One he sent north under Meleth of the Mossy Bower's command. He gave her a written message to Gilmar, telling her: "Deliver it to him when his proudest stronghold lies smoking." He himself led the second army west across the Copper River.

Most storytellers agreed that Senerthan's letter to Gilmar said something like this: "I punish you, Old First of the North, and the gods my father, aunts and uncles punish you for dishonorably and impiously striking out of season to wound the lands of my beloved." This conjecture could never be proved, since the piece of bark fell into Gilmar's hands when he routed Meleth's force near Meadowsedge on Ondarstream, the narrow tributary that Gilmar's grandfather had accepted as his southeastern border. Most of the eastern army died in that battle, and storytellers sang of how Meleth herself only escaped by casting Senerthan's message into Gilmar's face as he was about to strike her down with his great sword, and slipping away while he paused to read it. When he had read it, he laughed, "for nine hours" according to later tales, and then threw the bark into the flames of Meleth's burning tent. Because the report of what was in that message seems to have originated in a lampoon traced to Tanris of Everywhere, it probably approximates the truth.

Meanwhile, Senerthan's half of the eastern army at first succeeded better. It destroyed the settlement at Deepspring and went on toward Middle Wells, roasting the western herds over the flames of their burning grasslands, until it found Dulanis at a watering place which afterwards came to be known as the Pool of the Third Meeting.

Dulanis had gathered her army at Middle Wells and brought it out to check Senerthan's invasion, but for once his scouts were better than hers, even in her homelands. The herders camped at the pool and threw up shield walls, bracing for the battle they expected in two day's time when the hunters reached them. Senerthan took the full moon in an unclouded sky as a message from his father, completed the march by night, and fell on the Butter-hair's camp before dawn.

For an hour, surprise promised to win the battle. Senerthan and his personal command of three hundred actually reached the Butter-hair's own tent and battered their way through the wooden wall panels. While most of them clamored outside, forming a living passageway of men and shields, Senerthan and six members of his chosen bodyguard burst into the tent itself.

Dulanis stood on her bed of woolskins and woven blankets, a short green and orange tunic thrown over her nightrobe, her hair tied hastily back and her sword in hand. Her nine personal attendants circled her, the five fighters in front, the four chosen for wisdom and conversation in back —these included her uncle Jokan One-arm, who was now grown too old for battle, and her favorite childbearer, Naris Ever-fertile, whose sons and daughters the ruler had half adopted and who was once again in her third month.

Even of the five fighters, only Ytran Younglegs and Orm Hardnails had been selected primarily for their skill with weapons. They and Dranis Lightbrows gave a strong, short fight, and were killed. So was old Jokan One-arm, who died helping Dulanis protect Naris Ever-fertile. Naris took a serious injury and lost her child, but finally recovered her own wholeness. The rest of the nine soon fell wounded, except for Marn Mole-cheek, who fled from the tent and was never heard nor spoken of again.

In a few moments, Dulanis alone stood uninjured among her enemies. Senerthan waved his companions back and went to meet her one to one. Their swords and hand-axes rang for about nine minutes—which in later tales became nine hours— until Dulanis slipped on the body of her uncle Jokan and fell. Senerthan sprang upon her, putting one knee on the flat of her sword and the other on her axe-arm to hold them on the earth, and after another struggle, muscle against muscle this time, he rose carrying her across his shoulders, her weapons gone, her ankles bound and her wrists caught in a noose which he held tight with his left hand.

(They later sang that he encircled both her small wrists in one of his long-fingered hands, and that for a while she lay across his shoulders as if on a bed of blissful cloud.)

As he bore her from the tent, amid the cheers of his bodyguard and personal command, Irinore and her company reached them.

The surviving hunters said afterwards they had been surprised from behind. When Irinore heard this claim, she did not deny it, but rubbed her chin and told the storyteller that they should not have let themselves be slipped upon from behind in a battle, no matter what their cause for rejoicing.

Irinore herself broke through to Senerthan and matched her sword and hand-axe against his sword until she forced him to drop Dulanis and draw his own hand-axe again. Senta Long-toes jumped down to free her ruler's wrists and ankles. Senerthan half-turned and sliced his sword through Senta's neck. Irinore sprang close and might have killed Senerthan, but hesitated when Dulanis shrieked. Senerthan whirled back and struck off Irinore's hand with his axe.

Dulanis caught up Senta's spike-club and Irinore's sword, and came at Senerthan again. They drove him back, Dulanis covered with Senta's blood and Irinore poking her stump at Senerthan's face to blind and choke him with the spurts of blood, as Irinore's company were driving back his personal command and the rest of the Butter-hair's people, those who had survived the initial attack, were driving back the rest of his army. Senerthan's people had struck without resting from their long march, and as their advantage of surprise wore off, their disadvantage of weariness told against them. Besides, although both rulers started with about the same number of trained fighting people, Senerthan traveled only with warriors, who cared for their own needs and supplies on the march, while Dulanis had many assistants and camp attendants with her army. These took whatever they could find for weapons and helped fight Senerthan's invaders that night.

When at last Senerthan and the remnant of his personal command retreated—the rest of his army had fled without waiting for the signal—the easterners killed all the enemy wounded left behind, while nursing their own wounded. So for every man or woman Dulanis lost in the Battle of the Third Meeting, Senerthan lost two. He had to march his survivors home with only snatches of rest, the herders harrying them across the Copper River, as Gilmar's northerners were harrying Meleth's survivors back into the forest.

Including Senta Long-toes, Irinore lost only forty-seven from her three hundred, while most of Senerthan's bodyguard and more than a hundred of his personal command lay with the Butter-hair's dead in and around her tent. Irinore fell from loss of blood even as Senerthan retreated, and the Butter-hair's physicians claimed it was only their cleverness in pouring fresh goatsblood down her throat that saved her life.

Dulanis would never say whether that shriek, the only one she was ever heard to give in battle, had been for Senta's death or Senerthan's danger. But when autumn came she gave Irinore a wealth of sheep and finely woven wool cloth and sent her to the artisans of the south, to have them fashion whatever replacement she chose for her right hand.

Irinore chose the design of an eagle's talon worked in metals from the mountain mines: iron for strength, a first coating of copper to keep out rust and a second coating of silver to guard against verdigris, and gold on the claws for decoration. The gold was the metalworker's fancy, and Irinore seemed indifferent to the idea but pleased with the result. She had three weapons made at the same time, a knife, a small axe, and a spike-club, their handles and her talon fitted to each other; and she learned to use her sword left-handed. She became Irinore Silver-claw, a name the storytellers usually shortened to Silver-claw when they ventured to sing of her at all in the North or East.

Chapter 16.

For three years, there were no major campaigns, and all the rulers seemed only to be sharpening their warriors as if on a whetstone in summer skirmishes along the edges of their lands.

One thing happened of special note. Tanris of Everywhere was found at Laniscleft with her head in the Copper River and deep bruises on her neck and body as if she had been held by force. All storytellers glanced more often over their shoulders after that, especially those who were spies.

Since Dathan of the South still refused to change his trait-name, Derinore, formerly "of the North," was elected to Tanris of Everywhere's place among the Nine. They brought a protest to each ruler, but Senerthan, Dulanis, and Gilmar all denied fore-knowledge of the drowning.

"Tanris had a harp with silver strings, however, and gilded tuning pegs in the shape of maple keys," Attaran told his fellow outlaws when he gave them the story around their woodland campfire that autumn. "And Dulanis of the West sent one of those tuning pegs to Senerthan of the Long Forest as a summer's-end gift, twined around in a ball of hair the same color as that on Tanris of

Everywhere's head and pressed into a ram's horn."

"And how did you learn that, old rhyme-tattler?" said Jokan Greenstick as he lounged before the fire roasting marrowbones.

"Ylith of the North had it from Mandar of the East, who was at New Crescent when Senerthan unwound the ball of hair."

Arileth began to feather a new shaft. "Ylith is one of Gilmar's spies, I think?"

Attaran shrugged. "I'm safe enough. Spies or free, my fellow storytellers still respect the old bond, even if Dulanis Butter-hair does not."

"I don't think that was Letha's meaning." Tilis the Supple, now usually called the Wise, stared into the fire and rubbed her left knee. "Tanris was a kinswoman of Gilmar, was she not? Accidents have a way of finding Gilmar's close relatives."

"Tanris was never unfaithful to the First of the North," said Attaran. "Not even to bearing a child. I know. I tried often enough to warm myself in her in years gone by, when we were young."

Arileth laughed. "Don't count your silver hairs tonight, Otter-man. Tanris was a troublemaker, and she loved to play dangerous games."

"Tanris of Everywhere was a great storyteller," said Attaran. "One of the greatest in all the Nine Ages. Derinore will never fill her place."

Watching the molecules at play in the blade of her sword, Wildraith smiled. "You rearrange your Nine Ages of History every few generations," she said. "Tanris used her talent well enough, and now she begins exploring everywhere in earnest."

Wildraith might not have said so much if Tilis were absent. The others seemed to accept her comments as beads of awe, and either forget or twist them in retelling. In a way, Wildraith envied the assassinated storyteller, but she thought not even Tilis the Wise would hear that in her remark. She mused on her companions' probable reactions were she to tell them that Yrn Long-grin and Ilith the Rust-haired, patrolling the New Growth where lightning had ignited part of the forest in the dry weather eight years ago, had found a stranger and brought her to Rada the Cautious, who was now interviewing her.

Attaran nodded over the Nine Ages of History. "Perhaps . . . perhaps. The autumn after Gilmar's first drive down the Copper River valley we agreed this War of the Chess Game marks the beginning of the Seventh Age. Nine years ago, that was, when we decided it. The free South should have entered the fighting by now, according to Ondaris the Second's interpretation of the Long Prophecy of Damis the Ancient. But I remember my grandmother Loris of the Vibrant Throat telling me her parents claimed their generation lived at the end of the Eighth Age."

"Aye, Otter-man," said Ethaan, who never appreciated Attaran's liberalism in sharing newsbringers' secrets, "recite us Damis the Ancient's Long Prophecy. It helps me doze."

"Doze without my help, Ethaan Half-Arileth." Attaran returned to the problem of who had killed Tanris. "Gilmar has enough to worry about this harvest, with two years of failing crops in the North."

"All the more reason he may suddenly have seen his last close cousin as a threat," said Arileth.

"Soris the Hook-chin is a closer cousin than Tanris," Attaran argued. "And she lives in comfort—"

"Because she's ninety years old, a shrewd land manager, and all her children and grandchildren died fighting in Gilmar's battles," Arileth replied.

"Not all," said Jokan Greenstick. "Not if it's true that Soris the Youngest survived the Old Mounds and escaped to Adrak's South." He looked at Wildraith as if hoping she would confirm the rumor, for Soris the granddaughter was said to have been very beautiful; but Wildraith only smiled and shrugged.

So Greenstick turned to Attaran and said, "Well, sing us a tale, rhyme-tattler. Sing us the loves of Ondaris the Handsome and Iama Gold-eyes."

"I'm a-doze." Ethaan closed his eyes and feigned several snores.

Attaran had been tuning his harp since supper, but he tuned it again. That was standard storytellers' practice before every sung tale. Before he had finished tuning, Rada the Cautious came to their circle of firelight and said, "Wildraith, Yrn and Ilith have found an Ylsa Iron-eyes in the New Growth. She claims a desire to join us."

Wildraith's blood circulated faster. Her creatures had not recognized this stranger as the widow who ran from Ironstead the summer Gilmar entered the war, but only a small proportion of the Long Forest's inhabitants had seen Ylsa of Ironstead, and in many species the generations had turned more than once. "Do you have any reason to doubt Ylsa Iron-eyes?" Wildraith asked Rada.

"She's too young to be Ylsa of Ironstead. She gave up her weapons readily enough when she saw she had to, but one of them was a sticker as long as my forearm and thin as my finger. She explained it as a roasting-skewer, but she carried it in a leg-sheath beneath her breeches, and didn't volunteer it until Ilith started the search."

"You yourself objected to be searched when you first came to us, Cautious-mind," said Wildraith. "So stubbornly that Tilis and Jokan let you keep your spear."

Rada flushed. "One doesn't use a longshaft spear to murder at close hand, only to defend one's own self."

"And can a woman named Rada blame one named Ylsa for doubting her reception among us?" Wildraith reached up to slap palms with Rada. "Bring her to me and we'll try if she listens to argument better than you did."

"Shall we let her keep her sticker?"

"That's your decision, Cautious-mind."

"No, then." Rada slapped palms with her leader and went to bring back the new arrival. Attaran brushed a chord from his harpstrings. Jokan grinned at Tilis and said, "I hope this Ylsa Iron-eyes is pretty all the way down."

Tilis frowned at the fire as if her own thoughts were louder than Greenstick's teasing.

"We're fortunate," said Arileth, with a glance at Ethaan, whose snores, though soft, now sounded genuine. "We four are the only companions Wildraith never tried to argue out of following her."

"Out of leading me and teaching me," said Wildraith. "You aren't fortunate. You were only first, and I was very much younger."

"Greenstick was fortunate, at least." Tilis shook herself and began to skin the last rabbit of the day's hunt. "Well, Iron-eyes will probably be hungry."

Having incarnated full-grown rather than putting on her flesh cell by cell in a mother's womb, Wildraith had neither begun to age yet nor gain a clear appreciation of the process in other humans. She had, however, watched Jokan Greenstick mature from a boy in his mid-teens to a young man in his mid-twenties; she had seen Tilis tighten and fill in somewhat (though part of this might have been more due to the change in how she lived than to the passing of years); and she saw Arileth, Ethaan, and others grow silver hairs. Some children had been born to the outlaws, too, and she was watching them grow. She understood enough to realize, on seeing Ylsa Iron-eyes in the firelight, that Rada was correct when she judged this one too young for the Ironstead widow.

Wildraith sighed away her evening's hope. "Well, Ylsa Iron-eyes. When did you decide to join us? When they found you in the New Growth this last hour?"

The young woman came around the fire, sat cross-legged before Wildraith, and held up her empty hands. She moved a little nervously. "I decided when I was eight years old, First of Outlaws. I was one of the farmers' children at the Middle Curve of the Copper River when you turned back Gilmar's first invasion."

Wildraith nodded. "I thought you looked not much older than Greenstick when he came with me."

"But I hear the North in your voice, Iron-eyes," said Attaran of Everywhere.

Still holding out her hands, Ylsa bowed her head. "My parents had come from the North, and returned there the following summer. We have lived deep in Old Gilmar's lands all these years, but I was only waiting until I ripened enough to escape and find you."

"And this famine in the North helped you choose your time, eh?" said Arileth Half-Ethaan.

Iron-eyes glanced around at her. "We've had crop failures before. It's one of the injustices of working hard with the gods of the soil to grow your food."

Wildraith laughed. "But you don't fear angering the gods. Or you don't believe the stories of people praying to me as if to a god?"

The newcomer seemed to flush. "If Senerthan can be the child of a god, so can you, Woman, First of Free People."

"But Senerthan is not the moon god's son," said Wildraith.

Iron-eyes shrugged. "Whatever he is, you are the greatest leader of all, Wildraith of Nowhere and Everywhere."

Wildraith would have been disappointed, but she thought that Ylsa Iron-eyes was not quite sincere, that there was a fine note of partial mockery in her words. "Have you heard the tale of how I bled and flinched at Ormrathestead?"

The newcomer nodded.

"It is based in solid truth, Iron-eyes."

The young woman's hands were trembling with the effort of holding them up. She rested her elbows on her knees. "I didn't disbelieve it. But Senerthan would have called you Great Dravama's daughter before you called him Ellusa's son, if he had been handled like that."

Iron-eyes used the northern farmers' names for the gods. That fit with her story. But if hunger had moved her more than ideals—and cynicism seemed likely to be among her ideals—then she might still be persuaded to return home. "Famine sometimes strikes herders and even hunters as well as farmers," said Wildraith. "Droughts and floods do not fall only on cultivated land."

"But farmers suffer the most."

"Aye," said Attaran. "That's why Gilmar hasn't grown an army large enough to crush Dulanis and Senerthan both at once."

"And poor people share their last grains with you," Iron-eyes went on. "I would have given you my whole dinner almost any night these past nine years."

Wildraith rejoiced at the word 'almost.' "But not every night."

"You wouldn't have asked it every night."

"Probably we could not have rested near your home long enough to share more than one meal," said Wildraith. "If we continue to eat when crops fail, we pay for it by living in more danger than a true army on campaign."

"That's a lie," said young Ylsa. "You've lost fewer people than any ruler's army."

Ethaan woke up. "A lie? Who is this skewmouth?"

"Rest, Ethaan," said Wildraith. "So you're not afraid to tell the 'greatest leader of all' that she lies, young Ylsa? But to live in danger is not always to be trapped in it. If we survive, it's because we take great and constant care."

"As we have to take with our crops," said Ylsa Iron-eyes. "Late frosts, early frosts, droughts, floods, devouring creatures, blights, fire and armies. Wildraith, I can tell you enough about

Gilmar's North to help you spearhead him from Forestedge to Waterstead. You can cripple him for years, with what I know!"

"Do you think that's our aim?" Wildraith asked gently.

The young woman seemed to falter. "Isn't it?"

"If we aimed to spearhead any of them, why not Senerthan, who outlawed us first?"

Ylsa lowered her hands into her lap. "Well . . . maybe the Butter-hair only outlawed you to please Senerthan, but the Old First of the North hates you for his own reasons. Besides, to stop this war . . ."

Wildraith shook her head. "Wars go on as long as leaders are foolish and followers loyal. My only aim here is to find Ylsa of Ironstead. My followers . . . I do not know their aim."

"To follow you. To help you." Ylsa Iron-eyes lifted her hands again. "Finding one woman's as good an aim as burning and destroying. And you're the only leader worth following."

"There is Adrak the Slow of the free South."

"Half a leader," said Iron-eyes. "Free is another trait-name for divided, and the South's too cold for me."

Wildraith smiled, shrugged, and took Ylsa's hands between her own. She worried sometimes what would happen to these followers of hers after she had found the Ironstead widow. But she liked young Ylsa, and perhaps the newcomer's cross-grain of cynicism would help temper the rest of the company. "We share that trait-name with the people of the South," she said. "You are free to stay with us or leave us." Moving Ylsa's hands apart, she slapped right palms. "Now eat, if you're hungry."

The new outlaw looked around. "When will I get
my weapons back?"

"When you've eaten and drunk and you're falling asleep," said Ethaan with a laugh.

Jokan looked at Iron-eyes with appraisal.
"You're lucky, Ylsa Limber-legs. Usually Wildraith gives a longer argument. I'm Jokan Hardstick," he added like a boast.

Ylsa returned his look and smiled. "I've heard of
you, Hardstick. That's a weapon they never take
away."

"No more than we took away your sheath," he
said in a lower voice.

Tilis coughed and held up the last skinned rabbit, ready for skewering. "We usually turn our own
meat roasting, Iron-eyes."

Iron-eyes took a few steps, squatted beside Tilis,
took the rabbit and long skewer. "I've heard of you
all, I think. Arileth the Hunter?"

Tilis shook her head. "Tilis the Supple. That's
Arileth Half-Ethaan. Ethaan Half-Arileth is the
one who told you to eat and drink and fall asleep."

Iron-eyes tested the skewer's point with her finger. "And that's Attaran of Everywhere tuning his
harp?"

"Getting ready to sing us the loves of Ondaris
and Iama," said Jokan. "You came just in time,
Ylsa Limber-legs."

Young Ylsa nodded, spun round, and drove the
skewer into Wildraith's chest.

The pulse of time seemed to stop. Then all was
confusion and a falling sensation, with pain that
grew sharper and sharper, after the surprise, until
all noises faded in a moment of darkness.

So this was the long climb through unguessed ages. It was a stairway, almost invisible but felt underfoot, and the climb was with humanlike legs, one slow step upon another. Sometimes the treads were hard and ringing, sometimes ankle-deep in sticky stuff as if the stair itself were turning into tar, sometimes slick, and each fall brought a stab of pain between the ribs. Galaxies or atoms or universes exploded and reformed around the stairway, but far in the distance. Someone waited at the top, and when she saw it was Attaran of Everywhere, she knew her human brain was not yet dead, but dreaming. She tried to fix on this awareness, but it left her.

Now the one who waited was Erthan of the Subtle Mind, and the stairs turned inside-out, so that he waited at the bottom, where she was bound and weighted down. He was scooping out the navel she never had before, but not where she carried the scar. Between two ribs, rather. He inserted a long tube through her chest, fixing each end in a great pool of water or stargases, and pumped the liquid back and forth from tip to tip in spurts and tides, now swelling up searing cold to strain against heart and lungs, now dwindling to an electron-thin filament to leave a sucking vacuum between the organs.

Now it was afloat in a chosen mother's womb, multiplying the first several hundred cells, not yet either definite male or female. Now it was feeling the surges of adolescence, now the first few teeth cutting through the milky gums, now climbing the endless stairs again with some vague regret in the dim memory that birth and childhood were no more than delirious hypotheses for this incarnation.

There were nightmares of purely human mental processes, and visions which only the gods' language could describe. Often the two fused together. No one but another incarnation could have understood the generality; not even to another incarnation could all the details have been communicated. This aspect was alone and totally individual in the immensity of large and small, reality and fear.

It was morning when she opened her eyes and saw two centimeters of snow edging the bare tree branches outside the burrow where she lay wrapped in furs and the aroma of simmering broth.

"The leaves were still falling," she said to Tilis, who sat between her bed and the mouth of the burrow.

"You've been unconscious for sixteen nights," Tilis replied.

"We should have left Iron-eyes her own sticker. It might have been clean of grease. Where is she?"

Tilis was silent.

"Where is young Ylsa Iron-eyes?" Wildraith repeated.

"Dead."

Wildraith did not sigh, because of the tenderness in her ribs. "I would not have had her killed."

"I know. I knew. But I . . . it happened too quickly."

"Did they ask who had sent her?"

Tilis shook her head. "Not even that. She died at once."

Wildraith closed her eyes and felt her sibling aspects until she found the knowledge of Iron-eyes wandering the regions of fog, searching for some passage that eventually she would find to clearer planes. Wildraith might have asked a sib to touch

Ylsa Iron-eyes' mind and thus relay who had dealt the death blow, Ethaan or Arileth, Jokan Green-stick or Rada the Cautious, Attaran or Iron-eyes herself. She did not think it would be Tilis, who must have been first to catch her before she fell and drove the skewer more deep.

But she decided to leave them their secret and let the incident be buried. She opened her eyes again and smiled at Tilis. "I smell hot broth."

Part III.

Chapter 17.

The winter following Tanris of Everywhere's death was no more than lightly snow-covered, with a little teasing rain in the north, and that next summer the two-years' drought spread. Those farmers who lived beside the Copper or other large rivers and who could cultivate enough land to raise crops for selling, prospered; but they worried because even the Copper River was low. Several smaller rivers and streams dried completely. There were tales of farmers on the northern shore who painstakingly boiled sea water to catch the steam for their fields, or who tried to irrigate with it while still salty. The deep western wells did not give out, but the plains dried and Dulanis Butter-hair's people killed and cured more and more of their herds before the animals grew too thin.

Four years ago Senerthan had won disaster by splitting his army, but now Gilmar tried the same plan. Conditions were different. No area could have provided forage for a large army, except perhaps the Copper River valley, and the Old Man of the North was still shy of being stung there a third time. But neither would his own territory feed all his warriors. And it only took a small force to kindle fires during drought.

About a third of Wildraith's followers had left her on seeing how vulnerable she was to a surprise assassin, and many who remained were nevertheless disillusioned—Ylsa Iron-eyes' attempt had weakened the outlaws by that much, at least. Moreover, gods tend to tamper very little with the course of nature once they establish it. But Wildraith's humanity revolted at this use of forest fire as a tool of war, and she called on her sibling aspects of the weather. The storms that saved the Long Forest eventually spread north and west to end the drought, and in a wet and burgeoning woodland Gilmar's hungry men were a poor match for Senerthan's hunters.

Some storytellers quoted long dialogues between Wildraith and Gilmar when they came face to face in the Long Forest, but these meetings were the storytellers' own invention. Gilmar had gone with the half of his army that invaded Dulanis Butterhair's herdlands.

This part of the northern force met better success, and the east was blackened from just south of Gandreth's Wells (which Dulanis had never won back from Gilmar) almost to the Old Mounds before the invaders met a counter-fire. The two armies came together in the Battle of the Flames, where as many died from heat and smoke as from enemy stone and iron. Gilmar and Dulanis did come face to face that day, and the later stories of what they shouted at each other from horseback were based in truth.

"Woman, First of Herders!" Gilmar bellowed.

"Man, First of Farmers and Fire!"

"Tanris of Everywhere was my beloved cousin!"

"Your troublemaking spy, Old Man!"

"Perhaps, and will I send you the head of your Gornith?"

"Aye, if you can keep your own on your ugly jaw!" Dulanis cried, and ran her dark red horse closer to his silver-gray. Her sword crashed five times on his shield and his sword four times on hers, while their mounts shied and whinnied at the fire around them.

But the dry grass burned away quickly; and the Butter-hair's horse was a strong young mare, Gilmar's a canny old stallion. Some newsbringers reported that Dulanis drove Gilmar back pace by pace until they reached her people's hastily dug ditch and long, loose earth wall, others that Gilmar's horse pursued the Butter-hair's into her camp. Most storytellers used whichever version would best please their audience. All agreed that when the fires burned out and the armies sank down too blistered and weary for further action, Gilmar the Old sat under guard in Dulanis Butter-hair's tent.

"Well, Old First of the North," she said.

"Throw my head out to my army," he replied, "and tomorrow they'll be over this crumbling earthwork to burn the rest of your brown herdlands."

"And in the autumn they'll return to a free and leaderless North. You've left yourself no heir to finish the vengeance, old man."

"Nor you, old woman."

Dulanis stood, her eyebrows pressed low together above her grey-green eyes.

But Gilmar went on in a calm voice, "Look at yourself, First of Herders. Aye, they can still call you the Butter-hair, but now more of it's the same shade as white winter butter than of yellow summer fat."

Dulanis sat again. "I think I may make that test with your head, old man. Perhaps your army will avenge you, or perhaps I and my army will beat them again as we did today."

"There remains the problem of my cousin Tanris," he replied as if the Butter-hair were a prisoner in his tent. "And she a storyteller, too."

"Didn't you kill her yourself, Silverhead, to guard against a storyteller becoming First of the North when you are dead?"

Gilmar held up his hands. "These have never killed anyone outside of honest battle."

Dulanis held her hands up across from his. "Neither have mine, outside of honest battle."

"Tanris was a good servant to me, but a troublemaker to you."

"Well," said Dulanis. "I do not say I ordered her death. Perhaps it was Senerthan. But your life for hers. If I let your own body carry your head back to your camp, will you leave this war to me and the moon god's son?"

"No. But I'll take my army home and leave your territory unharmed for the rest of this summer."

"It's a cheap promise," she said. "And you'll lead them home on another horse than your silvergray."

"I have ridden no other horse for thirteen years," Gilmar replied.

Nevertheless, they slapped palms, both the right and the left, and next morning Gilmar returned to his army. Dulanis kept his stallion, and storytellers loved to tell how Gilmar in his seventieth year led his army the whole distance home on foot, bearing his great sword and ceremonial scabbard before them all the way, even through the black, sooty mud that mired them when that summer's rains reached the herdlands.

The following year Dulanis Butter-hair travelled north with her army, Gilmar's stallion, and a foal he had sired on her own red mare. Dulanis gave Gilmar the foal as a wedding gift when she married him by his people's rites and hers at Waterstead, and he gave her the right to choose his heir after he was dead.

Chapter 18.

Rom the Moody had earned command of three hundred in the northern army just before Gilmar sent his half of it to burn the Long Forest. Rom and his men had been at their work, sword or spear in right hand and torch in left, when a shift in the wind cut him off from the rest of his company. Stumbling into a little glade only a few paces ahead of the smoke, and feeling a traitorous hope in the sudden dark clouds overhead, he had found himself facing a score of strangers.

"Veil-eyes!" he had cried, guessing who the leader was by her sword. Though he had never seen it, it matched storytellers' descriptions—a pale blade that shone more like fluid than metal.

"Dig up the ground and bury your torch," said Wildraith Veil-eyes.

"There's no time!" he protested. "The forest blazing around us, and you want—"

With one sweep of her sword, she turned up a furrow of earth. "Bury it."

He hesitated, then thrust the torch at her face. She cut it from his hand, knocking it into the furrow. "Cover it," she commanded.

His torch hand aching, he leaped across the furrow and tried matching swords with her. At the first clash, she sent his weapon flying.

"Now," she said. "Cover your flame with earth before my people drown it with your blood."

Clutching first one wrist and then the other in his pain—he later found that two of his fingers had been broken—he kicked the loosened dry earth over his torch. The storm broke before he finished. . Wildraith and her outlaws disappeared into the forest as if they had melted in the heavy blades of water.

Rom found his way back to his own people, but he could not forgive the outlaws for humiliating him and then sparing his life. He was nineteen years old and most of his life had been dominated by the dream of holding a command in Gilmar's army. Now that this dream was achieved and already tarnished, instead of replacing it with the dream of commanding a thousand, he replaced it with the dream of capturing Wildraith Veil-eyes.

In the mixed rejoicing at that summer's rains and trembling at Gilmar's proclaimed dissatisfaction with his warriors' performance in the invasion attempts, Rom dared approach his ruler and ask leave to take his three hundred and search for Wildraith. Gilmar told him to go, and return neither earlier nor later than the nights of the first dark moon of spring.

In Old Ironstead and the few other Long Forest settlements that still survived free of allegiance to Gilmar or Senerthan, Rom heard some of the tales about the northern ruler's supposed meetings with the First of Outlaws that summer. Rom had never told anyone of his own encounter with Wildraith, but he assumed that the outlaws must have told and that these ballads were based on his own experience, transferred to Gilmar. Once he wounded a young Ironsteader he heard repeating a ballad on the subject.

In his personal bitterness, Rom searched until after the spring's first dark moon. Now his only hope of buying Gilmar's pardon was to succeed in his project. Eighteen of his men died from sickness or skirmishes with stray bands of Senerthan's hunters; he had to leave thirty-two more sick and wounded with friendly or neutral settlers here and there; and some of his remaining warriors spoke of turning back without him, but they could not be sure whether the First of the North would reward their obedience to the supreme ruler or punish their disobedience to the immediate captain.

One night as Rom sat drinking and brooding with his third in command, Arik the Split-chin, in the only tavern of a small town called Gorlan's Glade that lay between Old Ironstead and Forest-edge, he heard yet another storyteller begin yet another ballad that glorified Wildraith at Gilmar's expense. Rom was about to throw a cup at the singer, careless of storytellers' privilege and Arik Split-chin's cautioning hand on his arm, when he remembered that years ago Attaran of Everywhere had joined the outlaws. When Rom was a child, before anyone had heard of Wildraith, he had seen and listened to Attaran once or twice. Now he squinted across the ill-lit room and thought this might be the same man.

Rom and Arik drank no more wine that evening. Rom sent Arik out to the rest of their men, who were sitting outside to eat and drink what the tavernkeeper had to sell them, and when the storyteller came out, Rom was behind him and the northern warriors were ready. They surrounded

him, silenced him at once to prevent any chance
that the villagers, if alerted, might come to his defense, and forty of them bore him deep into the
forest while the others kept to their camp in
Gorlan's Glade as if nothing had happened.

At first the storyteller denied who he was. Finally, when Rom held a knife to the joint of his right
forefinger, he said, "If I am Attaran, will you maim
me—a storyteller and one of the Nine—so that I
can never play my harp again?"

Rom held the knife in place. "You'd better be
Attaran, or you'll lose your fingers, innocent or
not, the way Senerthan's cousin the torturer lost
his. Where is Wildraith Veil-eyes?"

"By your accent," said Attaran, "you're northerners. Gilmar's men?"

"Where is Wildraith of Nowhere?" Rom repeated, and drew his knife across the skin.

Attaran gasped and said, "Listen. I'm Gilmar's
spy. I've been working for your own First all these
years, spying among the outlaws."

"You've made useless work of it," said Rom.
"And Gilmar sent me to end this and take her."

"We're . . . on our way to Forestedge," said Attaran. "This is luck. I was looking for the chance to
send word."

"I don't care where she's going. Where is she
now?"

"Listen," Attaran said again. "We've heard
there's an Ylsa Ironmouth in Forestedge?"

"There could be. Ylsa the Maimed-face. She was
one of the captains who stayed to help guard Waterstead last year."

"She's the bait. You see? Gilmar must have sent
her to Forestedge this year as bait. Let me go back
to them, don't let them suspect anything. We'll

take them all in Forestedge."

"I'll take Wildraith now, and I won't share the praise for it with anyone but my own three hundred."

"Three hundred? You hope to take them all with one company? Listen, with Ylsa Ironmouth's three hundred in Forestedge, and Gilmar himself maybe on the way to help spring the trap—"

"Good. I'll have Wildraith there waiting for him as a gift." Rom made another sawing cut with his knife, and he used the edge that needed to be re-sharpened.

So Attaran, cursing the bad example given by Tanris of Everywhere's assassin, agreed to help capture Wildraith.

"Tonight," said Rom.

"Impossible. She can't be taken in the forest. Every bird, beast, and insect would come to her rescue."

"Tales."

"Truth." This time Attaran's sincerity was hard to doubt. "I've lived with them for eight years. I was at Ormrathestead that same Sunrise of the Animals when Senerthan's cousin lost the fingers from both hands."

"It might be too big a risk," said Arik Split-chin. "Remember the storms last year."

Rom turned on him. "They were overdue to break!"

"Well . . ." said Arik.

"We could barter you for her, outlaw storyteller," said Rom. "It's true she gave herself up to the moon god's son in trade for that captain of hers? The Hardstick?"

"For a night," said Arik. "So the ballads say. I don't think this one would be worth half a night."

"Set your trap in Forestedge," Attaran pleaded again. "Let me go, and I'll lead them into it."

"Between the woods and Forestedge," said Rom, "there are a couple of farmsteads. Do they welcome you there, outlaw?"

"As storyteller, I have been welcomed everywhere."

"Unh," said Rom. "Well, we won't haul the farmfolk to Gilmar for sheltering outlaws, if they don't try to hinder us this time. We'll take this one to Orimar's Stead," he went on to Arik, "and trap her when she comes to save him."

Attaran shook his head. "She'll come with all our people—more than half a thousand—and her animals, too. Your only hope is to let me go and bring her . . . to Orimar's Stead, if you must. We travel in small groups. We planned to gather near Forestedge."

It took much more argument, with pleading and persuasion, but at last Rom agreed to trust the storyteller.

On reaching his outlaw companions once more, Attaran could have told Wildraith everything, as Rom the Moody more than half expected. Why he did not was argued ever afterwards. Most agreed that the storyteller spy had been sincere when first he brought Wildraith his loyalty, though many guessed that at some time during these eight years with her he had already begun to play his old double- and triple-edged games and watch for the chance of betraying her to one ruler or another for his own best profit. Some thought he was loyal in desire but weak in will, frightened by Rom's threats and corrupted by Arik's promises. Perhaps he expected Wildraith to understand the meaning of his capture and release that night, as she under-

stood so much of what happened within reach of
the forest's senses, without being told by her fellow
humans.

But it had not been sufficiently obvious to the
forest creatures why Attaran spent those hours
with the strange men. Wildraith was aware of the
incident, but not that her storyteller had been
forced; he often mingled with strangers to exchange news, drink, and play rough, simple games
like arm-wrestling and knife-clicking. The
creatures had seen little difference, and there had
been forty men smelling of triumph and eagerness
to the one who smelled of fear. Attaran told Wildraith the cut on his finger was accidental, and she
did not question him further.

Orimar's farmstead was large but no longer
prosperous, not yet recovered from the last long
drought and Gilmar's most recent claiming of men
for his troops. Wildraith brought only thirty followers, and they carried some of their own supplies
from the forest to supplement Orimar's hospitality.

They slept four to eight in the various barns and
sheds. The outlaws' practice, whenever more than
six of them were in the group, was to keep two on
watch, staggering the turns so that one was always
rested. Attaran began his turn an hour after midnight, when Ethaan Half-Arileth was in the second
part of his. Attaran met Ethaan patrolling the
farmyard, exchanged greetings, and when they had
separated to continue their different rounds, Attaran slipped away and found Rom the Moody,
who waited with his men some minutes' march
from the farm on Orimar's road to the town.

Rom took eight men at once, having already
counted off the rest to follow in groups of thirty.
Attaran led Rom's group to the barn where Wild-

raith slept with Arileth Half-Ethaan, Ondreth of Laniscleft, and three others. Jokan and Tilis were each leading other groups of thirty and forty by different paths to Forestedge, but the original four had ever insisted on keeping at least one or two of their number close beside Wildraith.

Not so adept in farmsteads as in forest, Ethaan nevertheless heard Rom's approach and came to check the noises. The moon was three-quarters full and unclouded. Ethaan rounded the back corner of a large, empty henhouse, saw the strangers, and cupped his hands to give the call. But Rom was younger and quicker, and cast his spear without asking if this were an outlaw or one of Orimar's remaining farm workers.

So Ethaan Half-Arileth died first of the original Five. In later years the more popular version of the tale was that the betraying outlaw had killed his comrade, but in fact Attaran had not even had time to identify him to Rom.

In the barn, some wild rats awakened Wildraith. Rom and his eight were already at the door. Wildraith ordered her five companions to escape and gather the rest from their various sleeping places. Only Arileth Half-Ethaan, who had been with her longest, obeyed this command and escaped through an upper window. Ondreth fell wounded and the others were killed trying to defend their leader, to Wildraith's grief, for she would have pushed them after Arileth and given herself up alive, if necessary, buying her followers time to rally from all parts of the farm. The barn rats had not known to warn her of the larger enemy bands approaching.

Of the thirty-one outlaws who had come late that afternoon to Orimar's Stead, Wildraith and

Ondreth were taken alive, Arileth and six others escaped, Attaran disappeared into rumor, and all the rest died. Those storytellers who could not bear that one of their profession had betrayed Wildraith Veil-eyes sang only of a "false-hearted male."

Rom had his men cut off the slain outlaws' heads for carrying to Forestedge as proof, and left their bodies for the farmfolk to burn or bury. Arileth returned about noon with Tilis, Jokan, Yrn Long-grin and their groups, hours too late to prevent Rom's departure. Orimar and his people were mourning the outlaws in silence, but Arileth wailed loud over Ethaan's body as she wrapped it with her own hands. She commanded Orimar not to bury it with the others, but to dry it and put it in a spiced coffin, and when she returned from the town she would bring back his head and carry him whole to be buried in the Long Forest.

Each overcaptain commanded a thousand war-riors, a hundred directly and three companies of three hundred through their individual leaders. The overcaptain who held Forestedge that year was Sormar the Short-legged. He had seven hun-dred in the town when Rom arrived. One company of three hundred had been ordered to Old Water-stead to help swell the rejoicing ranks for Gilmar's marriage. With such a prisoner as Wildraith First of Outlaws to guard, Sormar was glad of Rom's warriors to replace those of Ylsa Ironmouth.

Gilmar's punishments, usually execution or dis-figurement, fell as quickly as his anger. Rumor said that Gilmar had secret underground places for questioning certain prisoners in all his important towns, but he shared the secret of where only with his trusted doctors, and if anyone else discovered such underground rooms, they said nothing for fear of being questioned therein. After some argument, Sormar and Rom decided it should be safe to keep Ondreth, who was weak and sick because of her wounds, in the common jail with the thieves, murderers and discipline-breakers whose crimes merited saving them for Gilmar's personal judgment. This jail was a stone-lined pit covered with a bronze grating and located beneath the scaffold where sentences were pronounced and executed. The grating allowed some air to circulate, and the scaffold usually kept out the worst rains. Between the thickness of the mortared stone floor and walls and the watchfulness of the guards, no one had ever escaped, even when Gilmar was a year and longer between visits. Rom insisted, however, that the guards be doubled, with instructions to be wary of woodland animals prowling near.

Sormar agreed readily to Rom's special precautions for the First of Outlaws. They took Wildraith to the cellar beneath the warriors' hall, had a smith fix both her ankles to an anvil and her right wrist to one of the stone columns that supported the roof above, and then built up a hasty shaft of stone and mortar around her from floor to ceiling, leaving only one small hole for air and a little food.

Because Rom had sent a few of his fastest-running men ahead to Forestedge with news of the capture, and Sormar had sent riders on to Waterstead immediately, Wildraith and Ondreth had only a few days to wait before the newlywed rulers came to town, attended by the most select companies of each army.

Irinore Silver-claw's three hundred were first in the Butter-hair's honor guard, Ylsa the Iron-mouth's first in Gilmar's.

These two captains had met in a street on the eastern side of Waterstead, just inside the gate, the evening before their leaders married. Gilmar and Dulanis had given orders that their armies take time to meet and mingle freely, western warrior with northern, to promote comradeship. In the fading light Irinore had recognized Ylsa first, by the mask over her scarred cheek. Putting her silver-coated iron talon on Ylsa's shoulder, Irinore drew her close, muttered, "We've never seen each other before," and pulled her toward the gate.

Had Ylsa lived a different life, she might have greeted Irinore aloud despite the warning. Being what she was, she accompanied her old comrade from town without a word until they stood on the bank of the Longstraits.

Then Ylsa said, "I've been wondering whether I'd trade my face for your hand."

"I would trade," said Irinore. "That, but not your place in Gilmar's army."

"It's a good enough place. Command of three hundred. If I hadn't taken it, I'd have been dead. Who else escaped from Darkpool?"

"Etaris Pinchbirth. Forty-four others." Irinore named them, not including Ondreth of Laniscleft. "And five townspeople."

"An army. Complete with followers. I thought those six children and I were the only ones."

"We assumed you were dead. We buried you in our thoughts six years ago. Ylsa Tightmouth—stay dead."

"Why?" said Ylsa. "Doesn't a free woman have as much right to rent her skills to one ruler as another?"

"In her own opinion, maybe." Irinore might have said, "In the opinion of the gods," if it had not been for Ylsa's old hardness on that subject. "In Gilmar's opinion, or Dulanis Butter-hair's, who can tell?"

"The Old Man of the North knows already," Ylsa said with a wry smile. "Do you think I got out of Darkpool first and then chased after the northern army to join it?"

"Still . . ." said Irinore, "I'd call it safer for you to stay a new-met northerner to us. I'll warn the others."

Irinore did not dare say anything to Dulanis, and possibly the Keeper of the Cauldron recognized one of her former minor officers, but she asked no questions and made no comment.

When news came that Wildraith and another outlaw were prisoners in Forestedge, Irinore found a private moment to tell Ylsa how the First of Outlaws had appeared on the edges of the fighting at Darkpool, looking for her. Ylsa shrugged and said, "Checking the fixed-name, eh? Well, she won't be finding any more Ylsas now."

"We will send Wildraith's head to the moon god's son," said Dulanis with a low chuckle. "Hers and those followers' of hers. We'll insist on the quarter-godhood and all the gems he offered eleven years ago. A fistful of gems for each head! It will beggar him."

"He may only give gems for the Veil-eyes' own head," said Gilmar. "But we'll have the pleasure of seeing it off."

"And if he fails to pay . . ."

The scaffold was large. At its north end two thrones of equal height were set up. The second had had to be made in haste, at news of Gilmar's

marriage, but woven cloths draped over both
thrones concealed the fact that one was fully decorated with carving and staining, the other not.
Sormar and Ylsa stood beside Gilmar's throne,
Irinore and a western overcaptain named Farn
Splay-finger beside Dulanis Butter-hair's. Rom the
Moody, flanked by his second and third in command, had a special place of honor on the
scaffold's east side. The permanent and temporary
equipment of execution, with three men and a
woman to operate it, filled the south half of the
platform. The heads of the twenty-three outlaws
killed at Orimar's farm, strung like blossoms in a
garland, festooned the gallows.

Sormar and Arik the Split-chin, mindful of such
tales as what had happened at Ormrathestead and
not quite trusting the distance between Forestedge
town and the forest itself, wanted to behead Wildraith in the cellar beneath the warriors' hall.
Dulanis might have agreed, but both Gilmar and
Rom the Moody insisted on a public execution.
Sormar suggested they could make a public display
of Wildraith's head and whatever execution they
chose for Ondreth (privately thinking that the
wounded outlaw, who had been allowed no care
except what her fellow prisoners could give her,
would not last long on the scaffold), but Gilmar
called it foolish to make a show of the underling's
suffering and not of the leader's.

So Arik and Sormar, whose ideas included the
theory that Wildraith might have power to whip up
creatures with her mind, made her drunk for the
occasion. She took the first cupful of wine willingly, for she did not yet suspect their purpose and
some of the stones had bruised her when the warriors knocked one side of the shaft away. The next

several cupfuls they had to force down her throat. The last one she again drank willingly, though they had to steady it against her chin. They surrounded her with nine guards to support her through the streets and tie her to one of the upright frames, hoping that the rulers and crowd would think her condition fear or the weakness of several cramped days with little food.

Probably they should not have made Wildraith drunk. Her humanity was weakened, but her godhood was not; only her thoughts were confused by the state of her physical brain, until she lost her perception of individuality in the pantheon of her sibling aspects. And though she witnessed that day's events through a vapor, she comprehended enough to feel the stirrings of rage. Heavy vermillion clouds began churning over the sky, and Gilmar called it bad luck that the weather should turn freakish at this time, but Dulanis told him it suited the occasion.

When Wildraith was secured, the guards went down for Ondreth. The wounds in her right side and left leg had festered; her makeshift bandages showed wetness through the dirt; she seemed partly delirious. Even with the best of care, she might have been doomed. The guards had to carry her up, and there was little chance that anyone would mistake the reason for her state.

"Behead her at once," said Dulanis with a look of disgust.

"No," said Gilmar. "First whip her bare and brand her. Give our people a show and Veil-eyes something to contemplate."

Dulanis looked at the clouds and at a number of birds, large and small, who were alighting on the roofs. A couple of dogs whined in the crowd. Some hooded onlookers held hounds that greatly resembled wolves. The First of Herders shrugged. "The full show, then," she agreed, "but let it proceed without delay."

The executioners bound Ondreth on the slanted frame for whipping. At the first lash, a bolt of lightning cracked, one of the wolflike dogs howled, and Ondreth's head snapped up. The new pain seemed to clear her mind a little—she looked across the platform and cried out: "Ylsa! Ylsa Unflinching!"

Wildraith turned her head as if trying to focus her dark eyes. Her voice slurred so that the name was hardly recognizable. "Ylsa of Ironstead?"

"Dead . . . dead at Darkpool." Ondreth went into the ravings of memory.

Gilmar looked at Dulanis. "Wife, if this outlaw was one of our warriors, my penalty for desertion is to slit the nose and hang by the ankles."

"If she survives the whipping," said Dulanis, as Ondreth's voice ceased. "But I think she is dead already."

Gilmar rose, crossed the platform, and put his hand beneath Ondreth's chin, holding up her face with its staring eyes. "She was not one of mine. I did not think so. Therefore, if she recognized Ylsa the Maimed-face, then Ylsa the Maimed-face must have been one of yours." He chopped his right hand through the air, and Sormar put his arm around Ylsa's chest and his spear to her throat.

"Sick ravings!" said Irinore.

"Or one of the outlaws." Rom the Moody joined Sormar to help hold Ylsa.

Beyond the edges of the crowd, a swarm of mice attacked a large, scarred cat. Two or three dogs howled, and thunder rolled, this time without visible lightning.

Dulanis looked at Ylsa and shrugged. "She may have been one of mine."

"Then she is a deserter," said the First of the North.

Ylsa screamed at him, "You knew when you took me into your army!"

"From her own mouth," Gilmar replied.

He nodded, and Rom drew his knife and slit Ylsa's nose.

A near bolt of lightning covered Ylsa's cry. Beyond the crowd, the mice killed the cat and turned on a townsman's ankles. He stamped and swore. One of the hooded onlookers stroked her howling dog.

"They say the moon god's son insists that once to offer Dulanis Butter-hair loyalty is to owe it to her forever," said Gilmar. "Can I give you less loyalty than he?"

"Husband," said Dulanis, "did you know?"

He returned and sat again in the throne beside hers. "If I did, First of the West, I am doubly bound to give you back the deserter I borrowed for a while when we were still enemies."

Dulanis frowned, but nodded. The executioners took Ylsa from Rom and Sormar and hauled her to an empty vertical frame. Wildraith shook her own hands, taut as they were tied. The wind rose, many of the birds flapped into the air, and thunder crackled redly.

Rada the Cautious had been chosen to give the signal. When Wildraith shook her hands and Rada's wolf strained and snarled in her leash, Rada decided the moment could not be held. She loosed

Wendy Adrian Shultz

the wolf and whooped like an owl.

Hooded and unhooded, disguised as storytellers, merchants, whores and wandering beggars, three-score outlaws had slipped into town and mingled with the crowd. They loosed their dog-wolves, those who had them, and caught up their weapons. The birds lunged, other outlaws and forest creatures that had gathered around Forestedge and already begun creeping closer abandoned stealth and swarmed toward the scaffold. Many of the dogs and cats, all the town's rats, mice, and other vermin and insects, joined the wild animals. Rain fell like blood and blood splashed like rain. The slaughter in Forestedge was far more terrible than that in the snow amphitheatre at Ormrathestead, for the god-woman was drunk and waking night-mares took the place of conscious control in her mind. Only Wildraith's outlaws were safe from the creatures, for the creatures themselves recognized the outlaws as friends.

Animals having killed or scattered the jail guards, Jokan Greenstick opened the jail. Many prisoners made their escape at once. Many others joined the outlaws both in that day's fighting and afterwards.

Dulanis and Gilmar led the defense on the scaffold. They saved their own lives, but could not stop Tilis, Rada and Arileth from freeing Wildraith. Tilis and Rada bore their leader away into the turmoil. Arileth found Ethaan's head, caught it and crouched over it for a few seconds on the scaffold, and Rom struck her down from behind, just before a wolf killed him. The four executioners, Farn Splay-finger, Sormar the Short-legged and Rom's second in command died there, too, as did many

others who climbed the scaffold to protect their
rulers. Arik Split-chin lost an arm and only saved
his life by plunging the stump into a brazier of
glowing coals to stop the blood. Irinore rushed to
the south end of the platform as if to prevent the
outlaws saving Wildraith, but instead of attacking
them she cut Ylsa free and slipped down with her
in the confusion. She found Etaris Pinchbirth, and
Etaris, filled with disgust at what Gilmar had done,
helped Ylsa away and became another deserter.
Irinore returned to the scaffold and used hand and
claw for Dulanis; she had learned not to expect ideals of any ruler.

When the storm turned from crimson to natural
black and crystal, and the fighting ended at last,
most of the dead were Gilmar's and Dulanis
Butter-hair's people, the bodies of only seven outlaws and several animals mixed among them. Wildraith, Tilis, Jokan, Rada, Yrn Long-grin, had all
escaped and disappeared. So had Etaris and Ylsa.
If Dulanis had seen or suspected Irinore's part in
helping her old comrade, she said nothing of it. Indeed, she offered Irinore command of a thousand,
but Irinore preferred to keep her smaller company
of women, most of whom had survived that Day of
the Bloody Clouds.

Tilis and Jokan took Ethaan's body from
Orimar's farm and buried it in the forest, carrying
out Arileth's plan as nearly as they could. Tilis
overheard Jokan muttering prayers in which he
begged Ethaan's forgiveness for not restoring his
head and for leaving Arileth's body to their enemies.

Chapter 19.

Of the continuous stream who had joined Wildraith over the years, fewer than four hundred now remained in her band. The rest had been shaken away, singly or in packs, by her vulnerability to assassination and capture, by the familiar way Attaran had shared storytellers' secrets and thus revealed the convenient shiftiness of historical record, even by the irony in Tilis the Supple's growing wisdom and the flaws in Jokan Greenstick's character. Splinter heresies had developed among the heretics. Wildraith was not displeased.

Yet even those stubborn ones who still followed her wanted something constant. They demanded that their captains remain Five. The day after burying Ethaan's corpse, Jokan and Tilis accepted Yrn Long-grin and Rada the Cautious to make up the number. Their most endearing qualification was that both Yrn and Rada showed they were aware they could never replace Ethaan and Arileth.

That night the New Five sat close around their small fire and tried to lay plans. "The northwestern newlyweds may not make any special effort to take Wildraith again for a while," said Yrn, "but they're sure to come down hard on Senerthan, or why glue themselves together?"

"The Copper River valley might be the best place for us these next few years," said Rada. "Or the West between Middle Wells and Laniscleft."

Jokan shook his head. "We've never run from the fighting."

"We've never found the whole of it, either," said Tilis.

"Is the fighting your chief business?" said Wildraith, partly to observe what effect her words would have on the discussion.

After a short pause, Yrn said, "Hardstick's right that we can do more here in the Long Forest."

"We save a farm yesterday, a merchant today, a breeding settlement tomorrow," said Tilis, "but the war goes on."

"We do enough, anyhow, to earn ourselves a good place in storytellers' ballads and a comfortable welcome when the warriors are gone," said Jokan. "And what if Gilmar and Dulanis try to burn the forest again?"

Wildraith smiled. "After I have found the Ironstead widow, trust me to keep Senerthan's forest safe from his enemies' fire as long as he lives."

She thought by their expressions that Rada and Yrn feared her a little crazed from what had happened at Forestedge.

"And we'll keep it safe in the meantime," said Jokan. "But what does Ylsa of Old Ironstead have to do with it?"

"Nothing," said Wildraith, "except that finding her has always been my chief business." And harder than she would have expected. By the time she had adjusted to mortal senses a decade ago, Ylsa had been gone from the Long Forest, and

Wildraith must depend on rumors, transferences, and those times when her quarry came within a patch of wild woodland. And always she must to some degree collate her followers' needs with her own.

"Was it her at Forestedge?" said Rada.

Wildraith looked at Tilis. "You are the only one of us who ever knew Tender-face by human sight."

Tilis lowered her gaze. "It . . . could have been. I had only a short look at her. Before they slit her nose. She already had that one scar-patch, and the crowd was tall around me . . . It could have been Ylsa Tender-face, it's been eleven years now, and we don't know how she's used them . . . but I can't be sure."

Wildraith stood. "I think it is the same. And she is vulnerable, too, and the years pass more and more quickly."

Putting her sword into its latest sheath, the new one Tilis and Arileth had made three winters ago, she left the fire.

"Well, that slit nose should make her a little easier to find again," she heard Greenstick say.

"Maybe she'll even come to us," Yrn replied. "That's what I'd do in her place. If she's still alive."

"Even if you suspected you were the one Wildraith's been looking for?" Rada put in. "After what you'd seen at Forestedge . . ."

Their talk told Wildraith they assumed she was only quitting them for a few moments to relieve herself. She nodded and paused, understanding why humans so often acted with emotion rather than reason.

Tilis alone guessed the truth and slipped away

from the others to follow. Wildraith was both disappointed and comforted. "You might have been more wise," she murmured when Tilis found her, "not to have looked for a leavetaking."

"Is it so important for me to become The Wise?" Wildraith embraced her.

"I've failed you," the younger woman whispered —except that Tilis was now about Wildraith's own bodily age, and would begin to grey sooner, for the incarnation had still some years before the time Wildraith had spent in this plane of existence equalled her apparent age on first shaping molecules into flesh. In human experience, Tilis had always been older. "Your only reason for taking me with you from Ironstead was for me to recognize Ylsa," she went on, "and now I cannot."

"But that was not your only reason for leaving Ironstead to come with me," said Wildraith. "Did you ever plan what you would do after we found her?"

"I never knew why we were looking for her."

"Tilla. When I find the widow of Ironstead, my purpose in living here is completed."

"You won't come back to us?"

"Not if I succeed at last."

By mutual agreement they pulled free of each other's arms, but Tilis kept her hand on Wildraith's shoulder.

"Tilla," said Wildraith, "we no longer help one another. You have taught me as much as I'll need, if all goes well, and I have made mistakes. Ormrathestead was the fault of my curiosity, Forestedge of my drunkenness. Already, you hear, the others make their plans with more mind to your own designs and prudence than to my need. And they are right."

"It's not only because of Letha and Ethaan?"

"They are still Of One Another. And Ondreth and the rest are safe, few of them unhappy. In some measure, I could envy them." Nevertheless, Wildraith's humanity mourned their deaths as sharply in silence as Arileth had keened aloud for Ethaan.

"Where is Ylsa Ironmouth now?" said Tilis.

"Not in forestland, or I would know. I think that one companion helped her out of town and that they went southwest, but all the images are confused." She also thought they were travelling toward Ondarstream, but creatures not native to the forest could spy for her only at secondhand. If Ylsa Maimed-face was hiding her head, so were other fugitives.

"And if you don't find her?"

"I may come back to you for a few years. But after that, it will be a very long time until I speak with anyone again."

Tilis gripped tighter for a moment. "Wildraith of Nowhere . . . Wildraith of the Forest . . . succeed."

She released Wildraith's shoulder, they pressed palms, and Tilis turned back while Wildraith went forward.

Chapter 20.

Dulanis and Gilmar sent forty heads to Sene-rthan, those of the twenty-three outlaws killed at Orimar's farm, Arileth's, and sixteen taken from Forestedge bodies that might have belonged to out-laws, for anything that strangers could prove. The moon god's son refused to pay a single gem, even for the heads of Ethaan and Arileth.

The headbearers also brought him his first hard news of Dulanis Butter-hair's marriage with the Old Man of the North, and Senerthan might have added the messengers' heads to the outlaws' in his rage. But Gilmar and Dulanis had been canny enough to choose storytellers for the mission: Der-inore, who had been named to the Nine in Tanris of Everywhere's place; Derinore's son and appren-tice Ilmar; and a lesser newsbringer, Yorn of the South, who had had the bad luck to be in Forest-edge the Day of the Bloody Clouds and the good luck to survive by slipping at once into the nearest house and bolting the door. On their way through the Long Forest with their burden, these three had met Derek of the West, who despite his trait-name was one of Senerthan's own secret spies, and Man-dar of the East. Storytellers' privilege was still

strong enough that the First of Hunters restrained
his temper rather than do violence to five of them
in a group.

He kept the outlaws' heads and gave the
storytellers a bag of animal droppings, which they
dared not deliver, bringing back instead a simple
translation in more respectful language of
Senerthan's message.

Senerthan's refusal gave Gilmar and Dulanis the
excuse, had they needed one, for a violent renewal
of the war. By now it was too late in the year for a
deep invasion, but, guessing that a quiet autumn
would not deceive their enemy, they sent large
forces to destroy his strongholds in the northern
part of the Long Forest. The attackers found most
of these strongholds already deserted, a clear sign
that the moon god's son was losing no time in making ready for the combined armies of North and
West.

The people of Warm-winter, the one stronghold
not deserted, claimed they had given up their loyalty to Senerthan and made theirs a free town. The
attackers destroyed it anyway, killing the men and
taking the women and children prisoner. The same
thousand warriors destroyed Hold-deep, a small
town with a long and unquestioned repute for self-
loyalty. Gilmar and Dulanis ordered the officers
responsible for the destruction of Warm-winter
and Hold-deep burned and their men whipped.
The two rulers had decided to court rather than
force the loyalty of the free towns. (But, the damage being done, they kept the captured women and
children.)

That was a winter of hard preparation both in
the warm North, where Dulanis and Gilmar drilled

their armies and promoted comradeship between herder and farmer, and in the snowy southern part of the Long Forest, where Senerthan tried to plan how, with an army not yet completely recovered from the disastrous campaign of five summers ago, he could hold his own against the united strength of North and West.

None of this made much difference to Ylsa, now doubly Maimed-face, and Etaris Pinchbirth, who travelled southwest, avoiding towns and stealing food from the outer fields of farms. Perhaps Gilmar's action and his bride's acquiescence on the scaffold at Forestedge had been more symbolic than passionate, for neither ruler showed particular interest in hunting them down. Indeed, some of the bodies had been mangled and scattered beyond easy recognition, and it was convenient to assume that Ylsa and the vanished Etaris were among these and burn them all in a common pyre, without making too strict a count, and afterwards concentrate on plans for crushing Senerthan and joining his East to their West and North.

This accomplished, the Copper River valley would have little choice but to accept Dulanis and Gilmar's rule as well, and the fate of the free South would depend on its ability to unite for defense and on whether the supreme rulers to the north judged it worth taking or too cold, poor and distant to merit the trouble. For the present, however, the South remained free and uninvolved.

Ylsa and Etaris had been officers long enough to understand that the next campaigns would almost certainly be fought in the Long Forest. So they headed for the Copper River, reaching it by rafting at night down Ondarstream until the waters

mingled. Following the great river south was upstream work, so they abandoned their crude raft
and kept to the western bank until they found a
small party of merchants camped on shore for the
night.

Ylsa wanted to steal one of the boats, but Etaris
argued her into approaching the merchants, three
men and two women, openly if not quite honestly.
Ylsa sat silent in the mask she had cut from her
cloak to cover her face, while Etaris persuaded the
merchants that even along the Copper River,
where trade was now comparatively safe, an extra
pair of trained warriors might be useful. She went
so far as to claim that Gilmar and Dulanis had released a few warriors to help guard free trading,
and the merchants did not question it. Probably
they were glad that these fighters offered their services instead of trying to loot.

The first payment Ylsa claimed was cotton cloth
to make a more comfortable mask. The next payment was wine. One of the three boats held nothing
but wine from the north, that always sold well in
the cold south. Ylsa travelled in this boat, spending
her days crouched beneath the canopy, where she
steadily drank the merchandise.

By the time they reached the Island of the Chess
Game, the merchants had decided that whatever
protection this pair might offer was more than can-
celled out by Ylsa's drinking. They camped on the
island, pretending to search for those long-lost
chess figures of jet and amber, and in the middle of
the night they pushed off, leaving Ylsa and Etaris
asleep in the place where once a hall had been
raised for that first meeting of Dulanis and Senerthan.

Etaris had offered to teach Ylsa to swim when

they made their raft for Ondarstream, but Ylsa had refused. Now she refused again, preferring to stay on the island. Etaris grew very tired of her company that summer.

Several days after the merchants had left, a few farmchildren rowed across for the traditional game of trying to find the chess pieces. Ylsa was hunting near where they came ashore, and when they caught sight of her face, unmasked, they fled back to their boat. Whether they spread a tale of evil spirits or dangerous fugitives, no one else came to the island. Ylsa and Etaris lived on game and wild growth, once or twice falling sick of some poisonous plant, until winter. Ylsa led the way out onto the ice dangerously soon after it had formed. When it held her up, Etaris followed and they continued south, generally walking on the frozen river but cutting overland at the major curves, sometimes begging hospitality at farms where Etaris passed them off as would-be outlaws looking for Wildraith, sometimes stealing food, blankets and furs when need and opportunity coincided. Ylsa's wool mask became welcome for warmth as well as pride, and Etaris cut a similar mask for her own face.

A little past midwinter a half-thaw and freezing rain caught them in open fields just north of Laniscleft. Throats cold-parched, they stumbled almost by chance to the nearest farm.

It was a small stead, held by a widower named Edrik Narrow-nose, his two grown daughters and one daughter's husband. They kept two mules for plowing, six or seven sheep for wool, and some cats. In summer they also kept additional sheep, some poultry, pigs, a goat or two and a heifer, or perhaps a cow with her calf, but they sold or slaughtered all these at harvest-time, to buy new animals each spring with the wool cloth they had woven and embroidered during the winter. All four of them were excellent clothworkers. They had used the southern style of building in their dwellings, storerooms, and winter shelter for the mule and sheep, so that with the fields harvested and empty the only sign that people lived here was a number of mounds, mottled white and brown with partly melted snow, and a thin column of smoke rising from the central one.

Edrik and his family nursed the strangers. Etaris was the more violently ill, but the quicker to recover. Well before the first true thaw of spring, she could sit up most of the day watching Edrik at his loom, and though still too weak to help with the earliest plowing, she had persuaded him by then to let her try her skill at embroidery. As her strength returned, she watched the sheep-shearing, helped with the haymaking, became competent with a spindle, and began to learn which herbs to gather for dye and how to color the yarn with them. Edrik was her principal teacher. He was not yet very old, nor she any longer very young.

Meanwhile, Ylsa changed her wool mask for the cotton one and sat brooding, drinking tea instead of wine but otherwise behaving much as she had in the merchants' boat. She watched friendship deepen between Etaris and Edrik, and perhaps she thought that she was more nearly his age than Pinchbirth was, though not yet too old to hope, even now, for another child. But Edrik had seen her mutilated face while he nursed her through the sickness. She seldom spoke, and the only help she offered the family was milking that year's cow and goats.

They heard from a minor storyteller that Dulanis and Gilmar had burned some farmsteads a little south of Ondarstream in an effort to taunt Senerthan out of the forest to a meadow battle. Only the outlaws had come out, and they were beaten back. No one could swear to seeing Wildraith herself among them. Senerthan refused to come into the open, so at last the northern and western rulers stopped burning farms and took their armies into the Long Forest, to find that here the woodland-trained hunters, though outnumbered, could hold their own.

At harvest time Etaris married Edrik and settled in to spend the rest of her life as farmer and clothworker. By then, Ylsa had left.

They had parted about halfway between midsummer and harvest. When Etaris voiced her decision to stay, Ylsa had told her, "You're a fool. We're still in the territory Dulanis claims."

"Within a few years, Dulanis and Gilmar may claim the South as well, and the only refuge will be the Whitepeak Mountains."

"Then I'll go to the mountains," said Ylsa. "With this face, the Tangletongues should worship me as a monster. Besides, it may be another generation before our great rulers conquer the South, at the speed they've fought their war."

"And with the northern and western armies combined, it may be a generation before they come this far again gathering new warriors. I'll take my chance."

Ylsa shrugged.

Two days later she had touched palms one last time with Etaris, given curt thanks to Edrik's family for nursing her, and gone on southward alone, refusing the gift of a new wool cloak.

She avoided all human contact even more strictly now, living on raw, ripening plants with sometimes a rabbit or a strayed domestic animal. Not liking to cross the Copper River, she kept to its western bank. She might have struck directly south for the mountains, but the river was her only assured source of drinking water. No doubt it had its smaller branches, and there must be wells and watering pools about, but she had never before been in this region. Moreover, autumn promised to close in early this year, and only by following the great river could she be sure of finding inhabited places to provide what she would need to stay alive in the Whitepeaks. By now a sort of numb persistency for life had begun to replace the desire for death she had felt the first seasons after that scene in Forestedge.

One day she crouched among old rocks and high grasses on the outskirts of a farm and watched a boy pasturing sheep. Late as it was in the year, unclouded sky and lack of wind warmed the afternoon until the boy took off his cloak and folded it for a cushion while he sat to eat. Several sheep kicked up a commotion at the far end of the field, the boy hurried to the disturbance, and Ylsa seized this opportunity to take his cloak and small bag of food.

The pasture was almost out of sight behind her when a tall young man came forward at a slant to block her way.

"That looks like Jan Turn-toes' cloak," he said.

"I begged it."

He took the bag from her, opened it, and pulled out a wedge of bread raggedly half-eaten.

Ylsa shrugged.

The young man said, "I think we have more to spare in Adrakstead than Jan's people have here."

"Bread or justice?"

"You left Jan unharmed," he replied, showing he had witnessed all. "Not every weapon-carrier coming south away from the war would do that. I'll return these. If you wait here, you can have a hot supper tonight."

"And an axe through my neck tomorrow?"

"I am Adrak Marthan the Simple, second child of Adrak the Slow. I promise you safety."

She had trusted no one since leaving Etaris, but she was tired and empty, the night would be cold, and Adrak Marthan the Simple was much the same age her own son would have been. She waited where he told her until he came back, went with him across the river to his mother's settlement, and sat alone in the shadows where she could take off her mask to eat her hot supper without letting her face be seen.

When they did not execute her as a thief, she stayed on six more days, helping with the work in return for a length of wool cloth, coarse and un-dyed but warm, and a skin of southern wine, made from berries, sharper than northern grape wine, but equally warming.

Chapter 21.

The storyteller Dathan of the South came to Adrakstead while Ylsa was there. This is a tale he told one sleety night to the company in the same small burrow where Ylsa sat mending leather harness:

Near the western edge of Senerthan's Long Forest, on a line with the Island of the Chess Game, thirty-two hunters sat around their campfire. Two of them, a young woman and a young man, were tightly bound.

A new woman came forward from the surrounding darkness. She was dressed much like the hunters except that her only weapon was a sword in a finely decorated scabbard. Her hair was caught up beneath a green cap, and her eyes seemed to be entirely black, even when she sat near the fire.

"You must be Senerthan's people," she said.

"I am his cousin Meleth of the Mossy Bower," said their captain. "Are you one of us, or a storyteller, or a merchant robbed of your goods?" For the dark woman had shown no fear. "Or are you of the South?"

"I am not Senerthan's enemy," the stranger replied. "In my own way, I am his ally. What have these two done?" She nodded at the prisoners.

"Cowards," said Meleth. "Afraid of Gilmar and false Dulanis who may try to hunt these woods next summer, this pair deserted from New Crescent."

"It must perplex your cousin to find adequate punishment," said the stranger, "since Erthan of the Subtle Mind died at Ormrathestead."

Meleth frowned and said, "We're to brittle the man like a deer, but more slowly, and carry him back swinging from a pole. The woman is to be kept underground, bearing children and forbidden to nurse them, until she dies or goes barren."

(Ylsa missed a stitch in her mending, and listened more closely despite her old indifference to storytellers.)

"Is cowardice so great a sin?" said the stranger.

"It's the only sin," Meleth replied.

"Perhaps," said the stranger. "For most people here outside the Free South follow their leaders in fear. But if all were brave enough to show their cowardice, like these two, where would the armies come from to fight your leaders' war?"

Meleth rose to her feet and drew her sword. "You're no ally to my cousin the moon god's son," she said.

The stranger smiled and stood, removed her cap, and shook free her hair, long, smooth, and shining black. She whistled, and wolf, badger, wildcat, porcupine and bear leaped or lumbered out of the shadows to her side, hawk, owl and bat flew down to circle the fire.

The stranger said, "I stopped the Old Man of the

North when he tried to burn your cousin's forest last summer."

Meleth whispered, "You are Wildraith Veil-eyes of Nowhere."

"I am Wildraith."

"Then call your beasts and kill us!" Meleth cried. "Finish what you began at Ormrathestead. We die brave and faithful."

But her men showed less courage, or greater sense. Many of them dropped their weapons and held out empty palms as if hoping Wildraith's animals would understand surrender. Others fell down and pretended to be dead already. A few edged away as if hoping to escape when the fight drew in around their comrades. Only three grasped their weapons firm, and they stepped close to the fire. But it was a small fire, and Wildraith's animals did not seem to fear it in the natural way.

"Yes, some of you would fight and die," said Wildraith. "Then I would free these two in spite of your deaths. Will you play one game of chess for them instead?"

Like many hunters, Meleth always carried a small set of chess pieces, ten of dark stone and ten of bright, strung on a silver chain about her neck. She drew a board in the ground beside the fire and unstrung her necklace. Wildraith chose the dark figures, eight of green jasper and two of jet, leaving Meleth those of amber and white onyx.

They played for three hours in silence, while the hunters trembled, the animals watched and the birds preened their feathers. From time to time owl or wolf dropped more branches into the fire. The wind died and the moon neared the western horizon.

Suddenly Meleth cried, "Cheat!" and caught up

her spear. The bear knocked it from her hand.

Wildraith stood, smiled, drew her long sword that rippled like translucent oil in the firelight, and pointed it at the chess game. "Perhaps I cheated. Or perhaps I mistook one shape for another. Or perhaps I was playing by the rules of another region. Will you scatter the game and create your cousin's war in miniature, or do you have enough courage not to act like a fool?"

Meleth scattered her chess figures with one foot. Some of them flicked into the fire. She watched the precious stone crack. Then she turned and cut the young prisoners free with her own knife.

Wildraith led them deep into the forest, all her creatures following. Some say she has changed their fixed names to Ethaan and Arileth in memory of the two who died in Gilmar's North. Others say that those two young hunters escaped to the Copper River and that Wildraith of Nowhere now walks alone and apart with her wild creatures.

"Now tell them how Wildraith held her wild creatures on a merciful rein at Forestedge," Ylsa muttered under her breath. She said nothing aloud, not because everyone else in the burrow applauded Wildraith and the Free South, but because she never spoke now when she could avoid it.

Chapter 22.

Ylsa could have wintered in Adrakstead, but she was restless among folk who treated her with tolerance, and the mask, which she wore sleeping and waking except when she lifted it to eat where she sat alone facing the wall shadows, crawled on her flesh.

So on a bright, warm morning in false autumn she crossed the short Narrows Bridge on the southeastern curve of the river and left Adrakstead behind.

Settlements were smaller, poorer, and more widely scattered as she went farther south. She preferred stealing, where she could do it quickly, to buying food with a few hours of working for people who looked curiously or sympathetically at her mask and sometimes offered her a winter home. She clung to the idea of wintering as a monster among the Tangletongues, though she risked freezing before she met them in their mountain range.

The last town she came to was a poor community called Streambottom, where she stole a capon to provision her. Unsure whether anyone had seen her, she followed the mountain path longer than was safe in the early darkness. The stream that gave the town its name ran alongside the trail. By now ice was starting to form on the lazier edges of the Copper River below, but this mountain water still flowed down too fast to catch crystals. When Ylsa heard its noise soften, she understood that the trail was rising farther and farther above the streambed.

By groping, she found a place where the path spread out to form a sufficient ledge. She struck her fire close to the mountain wall, feeding the spark with twigs, branches and chips she had picked up on her way. Her bag was heavy with fuel; she was strong enough to carry a good weight. She pulled off her mask to enjoy the free air—cold drafts mixing with the fire's warmth. She plucked and spitted her capon, drank her last mouthful of wine, and began roasting her supper.

The next time she looked up, she glimpsed a figure standing just beyond the firelight.

She said nothing and continued turning the capon.

The stranger moved into the firecircle. She was tall, dark, whole of face and body. Her hair blew unbound and unhooded, her cloak flapped open, a long sword in a finely decorated scabbard hung at her hip. Even when she sat near the fire, the circles in her eyes seemed to be entirely black, with no difference between the sightpoint and the colorring.

"Ylsa of Ironstead?" said the stranger.

"Ylsa the Maimed-face." She lifted her head and grinned, guessing how grotesque it must make her scars.

The newcomer put her hand over Ylsa's on the spit and helped turn the roasting fowl. "I know. I saw it done."

"Wildraith of Nowhere, are you?" Ylsa nodded. "Aye, trussed out waiting your turn."

"Why not curse Gilmar? Twelve years ago, you cursed a god."

"Twelve years." It seemed longer.

"You cursed the god of the forest for accepting your sacrifice and taking your son nevertheless. The god did not accept your goat, only permitted a wolf to eat. The wolf was hungry."

Had Wildraith not been turning the spit with Ylsa, the capon would have burned black on one side.

"Wildraith . . . Wildrava," the widow said at last. "Yes, I cursed you then, and I curse you now."

"I think this is fully roasted." Wildraith removed the capon from the heat and laid it on a rock. "One of us may be the gladder for a meal when this next hour is past." She stood and removed her cloak. Wind pressed her linen tunic and light wool trousers close to her body, but she did not shiver. She plaited her hair and twined it up around her head.

"So the goat was blemished," said Ylsa. "She was the only creature left to me in the world. *She was all I had.* You have all the creatures of the woodlands for your pets."

"I have left them behind this time." Wildraith drew her sword, which did indeed gleam as in the tales. "But why not curse Gilmar and Dulanis as well as me?" she repeated.

"I might, if I thought they were gods and could hear me." Ylsa drew her weapons and dashed through the fire.

Wildraith stepped back, half turned, and tripped her opponent with a soft kick to the lower leg. Ylsa fell on hands and knees. Her hand-axe jolted from her left hand and she heard it fall into the rocky stream far below. Her left palm was resting on rock while her fingers dangled in air.

"A narrow battleground for a night with one quarter of the moon," said Wildraith, pointing her sword at the partially scattered fire and the mountain wall behind it, her other arm at the chasm.

"You fear the heights, god?" Ylsa slashed her sword at Wildraith's knees. The god leapt high, coming down a pace or two farther from the edge.

Ylsa saw her advantage. Fighting on her knees, she gave herself a surer balance and made the angle more awkward for Wildraith. In this small area, the god could not circle around to the human's back without coming dangerously near the edge.

Wildraith got down on her own knees and slid toward Ylsa.

The two women faced each other at arm's length. Wildraith raised her sword. Ylsa shifted hers to counter it. Neither woman had a defensive weapon in her left hand. One well-placed blow from either sword could end the fight with death or a mortal wound.

Ylsa feinted. Wildraith seemed to know it for a feint. Instead of countering, she lofted as if for a blow to the head, but so slowly that Ylsa had time to bring her own sword back around and up. Metal clashed on metal for the first time. The women knelt a moment, blades touching and muscles straining.

Ylsa's knees were sore and, she guessed, bleeding from the rocks and sharp stone. Were her opponent's? She risked a glance at Wildraith's knees and thought she saw dark stains where trousers touched ground.

They slid their swords apart. Wildraith turned and struck hers against the cliff edge with sufficient force to make sparks dance like tiny roots of lightning. Bits of rock loosened and fell down into the stream. She lifted the blade again and twisted it in the light of the quarter moon. It shone like a thin mirror. She ran it along her left sleeve, and Ylsa heard the linen shirring.

"Forged on the anvils of hell," said the god. Then, glancing at Ylsa's blade, she smiled and threw the hell-forged weapon behind her. It struck the mountainside and fell near the fire. Wildraith leaned forward and seized Ylsa round the waist.

Ylsa cast her own sword after the god's and caught her round the head. They squeezed. The god's grip was strong, choking, but a middle could hold out longer than a neck. Ylsa threw her weight forward, trying to bend Wildraith's head beyond the breaking point. Still they fought in silence, save for their panting.

Wildraith collapsed backwards, Ylsa falling with and atop her. At last the god moaned, but no bones gave way. Her head was now on the ground—the neck was safe. Ylsa shifted her grip, grinding downward, hoping the rocks were sharp beneath the god's skull, trying to get her fingers into the colorless black eyes.

Wildraith loosed her arms and brought her knees up sharply beneath Ylsa. The human was thrown forward, over, to land in the fire.

She rolled clear. But she had screamed. She had never felt shame at crying out in battle with her own kind, but she felt shame before this god. Shame because the god delighted in her suffering. She snatched up Wildraith's sword, turned, and lunged.

Wildraith uttered a cry and jumped as if to meet her. Another trick? Ylsa stepped around, changing her thrust to a swing.

A rock turned beneath her foot. She pitched forward.

Wildraith caught her. They were grappling again. This time on their feet. And this time Ylsa did not throw away the sword. But it was not a weapon for such close quarters. She slapped it again and again at her opponent's back, sometimes hearing cloth tear, hoping flesh was being sliced as well, but unable to lever for a thrust . . .

A sudden lurch downwards, a sound of more falling stones. Wildraith flung her arms wide—she had stepped off the edge. Ylsa broke loose and rolled to safety. Wildraith screamed and fell.

The scream echoed for a long time. Ylsa crawled back to the embers of her scattered fire, scraped them together with the god's sword, added more bits of fuel and blew them into flames. She managed to eat one of the capon's wings before reaction drew her stomach too tight. She coughed, choked a little, and lay down between the mountain wall and her fire. She still heard Wildraith's scream. If she slept that night, it was only to dream that she lay awake.

Chapter 23.

Fall free now, said the god of weather. *Fall home to our own plane.*

No, said the god of soldiers, pointing to the deep chasm. *The sword I gave you has not yet fulfilled its purpose.*

The woman Ylsa stole one of my capons! cried the god of domestic animals.

Come join me, Wildrava! Come climb in pain with me, said Erthan of the Subtle Mind. But his voice came out of the chasm, and humans did not fall into the chasm. Erthan was groping through the hot, heavy fog. Thus Wildraith knew that some, at least, of the voices and presences were false.

It is completed, said the god of birth. *You fought her, and die in the result.*

It is not completed, the god of soldiers said warningly. *You fell, she did not push you. Neither cliff nor rock, water nor cold can complete Ylsa's own work.*

Which shall I believe? cried Wildraith. *Are you all no more than dreams in my human brain?*

They all clamored at once, ungodlike, and their voices merged with the fast-flowing stream around her. She lay face up on a boulder that happily kept her from drowning, but she thought it had broken her back, and the water that rushed over most of her body seemed colder than frozen, when she felt it at all. To sleep . . .

Sometimes she was once more in the snow amphitheatre at Ormrathestead; sometimes she stood spread-eagled and drunk beneath the vermillion sky of Forestedge; sometimes she lay dying and delirious from Ylsa Iron-eyes' knife, and that was when she was in greatest danger of trusting the voices which called her home, for Iron-eyes became one with the other Ylsa, and only this confusion warned the god.

But is it only Wildrava who falls into the chasm? she cried. *Or is it the god of the forest in all the names that humans use? Am I Wildrava of the Longforest, or Wildraith of Nowhere and Everywhere?*

Do you fear? said the Overgod.

Yes, I fear, said Wildraith. *And I am eager.*

In the morning all seemed quiet at last. Ylsa ate the cold capon and examined Wildraith's sword. It was a good weapon. The blade did not dull. She had that much from the god.

She carried the chicken bones to the edge of the cliff. By daylight it proved less high than it had seemed in the darkness. Ylsa could see the line between Wildraith's lips. Her body was bent to an unnatural angle in the water, her limbs twisted over the rocks of the stream bed, but her face, resting on a rock above the surface of the stream, was still beautiful. Ylsa had not seen more than a suggestion of its loveliness last night, with the flames casting their uneven glow. But only a god could stay beautiful in a death like that.

The flowing stream had washed away most of the blood. Ylsa was unsure whether Wildraith's chest moved up and down or whether it was an illusion of the water, but the eyes were closed, and she had never seen the dead close their own eyes.

Maybe gods died differently.

Ylsa thought she saw her lost hand-axe in the stream, lodged between rocks some distance from Wildraith. Besides, the scabbard was still buckled round the god's hips and might be worth salvaging. Ylsa took both swords and began the descent.

When she reached the stream, she saw that Wildraith was breathing. She stood and considered whether or not to try for the hand-axe and scabbard.

The god opened her eyes. "Ylsa." She whispered the name, yet it carried clearly over the sound of the stream.

Ylsa carried one sword in each hand as she waded out.

Wildraith nodded and smiled. "Thank the Overgod. To have missed by so little . . . Now strike, Ylsa of Ironstead!"

"The overgod?"

"We are many, but it is one." Wildrava's voice was low but steady, as if the mangling of her corpse had no control over her throat. "This is your satisfaction and my instruction: I must die by your effort. Now strike, Ylsa of Ironstead . . . or take a revenge longer than you can comprehend." For the first time, her voice had faltered a little. She stretched out one hand toward Ylsa's face. "Strike!"

Ylsa had not realized how close she was bending until she felt Wildraith's fingers touch her skin. It was like a plea. She drew back and struck twice, once with each sword, through stomach and heart. She knew by the staring eyes that Wildraith the warrior was finally dead. But Wildrava the god of the woodlands?

"And me?" she shouted. "What about a human

who could not forgive a god?"

Leaving the swords in the body, she buried her face in her hands. Her fingers did not contact the accustomed scars. She felt her face, then withdrew the god's sword, rinsed it in the stream, and held it close. It was narrow and almost transparent, but smooth and ungrooved, a fair mirror to confirm her sense of touch. Her face was whole again.

For a few heartbeats the vision rose in her brain of taking Wildraith's place. With the god's sword and Ylsa's own fighting skills, the other outlaws would surely accept her as chosen by Wildraith herself to be their new First Captain. To carry on the work that had earned Wildraith such honor and affection in the storytellers' ballads, the work that Ylsa had indulged in once already, when she saved the six children at Darkpool . . . to strike back at Gilmar and Dulanis with her own force of seasoned outlaws . . .

She became aware that it would be wise to move out of the cold water, and almost at the same moment another plan took shape in her mind. One lawful ruler remained to whom she had not yet sold her services. He was outnumbered and should welcome a skillful captain who knew his enemies' style and who had proved able to kill the great Wildraith. He was a man newly frustrated in his lifelong desire and might welcome a woman restored to her old beauty.

She would not take him Wildrava's head. She owed the god that much, and if Senerthan would not believe the evidence of Wildraith's famous sword, he would still accept and pay Ylsa for her own worth. She closed Wildraith's eyes, retrieved her own sword, the scabbard and her hand-axe, and waded from the stream.

Wendy Adrian Shultz

Epilogue.

The story of Wildraith ends here. What follows is taken largely from Dathan of the South's last great epic, the Song of Peace:

In the third summer of their marriage (which was the first summer following Wildraith's last battle), Dulanis and Gilmar tried again to burn the Long Forest, but drenching rains met them everywhere, and rust destroyed more weapons than weapons destroyed lives. In the fourth summer of their marriage, which was the thirtieth of the war, Gilmar suddenly died. Dathan hints that Dulanis was responsible. Gilmar was seventy-five years old, but had seemed strong to the end.

Widowed Dulanis attacked the northernmost edge of the Long Forest, where it came within a half day's march of the seacoast. Turning her warriors into woodchoppers and woodland into fields for plowing, she finally lured Senerthan to one last open battle. Some say—and here Dathan records it only as rumor, without committing himself to one version or the other—that Dulanis had planned from the day of her marriage to kill her first husband and wed the moon god's son, combining

North as well as West with the East, and their last meeting began as one more attempt at reconciliation, but the Butter-hair went into a sharper fury than ever when she discovered that Senerthan's new overcaptain, Ylsa the Handsome of Nowhere, who claimed to have killed Wildraith, was also Senerthan's lover.

So they fought the last and bloodiest battle of their war on the sands between forest and northern sea. At the heart of the battle, Senerthan's chosen command and Irinore Silver-claw's company of women fought and fell, warrior by warrior, until Senerthan and Dulanis were left alone, and then they killed each other. Some say that Irinore of the Silver Claw and Ylsa of Nowhere also fought to the death, and Ylsa cast her sword, which was either Wildraith's own weapon or its twin, into the waves with her dying strength. Others say that Ylsa and Irinore touched palms and slipped away together as comrades when the rest of their warriors and both their rulers were dead, that they made a boat and rowed away to find the forgotten lands beyond the sea, or went into the forest, or made their way to the mountains, or hid themselves to work a small farm in obscurity. A very few like to believe it was Dulanis and Senerthan who went away together, but Dathan records this notion only to scoff at it.

After the battle (and here Dathan was closest to the events), Adrak Marthan the Simple, Adrak the Slow's younger child who had two fixed names because his sister was also called Adrak, and Gilmar's distant kinswoman Soris the Beautiful, who had fled south after the battle of the Old Mounds, married and boated north down the Copper River, coming ashore often. Everywhere the war-sated people offered them loyalty in return for peace. Meleth of the Mossy Bower brought them her cousin's ceremonial Moon Spear of silver and bronze, and the oldest son of Naris Ever-fertile brought them the Cauldron of the Ancient Hearth.

Rada the Cautious had been killed fighting to save one of Senerthan's forest breeding-places from Gilmar and Dulanis. Jokan Hardstick, Tilis the Wise, and Yrn Long-grin had taken Ilith the Rust-haired in Rada's place. When Soris and Adrak offered truce to the outlaws, these four captains accepted it in Wildraith's name, though pointing out that it was a mere unnecessary form since the rulers who had outlawed them were dead. The two young hunters Wildraith had saved from Meleth joined the new rulers' companions, some of the outlaws returned to farming or herding, but most continued to live freely in the Long Forest as nominal captains for Soris and Adrak Marthan. For the most part they enjoyed truce and even comradeship with the hunters, who were largely reverting to their old clan loyalties, though there was an occasional small skirmish. Jokan recovered the heads of Ethaan and Arileth from Ormrathestead and buried them with Ethaan's body. Some say the former outlaws maintained that they often saw the spirits of Ethaan and Arileth and other dead comrades and that they always believed Wildraith would come back to them someday, but neither Tilis nor Jokan could ever be proved to have made these claims. (In an addition to the epic made after Dathan's death, an anonymous storyteller records that in her old age Tilis the Wise became advisor to the heirs of Soris and Adrak Marthan.)

After completing their trip from Adrakstead to the northern mouth of the Copper River and adding the Ceremonial Scabbard of the North to the Ancient Cauldron and the Moon Spear, Adrak and Soris returned midway and made their principal center on the Island of the Chess Game, building wide bridges to either bank. Some of the gifts they received during their various journeys through the united lands were so notable that Dathan recorded the names of the givers. Among them were a pair of fine woolen tunics, light and soft as linen or cotton, made and presented by Edrik Narrow-nose and Etaris of the Nine Supple Fingers, farmers and clothworkers from near Laniscleft.